Boc

The Trident Trilogy

Eight Years

The Only Reason

Wild Card

The Grand Slam Series

Truth or Tequila

Raine Out

Leave it on the Field

The Blitzen Bay Series

The Runaway Bride of Blitzen Bay

No One Wants That

Pretty Close to Perfect - December 2022 - Preorder on Amazon.

LEAVE IT ON THE FIELD

DONNA SCHWARTZE

This book is a work of fiction. Names, places, characters, organizations, events, and incidents are either products of the author's imagination or are used fictitiously. Any resemblance to actual persons, living or dead, or to businesses, companies, events, institutions, or locales is completely coincidental. Any trademarks, product names, service marks, and named features are assumed to be the property of their respective owners and are only used for references. This book is intended for adults only due to sensitive language and sexual content.

Copyright © 2022 by Donna Schwartze

All rights reserved. No part of this book or any of its contents may be reproduced, copied, modified, distributed, stored, transmitted in any form or by any means, or adapted without the prior written consent of the author and publisher.

ISBN: 9798831768725

Published by Donna Schwartze, 2022

donnaschwartzeauthor@gmail.com

❦ Created with Vellum

LEAVE IT ON THE FIELD

DONNA SCHWARTZE

For the beautiful rowdy prisoners.

"When I saw you first, it took every ounce of me not to kiss you. When I saw you laugh, it took every ounce of me not to love you. And when I saw your soul, it took every ounce of me."

—Atticus

Author's Note

Leave it on the Field can be read as a standalone novel, but there are character appearances from past books. If this is the first of my books you're reading or if it has been a while since you read my other books, please use this guide to understand how the characters connect.

Couples:

1. Sophie (Introduced in *Truth or Tequila*, public relations consultant) and Seb (Introduced in *Truth or Tequila*, professional baseball player). They met in *Truth or Tequila*.
2. Millie (Introduced in The Trident Trilogy, former CIA agent) and Mason (Introduced in The Trident Trilogy, former Navy SEAL). They met in *Eight Years*.
3. Raine (Introduced in The Trident Trilogy, CIA agent) and Alex (Introduced in *Truth or Tequila*,

Author's Note

professional baseball player). They met in *Raine Out*.
4. Elle (Introduced in *The Runaway Bride of Blitzen Bay*, law student) and Nash (Introduced in *The Runaway Bride of Blitzen Bay*, former Army Ranger). They met in *The Runaway Bride of Blitzen Bay*.
5. Kit (Introduced in *The Runaway Bride of Blitzen Bay*, teacher) and Butch (Introduced in The Trident Trilogy, former Navy SEAL). They met in *No One Wants That*.

How other characters met:

- Raine and Sophie were neighbors growing up. (*Raine Out*)
- Alex and Seb play on the same professional baseball team. (*Truth or Tequila* and *Raine Out*)
- Millie, Mason, Raine, and Butch met working together. (The Trident Trilogy)
- Elle and Kit are cousins. (*The Runaway Bride of Blitzen Bay*)
- Raine and Butch met Alex at a wedding and introduced him to The Trident Trilogy characters. (*Raine Out*)

Other series characters:

Author's Note

- Drew - General manager of the baseball team. Introduced in *Raine Out*.
- Joe - Head of security for the baseball team. Introduced in *Truth or Tequila*.
- Dottie - New owner of the baseball team. Mentioned in *Raine Out*.
- Maisie - Sophie's best friend, married to Ryan. Grew up with Sophie and Raine. Introduced in *Truth or Tequila*.
- Ricky, Paul, and Stone - Seb's childhood friends. Introduced in *Truth or Tequila*.
- Jack and Adie - Seb's parents. Introduced in *Truth or Tequila*.
- Bob and Deb - Sophie's parents. Introduced in *Raine Out*.
- Roman - Sophie's friend and former client. He owns hotels in Miami and St. John. Introduced in *Truth or Tequila*.
- Sam - Nash's neighbor in Blitzen Bay. Introduced in *The Runaway Bride of Blitzen Bay*.

Prologue

Twitter **@miamibballbabe**
(October 30, 2021)

Seb Miller just married a gold digger - @sophiabankspr I guess he married her because she's hot, but she's so phony. Sophie+Phony #sophony The perfect name for her. Seb and #sophony. It's not going to last. He'll come to his senses.
@realsebmiller

Twitter **@miamibballbabe**
(November 15, 2021)

Seb and #sophony are on their honeymoon. Someone posted this pic of them in Italy. Look how his hand's all over her ass. Lol. I mean that's why he married her, right? And I'm guessing her hand's all over his wallet.
@sophiabankspr @realsebmiller

***Twitter* @miamibballbabe**
(February 18, 2022)
Seb's finally back where he belongs - on the field at spring training. Of course #sophony is with him. She can't let him out of her sight for more than a second - worried he'll find someone better. Everyone's better. @realsebmiller @sophiabankspr

Lol. #sophony made her account private and blocked me. Whatever. She's nothing without Seb. She'll find that out soon. @realsebmiller You bored with her yet?

***Twitter* @miamibballbabe**
(April 14, 2022)
Opening night in Miami. Got the W on a @realsebmiller homer. The only bad part was the fans yelling Princess Sophie's name during the game. You just know she LOVES the attention. She's such a little ho. #sopHOny Lolllll.

Chapter One

SOPHIE

June 9, 2022

"I love that you married Seb."

Ryan stretches out his legs as far as they'll go and sighs.

"Seriously, Soph. These seats are amazing. I mean look at the leg room. Look at it! My legs are fully extended and my feet barely touch the seat in front of me. And the seats are cushioned. Cushioned!"

"Babe," my best friend, Maisie, taps her husband's leg. "I'm sure you meant to say you love that Sophie married Seb because he's such a good guy."

Ryan sits back up quickly. "Oh yeah, Soph. That too. Seb's awesome. Way more awesome than these seats."

"Ry, it's fine. You can love Seb and the seats at the same time. I do. Well at least I used to—"

"What? You don't love Seb anymore?" Ryan whispers as he leans over Maisie's body to get closer to me.

"The seats, babe." Maisie pushes him back. "She doesn't love the seats anymore."

"Oh," he says, stretching out again. "Why? They're the best seats in the stadium—right by the dugout and like ten feet from the field. I could almost touch the players."

"The seats are fine." I lean over Maisie and whisper to him. "It's just that people have started recognizing me since that miamibballbabe bitch started posting pictures of me on *Twitter*. It's weird. I just want to watch the games, but people are always trying to take pictures of me—or worse *with* me. I hate it."

"Do you two want to sit by each other?" Maisie pushes me back and slides her arm around my shoulders. "Soph, you know how passionate Seb's fans are. They think getting close to you will make them closer to him somehow."

"I know," I say, laying my head on her shoulder. "Most of them are cool, but it's still weird. Seb's the famous one. I don't want to be famous. I don't want people to notice me."

"Is that why you've started dressing like the Unabomber at games?" Maisie flips up the bill of my baseball cap. "I can barely see one square inch of your face."

I shove her hand away and pull the cap back down. "It's good sun protection. That's all. Pay attention. Seb's coming up."

As if on cue, Seb walks out of the dugout toward the on-deck circle. I've seen him do this hundreds of times now, but I still get stupid turned on when I see how good his butt looks in the uniform. He takes a few practice swings, then turns around and smiles at me. He does that every time—every single time—and it still makes my heart skip a few beats. I blow him a kiss.

"You've been married almost a year," Maisie says, nudging me. "I thought your mutual obsession with each other would have faded a little by now."

"Nope. I think I'm even more obsessed with him now."

"Me too," Ryan coos as he starts fanning himself.

"Shut up, weirdo." I reach across Maisie to slug his shoulder.

"Honestly," Maisie says, "I think Ryan will divorce me and try to marry Seb if you ever break it off."

"He'll need to get in line," Paige chimes in from my other side. She's dating Seb's teammate, Manny.

"What?" Maisie looks over at her. "I thought things were going well with you and Manny."

"They are. Really well. I'm not talking about me," she says, patting my leg. "Seriously, Soph, I don't know how you handle it. Every available woman in America wants to be with Seb. Frankly, most of the unavailable ones too."

Maisie scowls over at Paige. "But he only wants to be with Sophie."

"I know. I know," Paige says, holding up her hand. "I'm just saying I'm glad Manny isn't as famous as Seb. I don't think I could take the extra attention. Your friend Raine told me she feels the same way. She can't wait for Alex to retire so she doesn't have to deal with the fan love quite as much, and she's not even at most of the games. You go to all of Seb's games, right? Even the road games?"

Seb heads toward home plate. The intro to "Especially in Michigan" by the Red Hot Chili Peppers blares through the stadium sound system. The team plays it before Seb bats to honor his home state.

"Yeah, I've been to almost all of the games this season," I say as I watch him dig in at the plate. "I like watching him play in person, but I'm not sure how much longer I can do it. I think I'm starting to be a distraction."

"You are not!" Maisie grabs my hand. "Seb loves having you at the games. He would be way more distracted if you weren't here."

"I'm not talking about him," I say, nodding my head backward as a man yells my name again. He's been yelling at me most of the game. "You know how it is now. Someone's always trying to get my attention. It's distracting for the fans who sit in this section, including the other wives and girlfriends."

"She's not wrong," our centerfielder's wife, Casey, says from behind us.

Maisie spins around. "Keep your opinions to yourself, Casey. You're jealous that you don't get this kind of attention."

"Mae, stop," I say, taking her chin and pointing it back toward the field. "Casey and I have made our peace since the St. John drama. Leave it alone."

Casey pats my shoulder. "I'm not coming at you, Sophie. You're one of us now, but really, you're getting as famous as our husbands. Everywhere we go, someone's trying to take your picture or get your autograph."

"Like I said—jealous." Maisie turns back around to face her. "Are you still in contact with Caroline? Is she the one who's trolling Sophie on *Twitter*? She's always had a really creepy obsession with her. Does she still blame Sophie for Manny divorcing her?"

"I don't know who she blames for what," Casey says. "I don't talk to her anymore. It was affecting my marriage so I stopped. Paige, does Manny still hear from her?"

"I have no idea. We don't waste our time talking about Caroline. She moved back to Orlando. Out of sight, out of mind."

"That's for the best," I say, smiling at Paige. "You're so good for Manny. He deserves someone like you."

"We're really happy," she says. "I told him if we ever have kids, we have to name the first one after you to thank you for setting us up."

"Lord help us," Casey says. "Another Sophie in the world."

"Sophie! Sophie! Turn around!" The guy's voice is getting louder and more insistent.

"God," Casey says, "it's so annoying."

"For no one more than me," I say, trying to concentrate on Seb as he fouls off another pitch. "I hate every second of the attention—here, on social media, at the grocery store. I hate it all."

"Speaking of social media," Paige says, "my mom said she tried to follow you on *Twitter*, but your account is private. Since when?"

"Since spring training. That's when miamibballbabe really started coming after me. I blocked her and made all of my social accounts private. She has like fifty thousand followers. I couldn't block them all. They're like weeds."

Maisie growls. "It's stupid that you can't have social media because people don't have lives. I swear if I ever find out who she is I'm going to bitch slap her into oblivion."

"You and me both, sister. I'm thinking about just deleting my accounts. I never post anymore. The comments are crazy. And I don't want anyone to know what Seb and I are doing anyway."

"He still posts though," Paige says. "I follow him."

"No," I say, laughing. "He doesn't post at all. That's his social media coordinator from the agency. She takes care of everything. I'm not even sure he looks at social media except to see what people are saying about me. I had to ask him to stop sharing the hateful posts with me. Like Paige said, 'out of sight, out of mind.'"

Seb fouls off another pitch. He's been working a full count forever. I can tell the pitcher's getting frustrated. My husband is stubborn. He's not an easy out.

"Way to hang in there, Seb!" some guy to the left of us yells. "This next pitch is all you."

"Do you think he hears any of that on the field?" Maisie asks. "The coaching tips and stuff?"

"He says no, although he can tell me word for word what I yell out to him, so maybe he has selective hearing."

The pitcher steps off the mound and starts muttering into his glove. The catcher calls a timeout and walks out to him. The third baseman joins them.

"Hey." I look up to see a strange man pointing at me from the aisle. He's wearing Seb's jersey. "Aren't you Seb Miller's wife? I've been yelling at you."

"Uh, I'm just trying to watch the game," I say, trying to hide behind Paige as I sink into my seat.

"Yeah, we all are," Maisie says, motioning around him to home plate. "You're in the way."

"It's a timeout," the guys says, spilling his beer as he tries to take a drink. He's obviously had a few too many already. "You're not missing anything. Sophie, can I get a picture with you?"

Paige motions to the usher assigned to our section.

"It's one quick picture," the man says, looking up at the usher who's now walking toward him. "It will take two seconds."

I try to keep my tone civil. "I don't really like pictures."

"What? Everyone likes pictures." He points to his jersey as the stadium usher tries to get him to move on. "Come on, I'm Seb's biggest fan. Quit being such a diva."

"Hey, man," Ryan says, "the game's starting again. Why don't you find your seat?"

I see Seb take a called third strike right before the guy grabs my arm and pulls me into the aisle. He puts his arm around me—his beer sloshing all over my shorts—then holds up his phone to take a selfie of us.

"Smile," he slurs as his hand slides down my body.

"Stop it!" I scream, elbowing him in the side.

As soon as I yell, I regret it. I know Seb probably heard me. I try to turn around to wave him off but the guy tightens his arm around me.

"Get off me!" I yell as loud as I can. This time I don't care who hears me. I've had enough of this bullshit.

Chapter Two

SEB

June 9, 2022

"Seriously, Jim?" I look at the home plate umpire as he punches me out on a called third strike. "That one almost hit the dirt. Remember what they taught you in ump school? Strikes are between the knees and the shoulders. Do you need help finding my knees? They're right here."

"Move it along, Seb," he says, waving his arm toward the dugout, "unless you want to watch the rest of the game from the clubhouse."

I look at him one more time and shake my head before I start walking away. As I'm headed back to the dugout—grumbling to myself—I hear Sophie's voice.

"Stop it!"

I jerk my head up and look to where she sits during the games. She's standing in the aisle. Some guy has his arm around her with his hand on her butt. She's trying to push him away.

"Get off me!"

Our friends Ryan and Maisie jump out of their seats and try to pull Sophie away from him. He pulls back. I drop my bat, throw my helmet off, and charge toward the stands.

"Everything I read about you is true," the guy says as I close in on the wall separating the field from the seats. "You're a bitch."

As I vault over the wall, I see Joe, the team's head of security, sprinting out of the dugout. I figure I have about twenty seconds to kill this guy before Joe pulls me off him.

"Seb!" The guy's face lights up with excitement when he sees me, then drops into panic as my hand crashes into his face.

"Seb!" Sophie says, trying to push me back. "Seb! Stop! I'm fine."

The guy's sprawled out on the stairs. I take another step toward him as he tries to crab walk away from me. Just as I'm bending over to punch him again, Joe, his right-hand man, Max, and a handful of Miami police officers grab me.

Joe puts his finger in my face as the cops circle around me. "Seb, get back on the field. Now."

"That asshole was assaulting my wife. I'm not going anywhere."

"I wasn't assaulting her!" The guy screeches as a cop pulls him up.

"Yes, you were!" Paige, my teammate's girlfriend, points at him. "You grabbed her butt, you little pervert."

"Enough!" one of the cops barks. She turns to me. "Seb, get back on the field. We'll take care of this guy."

"I'm not leaving without my wife," I say, wrapping my

arms around Sophie. "Come on, Soph. You can leave through the dugout."

"Absolutely not," Joe says, trying to separate us. "She's not coming on the field. You've caused enough of a spectacle already. Max will get Sophie into the offices."

"Seb, I'm fine," Sophie says, her voice shaking a little. She puts her hands on my chest and smiles up at me. Her eyes are glassy and her lips are starting to tremble. "I just want this to be over, okay? Please get back to the game."

"I don't care about the game." I pull her tighter to me. "You're way more important."

"I'm fine." She circles her arms around my waist. "I promise. Go back to the field. I don't want any more attention. I just want to go home."

"I've got her, Seb. Go," Max says, nodding toward the field. "Trust me. No one else is going to touch her."

I consider my options for a second, then nod. "No one gets near her, Max. Ryan, Mae, will you go with her? Take her home. I'll be there as soon as I can."

"We're on it, Seb," Ryan says. "I'll text you when we're out of here."

Maisie puts her arm tightly around Sophie's shoulders as they start walking up the stadium stairs. Ryan is glued to her other side with Max following them.

I look back at the assaulter whose nose is now bleeding.

"Don't touch my wife again," I say, taking a step toward him. "And never wear my jersey again."

Joe grabs my arm. "Now, Seb. Move or I'm going to move you."

I look at the guy for another second, then turn around and walk back down to the field. Jim's waiting for me.

"Seb," he says as I climb back over the wall, "you know I have to eject you for leaving the field of play."

"Yeah," I say, nodding. "I'm leaving."

I glance back up to see if Sophie has made it to safety. Just as I head into the dugout, her blonde ponytail disappears behind the doors that lead to the private offices.

"What the hell was that?" Our manager, Bud, has his hands in the air like he's signaling a touchdown. "You know we're in a playoff run, right?"

I ignore him and start walking up the tunnel to the clubhouse. He follows me.

"I mean, you're an asshole on your best day, but maybe think about the rest of us before you jump into the stands and punch one of our fans."

"He grabbed Sophie," I say without turning around. "No one gets away with that."

"I'm sure he's not the first guy to grab her—"

He stops dead in his tracks when I spin around. Joe steps between us.

"Seb," Bud says, taking a few quick steps away from me, "I'm just saying, you can't react like that. You're out of this game, and you're probably going to be suspended for a few more games, not to mention the hefty fine that's headed your way. We need you down the stretch. You have to keep your head on the field during the games. If Sophie's becoming a distraction, maybe she doesn't need to come to the games anymore."

"Sophie's not a fucking distraction," I say, pushing Joe out of the way. "The guy who grabbed her ass is the problem—not her."

Bud takes a few more steps back. "We can talk about

this later. I have a game to manage. Don't leave the stadium before the game's over. You need to be here for your teammates. Not to mention, the media's going to want to talk about this bullshit. Ken, do you think you can come up with something for Seb to say? Maybe that he went temporarily insane after he got called out on that bullshit pitch."

I turn around to see our PR guy, Ken, standing right behind me. "I'll work on it. Come on, Seb. Officially, you have to be in the clubhouse when you get kicked out of a game. No lurking in the tunnels."

I start back up the tunnel—Ken and Joe following closely behind.

"Will you find Sophie for me, Joe?"

"I checked on her on the way down here from the press box," Ken says from behind me. "She was already leaving the stadium."

"Was she okay?"

"Uh," he says, blocking me from a few television cameras that are shoved in my face as we emerge from the tunnel. "Not now, guys. Seb will talk after the game."

A few reporters yell questions at me. I walk by without looking over at them.

Our clubhouse guard, Chick, daps me up and whispers, "Glad you got a piece of him, Seb."

"Not helpful, Chick," Ken says, pointing at him. Chick shrugs.

"Ken, you didn't answer my question. Is Sophie okay?"

"She isn't okay," he says, looking at his phone as it beeps again. "She was crying. Max said people were yelling crap at her as she left the stands—like it was her fault you got ejected."

"It wasn't her fault!"

Ken looks up from his phone. "Damn, Seb. Just the messenger. I know it wasn't her fault. I need to get back to the press box. You have to stay and face the scrum after the game."

"I know," I say, sitting on the chair in front of my locker. "I'm staying, but I won't talk about Sophie. I don't talk to the media about my family."

"You don't have to," Ken says, backing toward the door. "I'll call on some friendlies and only take three or four questions. You know I've got you."

I watch him leave, then turn back to Joe. "How many games do you think I'll get?"

"More than one, less than five," he says. "You're Seb Miller so the league's going to give you a break, but you know they have to suspend you. You can't be doing shit like that."

"I know," I say, looking at the ceiling, "but how would you feel if that were Darcy? Some guy grabbing her ass. Tell me you wouldn't kill him."

"Oh, he would definitely lose a hand at least, but I'm not Seb Miller. No one cares what I do."

"So because I'm famous I can't protect my wife?" I throw my towel across the room. "I mean, I've been pretty tolerant so far. People yell at her. They post horrible stuff about her on social media. She didn't sign up for this. I've tried to let it roll off, but touching her is different. I'm not going to let her get assaulted."

He sits down in the chair next to me. "Sophie's tough. She can handle it."

"I know she's tough. She handles all of this way better

than I do, but everyone has a breaking point. I can tell it's starting to get to her. She says it's not, but I know it is. And all of this because she married me. I just want to make her happy. Every day. And instead, my fame is bringing this crap down on her."

"You make her happy, Seb." He puts his hand on my shoulder. "You're the happiest couple I know. She's not going anywhere. You'll get through this. In a couple years, you'll be retired and bringing up your kids. You both will forget all about this."

"It can't come soon enough for me." I look in my locker for my phone. "Damn. I left my phone in my office. I want to call her. I'll be right back."

He jumps up. "Sit your ass down. You're not leaving this clubhouse. You know the vultures are circling right outside the door. I'll get your stuff. Get in the shower. I'll be back in a few minutes."

Joe walks to the door and turns around. "Seb, I'm telling Chick to tackle you if you try to leave. He's a hundred years old and will break every bone in his body if he tries, but he'll try. It's on you if he ends up in traction."

"Go," I say, kicking off my cleats. "I'll be here when you get back. Tell Chick he's safe for now."

Twitter @miamibballbabe
(June 9, 2022)

A fan tried to get a picture with #sopHOny during the game tonight. She FREAKED! Settle down, Princess. He just wanted a picture. @realsebmiller went into the stands to defend her dramatic ass and was ejected. She's such a distraction. I want her to go away!

Chapter Three

SOPHIE

October 29, 2022

**Twitter @miamibballbabe
(October 29, 2022)**
The World Series starts tomorrow! The players are staying in a hotel before home games. I'm glad @realsebmiller is getting away from #sopHOny. I'll kill her if she tries to distract him from bringing us home the championship. No drama. Just baseball.

"Seb! Stop. Joe will be here in fifteen minutes."

"Thirty," Seb says as he backs me up against the kitchen island. "We have plenty of time."

I grab his hands as they start pulling up my dress. "You know he's always at least fifteen minutes early."

"Okay, he'll be here in fifteen," he says as his face plunges into my neck. "Like I said—plenty of time."

"Stop." My body arches into him like it always does when he gets anywhere near my neck. "You know the neck thing makes me crazy."

"Really?" He starts nibbling. "I had no idea."

"You did too," I say, running my hands down his back. They land on his butt. "And stop flexing. You know how I feel about your butt muscles."

"They like you too," he whispers as he continues to flex underneath my hands. He knows exactly what to do to put me in the mood. Honestly, it doesn't take that much. Just looking at him does it for me most of the time.

I unzip his jeans and pull him out. Hard again. "We already had sex last night *and* this morning."

His hands dart under my dress. "Not even close to our record for a twenty four hour period."

"I swear you have more than two hands." I sigh as I feel my body pass the point of no return. "And you're way hornier than usual."

"Incorrect. I'm always this exact same amount of horny." He lifts me onto the island.

"Not here," I say, trying to get down. "I'm entertaining later."

"We've had sex on every surface of this house including this one. We can clean it."

He continues the neck work as he pulls my legs around his waist. He fingers me a little before he slides inside. I let out an extended moan as he fills me up.

"That's better," he whispers. "I knew you would come around to my way of thinking, eventually."

I wrap my arms around his neck as he starts pumping. I know it will happen like it always does. The tingling starts in my toes and shoots up my legs. Then my entire body starts shaking. It's such an intense sensation that sometimes it's all I can do not to pass out.

The intercom beeps to announce that security has cleared someone through the gate. "Joe Porter," the voice announces.

"Seb." I groan as he starts panting against my neck. "He's here."

"Take your time." He slides his hands under my butt and picks me up. "He's not getting in until I let him in."

He pushes me against the wall. The shelves to the left of my head start shaking. I think something falls off. My head drops to his shoulder as he whispers something to me. I can't hear him. The roar has started in my brain like it does just before I'm about to lose control.

I hear a knock on the door just as my body releases. I bury my mouth against Seb's neck to try to deaden the long series of sounds pouring out of my mouth. He pumps hard a few more times before he erupts inside of me with a loud grunt that rattles around inside my head as I collapse against him.

He pants into my hair for a few seconds, then whispers, "You had perfect timing, as usual."

"I'm not sure I should get much credit for the timing." I shiver as the sensations continue to tingle through my body. "You know I pretty much lose control once you're inside."

"Really?" He wraps me up tighter. "I had no idea."

"You're such a liar. I really horny liar," I say, laughing as I rub my head against his chest to try to get it to stop spinning. "Joe's waiting."

"He can wait." He kisses the top of my head as he starts rubbing my back. "You need your recovery time."

"Since it usually takes me about an hour to recover from all that, you might as well let him in now."

He presses me more firmly against the wall as his tongue parts my lips. My head starts spinning again as he takes a slow, deep kiss.

"Stop," I say when he finally pulls back. "That doesn't help my recovery."

He brushes his cheek against mine. "I'm going to miss you so much."

"It's only a couple days," I say, running my fingers through his hair.

"It shouldn't be any days. I've played for this team for nine seasons. They've never made us stay in a hotel before home games."

"This is your first World Series. I guess they think it's different."

Another knock at the door. Well, really more like a pounding.

He carries me over to the intercom. "Be there in a minute, Joe."

"Yep," Joe gets out before Seb clicks it off.

He sets me back down on the island and nuzzles his face into my hair as I start to unwind myself from his body. "You're everything to me. I'd quit baseball today if you wanted me to. You know that, right? If this all gets to be too much for you, just tell me and I'm done that second."

"It's not too much. I don't want you to quit." I nod toward the front door. "You need to let him in before he breaks down the door. Go."

He brushes his lips over mine, sighs, and then heads toward the front door.

"What took you so long?" Joe's gruff tone vibrates through the house. "We're already running late."

"Do we really have to do this?" Seb asks as he walks back into the kitchen. "It's bullshit."

"Hey, Soph." Joe follows Seb around the corner. "You ready for this week?"

"Hey, Joe." I glance up at him as I'm picking up the book that fell off the shelf. "Yeah, I think. It's going to be crazy."

Seb pulls me back against him. "It would be less crazy if the team would let us stay with our wives like we're grown-ass men."

"I'll be fine," I say as he circles his arms around me. "Really. Just worry about baseball for the next few weeks."

Joe points toward the front door. "Seb, we need to leave. Drew said everyone had to be in the hotel by two. It's 1:28. With traffic, we'll be lucky to even make it on time at this point."

Seb doesn't move. "I play better when I spend the night before a game with my wife."

"Why are you arguing with me?" Joe throws up his hands. "You know it's not my decision. I'm paid to get you where you need to go safely. And right now, where you need to go is that fucking hotel."

"Babe, you have to go." I take Seb's hand and pull him

toward the foyer. He follows me, dragging his feet. "I'll see you at the party tonight."

"For what? Like twenty minutes?" He picks up his suitcase as Joe opens the front door.

"Babe," I say, squeezing his hand, "it's not like we'd be alone here anyway. Our parents are arriving in the next few hours. And your sister and my brothers come in tomorrow. Our house will be packed."

"I'm here!" Maisie bursts through the front door. Joe grabs her and pushes her against a wall. She screeches. "Jesus, Joe! It's me. Lighten up."

"Have you ever heard of knocking?" Joe releases her slowly. "Don't surprise me. You know I hate that. How did you even get in here? Security didn't call to clear you."

"The door was open. And I'm on the no-ring list. You know how much Sophie hates that intercom going off." Maisie pats his back. "You really need to settle down. I mean, you're hyper most of the time but the World Series is going to kill you."

"Sophie," Joe says, narrowing his eyes, "what did I tell you about the no-ring list? The more people you put on it, the more confusing it gets for the guards. They make more mistakes as the list grows longer. I don't want anyone surprising you—not even your best friend."

"Maisie's the only person I've added," I say, pulling her away from Joe and hugging her to my chest. "But yes, this is a surprise. What are you doing here?"

"What do you mean?" She looks at Seb who's trying to subtly shake his head at her. "Seb asked me to come over and hang with you until his parents get here."

"Seb." I look back at him—my eyebrows raised.

"Really? I don't need a babysitter."

"I'm your husband. I get to be worried." He puts his suitcase back down. "Too many people are talking about you right now. The social media stuff has gotten out of hand. That one bitch said she would kill you—"

"It's a figure of speech," I say. "She didn't mean it literally."

"Joe," Seb says, "has she posted anything since this morning?"

"No. And I agree with Sophie. It's just smack talk. You should be used to it by now."

"I'm used to it for me, not for Sophie." Seb pulls me back over to him. "I'm going to lose it if people don't stop talking about her."

"Babe," I say, rubbing my forehead against his chest. For some reason that usually calms him down. "It's gotten so much better since I deleted my accounts. I don't even look at it unless you show me."

"Seb." Joe points toward the door again. "Now. Let's go."

"Okay." Seb's voice is as tense as his body.

"I'll be fine," I say, looking up at him. "I'll see you tonight."

"I wish you would let me hire a bodyguard—"

"Seb, no. We talked about that. I don't want a stranger following me around." I nod back at Maisie. "She can be my bodyguard."

He grunts. "Well it's better than you being alone. Mae, will you stay until my parents get here?"

"I'm not leaving her side. And who's going to get to her in this house? It's on an island with only one way in."

"No one monitors the bay," Seb says. "They could come off the water."

"Your security system—including on the bay side—is almost better than what they have at the White House," Joe says. "All we're missing is Secret Service agents."

"Okay." Seb takes a deep breath and slowly exhales. "Soph, remember to text me when you leave for the hotel."

"I will. Go. You're playing in your first World Series. I'm so proud of you, baby. Promise me you'll enjoy every minute of it."

He nods and finally smiles. "I promise, but just for you. Come on, Joe. Hurry up. We're late."

"Unbelievable," Joe says as he watches Seb walk out of the door. He turns to me. "I'm going to kill him by the end of this."

"You're a saint, Joe." I pat his shoulder. "Not many people could deal with him when he gets this way."

I close the door and turn back to Maisie. "Good Lord. I didn't think Seb would leave. He's been pacing around all morning."

"He's worried about you." She takes my hand and pulls me into the kitchen. "I didn't think he would recover after that guy grabbed your ass at the game in June."

"The only reason he recovered is because I agreed to sit in the owner's suite for games now. There's no way he could concentrate if I was still sitting in the stands." I take a bottle of wine out of the refrigerator. "Too early?"

"Never. What time are you leaving for the sponsor party tonight?"

"I need to get there around six to help Dottie prep her speech."

"I'm still confused." Her forehead crinkles up. "Are you officially working for the team again?"

"No, but this is Dottie's first year owning a team and she's already hosting a World Series." I give the island an extra wipe down before I place a charcuterie plate between us. "She's freaked out. I told her I would help her through the postseason."

"Dot seems like a tough old broad. I can't believe she's letting this rattle her."

"She is tough, but I think since her husband died, she feels more exposed. You know? She doesn't have that backup."

Maisie grabs a piece of cheese. "Well, I hope she doesn't die for a while. Seb seems to like her."

"*Loves* her. The entire team does. She's so sweet. She's like a grandma to them. I was going to tell her no when she asked me to help out in the postseason. Seb talked me into it just so Dottie would feel more secure."

She sticks out her tongue as she takes a bite of the Limburger. "This tastes like butt."

"It's Seb's dad's favorite," I say, handing her a napkin. "It smells awful."

She spits out the cheese and rinses the bad taste out with a swig of wine. "We're sitting in a suite for the games, right?"

"Yeah, it's so much easier than buying individual tickets for everyone. With our family and friends, we have twenty-seven people, and that's after cutting the list several times."

She drains her wine glass. "Don't players get free tickets?"

"Only six for postseason games. Seb's are right behind the dugout. He's giving them to his parents, his high school coach, and his Michigan friends. They've been with him from day one. He said they deserve those seats more than anyone."

She smiles. "That Seb is just a good guy."

"Yes, he is. He's the best guy."

Maisie jumps when the security booth intercom beeps. "God, I don't know how you've gotten used to that thing. It's so loud."

I shrug as I answer it. "Hey, this is Sophie."

"Hey, Mrs. Miller. It's Steve. Seb's parents are at the gate. They're on the permanent clear list, but they wanted me to call you before they came in."

"Thanks, Steve. Send them up."

"Done. They're headed your way."

"You drink way too slowly," Maisie says as she grabs my wine, drains it, and then puts our empty wine glasses into the dishwasher. "Hide the evidence. I don't want your in-laws to think you're a drunk."

"They both drink way more than I do. His mom always thinks I'm pregnant when I turn down alcohol. She can't accept that I'm just a lightweight."

"She hopes you're pregnant," Maisie says, rolling her eyes. "I've been married longer than you, but I don't have near the amount of pressure you have to reproduce."

"Right? And it's from all sides. Everyone wants the heir to the great Seb Miller to be born."

"Except for the great Seb Miller," she says as we head toward the front door. "Does he still want to wait?"

"Yeah, and I get it. He wants to spend as much time as possible with our kids. He can't do that while he's playing. I'm ready now, but we're waiting. We're trying to time it with his retirement in a few years."

I open the door just in time to see the Millers turning into our driveway. Seb's mom, Adie, has her arm out the window—waving at us.

"I'm leaving," Maisie says, hugging me. "I can't take too much of Adie's enthusiasm until I've had more to drink. I'll see you at the game tomorrow night."

Chapter Four

SEB

October 29, 2022

"Damn. Tell me again how this is supposed to help us focus better than staying at our own quiet homes."

When we arrive at the hotel, the Miami police have the street blocked off with concrete barricades. Their armored vehicles—with lights flashing—are surrounding the perimeter, and there are at least ten cops patrolling the only entrance into the fortress.

"I don't know, man," Joe says, rolling down his window as three cops approach our car. "Let's just make the best of it."

"Was the hotel Drew's idea?"

"I don't know whose idea it was. And it doesn't matter." Joe points toward the hotel. "Drew's the general manager. If he says you have to stay in that hotel the night before the games, then that's where you're staying."

"This street's closed," one of the cops says. "Turn around."

Joe points at me. "I have Seb Miller."

"Oh. Hey, Seb," the cop says, leaning into Joe's window. "I thought all of the players were already inside."

"What's up, man?" I nod at him. "Kind of a circus down here. You expecting the president or something?"

"Yep, and he just arrived. Bring us home that championship, Mr. President."

"I'll try my best," I say as Joe rolls up the window. "No pressure or anything."

Joe laughs. "You seem to think since this isn't a big deal for you that everyone feels that way. This town is hungry for a championship."

"It's a big deal. I've wanted to play in the World Series since I first picked up a baseball." I wave at the other cops as they remove the ropes across the parking lot entrance. "It's just not the biggest deal. You know how I work. My family, especially Sophie, is way more important to me than any baseball game."

"As they should be," Joe says, pulling into the parking spot with my name on it, "but I also know when you get on the field, you'll bring your best stuff like you always do."

"Well, yeah. You know how much I hate losing. Like I really fucking hate it."

"Yep. That's what makes you a great player."

Joe waves to Drew, who's bounding down the steps from the hotel lobby. He's taking them two at a time—his short, little legs just barely landing each leap.

"You're late," Drew yells before I even get my door open.

"We left an hour ago," Joe says, patting Drew's back. "Almost an hour and a half. Have you been out lately? South Beach is crazy. Everyone's so excited about this series. Good work, man."

Drew's face turns a little less sour. He loves being complimented. "Yeah, it does seem like it's going to be epic. Just get inside before everyone loses their minds."

Drew heads back up the steps—taking them one by one this time. When he gets to the top, he turns around and surveys the pandemonium. He looks like Scar in *The Lion King* when he called forth the army of hyenas.

"He's such a tool," I say, turning to Joe. "Please teach me how to lie to his face like that. It's a thing of beauty how you turn it on that easily."

"You would never pull it off, man." He shoos a porter away who's trying to grab my bag. "You have absolutely no filter. Or patience. Or really anything that's required for successful diplomacy."

"Bryan, Mr. Miller doesn't want help with his bags." The hotel owner, Roman, points the porter away from us and shakes my outstretched hand. "What's up, Seb?"

"Hey, Roman. It's good of you to shut down your entire hotel for the team."

His deep laugh rumbles through the lobby. "Good, my ass. The team's paying twice my rate for this time of the year."

"Glad to hear it," I say, nodding. "Always look out for number one."

My teammate Alex walks across the lobby to join us. "Can you believe this zoo? How are we supposed to get more rest here than at our houses?"

"Right? That's what I told Joe. It's crazy," I say, watching the hotel staff fly around as Drew barks orders at them. "Has Raine gotten in yet?"

"Yeah," Alex says. "She got here a few days ago so we could spend some time together before the games started. She's at the pool now. I'm headed up there."

"What?" I spin around to Joe. "Is she staying here? I thought no girlfriends or wives allowed."

"Man, keep it down," Alex says, shoving my shoulder. "She snuck in with Butch and the California crew. None of the front office staff really know who she is. We've done a good job of keeping everyone out of our business."

"You have to get Sophie in here," I say to Joe. "If Raine—"

"Stop," Joe says. "No one knows who Raine is. Sophie can't even leave the house without being recognized. It's not the same. Although Raine shouldn't be staying here either."

"Don't give me up, Joe," Alex says. "You either, Seb."

"No one will give you up. Right, Joe?"

Joe scowls at me but finally nods. "Fine, but if I get one complaint, Raine's out."

"Do you want to come with me to the pool, Seb?" Alex nods toward the elevators. "The Cali group is up there."

"Later. I want to call Sophie. Who all made it in?"

"Mason, Millie, Nash, Elle, Sam, Butch, and Kit," Alex says. "Hey, did you know Kit was pregnant? Raine just texted me. Butch is going to be a dad."

"God, help us all," I say, smiling. "No, that's great, man. Tell them congrats for me. I'll catch up with everyone later."

After Alex walks away, I turn to Roman. "Is the California group staying here too? I thought the team bought out the entire hotel."

"Sophie asked me to let them stay here, and you know I can't say no to her," Roman says. "Besides, the team's not using all of the rooms. Drew's so pissed. He went up to the pool and yelled at them. I thought Butch was about to take his head off."

"I'd pay to see that," I say. "Drew needs to be taken down a few notches. He's become a huge pain in the ass."

"He threatened to move the team to another hotel if I didn't kick Butch and his crew out," Roman says, chuckling. "I told him to have at it. The team paid everything upfront. He can leave any time he wants. I'm still getting paid."

"If he tries to move us to another hotel, I'm going home. Do you have my room key? I want some privacy to call Sophie."

Roman hands us our keys. "Seb, you're in the penthouse suite. Only you and Joe have a key to unlock that floor. Joe, your room is a floor below him, but there are two beds in the suite if you want to stay closer to Seb. Let me know if you need anything."

Joe nods at him as he walks away. "Appreciate it, Roman."

"You're not staying in the suite. Don't get any ideas."

"Believe me, no one except Sophie wants to sleep that closely to you." Joe points me toward the elevator. "So, wait, Butch is in town? The Butch that I met at your wedding?"

"Yeah. I told you we bought that town in California.

Remember? Blitzen Bay. Butch and all of our co-owners are here. They're becoming really good friends. Great group of people."

"Why didn't you tell me Butch was coming in?"

"Why would I?" I punch the penthouse button on the elevator. "I don't remember you guys being all that tight."

Joe looks at me like I'm about half stupid. "Seb, he's a former Navy SEAL."

"I know what he is. So is his buddy Mason who's also on this trip. And their friend Nash is here too. He's former Delta Force."

"Damn," he says, letting out an extended sigh, "you really are as dumb as you look sometimes."

"I've been telling you that for years."

He backhands my arm. "You're worried about Sophie's security when you have three former special forces operators at your disposal. And Sophie knows them, so she won't feel weird about them following her around."

"Son of a bitch. That didn't even cross my mind. Do you think they would help out?"

"You're treating them to World Series tickets." Joe starts to sweep the suite to make sure no one's hiding in the closets. It's happened twice before. "I'm sure they would like to pay you back in some way."

"No, I don't want them to pay me back. They're our friends now and they're really cool. It's been so long since I've felt like I could chill with a group of people without them wanting something from me. They don't have to pay me back for anything."

"I understand that," Joe says, starting the second round

of his sweep to make sure the doors and windows are locked. "But I worked with a lot of special forces guys when I was in the Marines. Believe me, these guys would have done that job into their nineties if their bodies would have held up. I'm guessing having a chance to use those skills again would be a treat for them."

"I think Butch and Mason are still active in some way." I plop down on one of the couches in the sitting area. "They're both retired from the Navy, but they have something going on with Raine and Mason's wife, Millie. They're really vague about it. I think Alex knows what they do, but he blows me off when I ask."

Joe looks around like someone else is in the room and then whispers, "I think Raine is CIA. We're probably better off not knowing exactly what they do. And it doesn't matter for our purposes over the next few weeks. If these guys are around, we need to use them. And if they're your friends now, they won't want anything to happen to Sophie. It's the perfect solution."

I consider it for a second, and then nod. "I think it is. I wouldn't worry if Sophie had one of those guys next to her when I'm not around. Let's talk to them."

"Call Sophie and see what she thinks. I'll bring them up here for a meeting." Joe smiles for the first time in days. "And remember to lock the balcony door every time you use it. We're only on the seventh floor. People can and will try to scale the building to get to you. You remember that guy in Houston who climbed thirteen floors to get Cole's autograph?"

"People are crazy, man. I wouldn't walk across the

room to get Cole's autograph." I open the terrace doors and gesture to the police who are still circling the hotel. "I doubt anyone's going to get past that."

"They can and they will. Lock the door every time." He points at my phone as he leaves. "Call Sophie."

I wait for him to leave, then call her. She answers on the first ring. "Hey."

"Hey," I say, laughing. "I'm guessing by the tone of your voice that my parents got in."

"They got here about an hour ago," she says, making her voice more cheerful. "We're sitting by the pool having a glass of wine. Say hi to your son."

"Hi, honey!" Mom yells. Dad grumbles something in the background.

"Did Mom give you the disappointed face when you poured yourself a glass of wine?"

"Yup."

"Well it's better to let her know immediately that you're not pregnant. At least she won't drop hints the entire trip like she did last time. I'm sure that's the first thing she'll talk to your mom about when your parents get in—if she hasn't already texted her."

"Yup."

"Soph, go inside so you can say more than one word to me at a time."

"I'll be back in a second. Jack, I'll bring out the rest of the Limburger," she says. I hear the patio doors close. "Okay, I'm inside."

"I'm sorry you have to deal with our families alone. I'm beginning to think being at the hotel might be better than being there."

"It's fine," she says. "You know I love your parents. It's just going to be a lot with everyone here at one time. How's the hotel?"

"Crazy. It's a shit show, but I'm in my room now. It's quiet. I just want you to be here with me."

"I want to be there too," she coos. "I already miss you."

I stretch out on the couch and look at the ceiling. It's painted a metallic gold color. I feel like I'm staring at the sun. "I miss you too. I can't wait to see you tonight. And you might want to pack an overnight bag."

"What? I thought I couldn't stay there."

"Joe had a good idea. He thought Butch, Mason, and Nash could be your security during the series. And if that's the case, you'll need to stay here, so they can keep an eye on you."

"Oh, babe, I want to stay down there, but we don't want to ask our friends to work while they're here."

"It wouldn't really be work. I mean their kind of work anyway. This would be easy for them. I know they'll want to help us out. Joe's bringing them up to my room to talk about it. In fact, I hear them in the hallway right now. Will you start packing, just in case? I'll call you after they leave."

"Okay," she says, hesitating, "but don't make them feel like they have to do this. I'll be fine."

"I promise I won't. I'll call you back in a few."

Twitter @**miamibballbabe**
(October 29, 2022)

The eagle has landed. @realsebmiller is at the hotel. And drumroll please… #sopHOny is NOT with him. It's a miracle. Let's play ball!

Chapter Five

SOPHIE

October 29, 2022

Just as I hang up with Seb, the security gate intercom rings again. It's Seb's childhood friends: Stone, Paul, and Ricky.

"I heard the alarm," Seb's dad says as he walks in from the patio. "Everything okay?"

"Yeah, it's the Michigan boys."

"Did you clear them?" His face drops from a smile into a scowl. He looks just like Seb when he does that. "Seb said he wanted the house to be family only."

"Yeah, I cleared them," I say, grabbing more snacks out of the refrigerator. "You know they would never let Seb hear the end of it if I didn't let them in. They still think I'm a guest in this house, especially Ricky."

Jack's scowl deepens. "Ricky's a pain in the ass. He has been his entire life. Don't let him bother you, and if he does, tell me and I'll put an end to it. This is your house as much as Seb's now."

"Thank you, Jack. You and Adie are always so sweet to me."

"We love you like one of our own." He grabs a few of the chocolate chip cookies I made yesterday. "Don't tell Adie. I'm supposed to watching my sugar."

"Our secret."

He takes a big bite and sighs. "Heaven. And don't let Adie bother you with her less-than-subtle hints about babies."

"It's fine," I say, laughing. "She's not as bad as my mom."

"I think it's a tie, and together, they're a nightmare. I'll run interference for you this week."

"Appreciate it."

I hear the front door keypad beep its first warning that the code was entered incorrectly. It only gives two warnings and then all hell breaks loose. I run to the door and fling it open. Ricky's tapping on the keypad.

"Stop!" I push him back and hit the abort key three times to prevent the meltdown. "We changed the code."

"Seb didn't give us a new code," he says, walking by me into the house. "Are you sure he changed it?"

"Yes, I'm sure *we* changed it."

"What's the new code?" Ricky pulls out his phone and gets ready to type it in. He glares at me when I don't say anything.

Jack walks over. "You don't need the new code, Rick, because you're not staying here."

Stone hurries toward us. "We definitely don't need the code. Hey, Soph. Hey, Mr. Miller. We just got in and stopped by to say hi before we check in at the hotel. We can leave if you have too much going on."

"Not at all," I say, accepting a hug from him. "I'm glad you made it in safely. We're hanging out by the pool. Join us. Hey, Paul."

"Hey, Sophie," Paul says, hugging me. "Hey, Mr. Miller. We won't stay long. I know it's going to be crazy the next few weeks."

"Where are the ladies?" I reset the security system and close the door.

"Shopping," Stone says. "They wanted to give us alone time with Seb. Is he still here?"

"No," I say, "he left for the hotel a few hours ago."

When we walk into the kitchen, Ricky's already in the refrigerator helping himself to a beer. He pops off the cap and heads toward the patio door.

"Hey, Rick. You don't just walk into someone's house and help yourself." Jack walks over and stands in front of him. "I know your parents didn't raise you to be this much of an asshole."

"Come on, Jack," Ricky says, rolling his eyes. "You know how many years we've been coming to this house. It's like our second home."

"Not anymore—"

"Jack, it's fine." I grab two more beers and hand them to Stone and Paul. "Will you guys see if Adie needs a refill? And take these snacks out."

"We're on it," Stone says as he and Paul grab everything and follow Ricky outside.

"I'll fix Ricky," Jack says. "Seb said he gave him one

last warning at the wedding about playing nicely with you. It doesn't seem like he's taking it seriously."

"Don't say anything to him. It's not worth it. If Seb finds out he's still being an asshole, he'll go ballistic and cut him off. I don't want that. They've known each other since they were five, right?"

Jack takes a deep breath and blows it out. "I won't tell Seb if you don't want me to, but I won't let anyone disrespect my daughter-in-law like that. Rick seems to think he has a free pass because he's been around for a while. Time doesn't have a thing to do with it. You have to earn friendships every day. You have enough going on without having to deal with his petty bullshit."

"Yeah," I say, leaning against the counter. I always feel exhausted the second Ricky walks into a room. "This past year has been a lot. And the World Series has amplified everything."

He pats my shoulder. "I know inheriting Seb's fame is difficult. We've had to deal with a little bit of that too. Seb told me about the stuff people are saying about you on social media."

"I figured. I know he tells you everything."

"I opened an incognito *Twitter* account so I can monitor it myself. Most of it seems like normal fame stuff, but there's that one account—miamibabe—that goes way too far. She's a stalker."

"Her handle is miamibballbabe and yeah, she seems to really hate me." I rub my temples and try to stop the headache that I know is on its way. It's Ricky symptom number two. "I don't read the stuff anymore. Seb's social media manager keeps an eye on it and sends him updates. I asked him not to share it with me."

"That's probably the best thing for your sanity," Jack says, starting in on another cookie. "And Adie doesn't know about any of it. It's better that way. She would be so anxious if she thought someone was threatening you."

"I won't tell her," I say, waving him off as he tries to refill my wine glass. "I really don't think it's that big of a deal."

"Seb does." He tops off his own glass. "He said you didn't want him to hire a bodyguard. I think you should reconsider."

"I don't want a stranger following me around, but speaking of that, did Seb tell you about our friends from California? The people who are our co-owners of Blitzen Bay."

"Yeah. He said they were a good group."

"They're awesome. Seb loves them. We both do. I'm not sure if he told you that three of them are former military special forces."

"He did. I met that one at your wedding. Butch, I think."

"Butch and his buddy Mason were SEALs and Nash was a Ranger. Anyway, they're in town for the series, so Seb's asking them to have my back while they're here. He's talking to them right now."

The patio door flies open and Adie bursts in. "Will you two please get back out here before I push Ricky into the pool? He's complaining that his girlfriend can't sit next to him at the games."

"I'll take care of that right now," Jack says marching

toward the patio door. He stops and turns back to me. "We can finish our conversation later, but I think that's the perfect solution."

"What's the perfect solution?" Adie pours herself another glass of wine. She grabs a cookie. "Don't let Jack have any of these. His triglycerides are too high."

"Noted. And we were just talking about who's sitting where for the series. It's a crazy puzzle. I feel like I'm doing a seating chart for a wedding."

"You thought you got away from that since you had a small wedding," she says, laughing, "but this might be worse. Every random relative and friend appear out of nowhere when Seb reaches another milestone in his career. His first game in the majors was a nightmare. Everyone wanted a ticket."

"I can imagine. Our phones haven't stopped since he made it to the playoffs."

"These are yummy. Send me the recipe." She grabs another cookie. "Are you sure you don't want one of the box seats for the games? I feel so badly that you're not sitting as close to the action as possible."

"Don't," I say, shaking my head. "Honestly, it's hard for me to sit there now. People try to take pictures of me, and they yell stuff at me. It's impossible to enjoy the game."

Her forehead wrinkles up. "What do they yell at you?"

"Nothing to worry about," I say, hugging her. "You know how passionate his fans are."

She takes my face into her hands. "Maybe it's better that you sit in the suite. I worry about you. Madison sends me the mean tweets people post about you."

Leave it on the Field

"She shouldn't be doing that," I say as she leans her forehead against mine.

"You know how my daughter is. She's the champion of anyone who's being mistreated. She wants to find the meanies and beat them up."

"I'd like to see that." I try to pull back from her but she pulls me into a hug. "Adie, we should go outside before Jack and Ricky get into it too badly."

"Okay," she whispers, "but promise me you'll take care of yourself. If anything happened to you, Seb wouldn't be able to go on. He just wouldn't survive it. None of us would."

I grab her hand and pull her toward the door. "I promise I'll be careful."

When we walk outside, Stone and Paul are sitting at the table with Jack. Ricky's lying on a lounge chair looking out at the bay. I hear him say my name just before Stone kicks his chair and he stops talking.

"Don't let us interrupt," Adie says, squeaking out a laugh, "unless Ricky's still complaining about his totally free, prime location seat for the World Series. Then we're happy to interrupt."

"I'm not complaining," Ricky says without looking back at us. "I just think our dates should be able to sit with us for the games."

"I didn't know you were even dating, Ricky. Anyone we know?" Adie's voice gets a couple octaves higher when she's trying to keep the peace.

"Yeah," Ricky says, finally looking back. He stares right at me. "Kaitlyn Barr."

Adie takes a sharp breath in and grabs my hand.

"You're dating Katie Barr? Well her last name is Houseman now, right?"

"She's divorced," Ricky says, grinning. "Well in the process of getting a divorce. Anyway, yeah, she's here with me. I know she would like to sit as close as possible to see Seb play. All of our dates would."

Stone grabs Jack's arm as he starts to stand up. "First, Paul and I don't have dates. We have wives. Second, our wives are thrilled to be sitting anywhere in the stadium to watch our friend play in the biggest games of his life."

"Yeah, but," Ricky says, lowering his sunglasses. He's still looking right at me. "Seb's the franchise player. Surely he can get more seats, especially for someone he loves as much as Katie."

Adie squeaks when Jack jumps up and lunges toward Ricky's chair. "Rick, I know you're slow but we've covered this. There are six box seats available. That's it. Seb decided who gets to sit there—me, Adie, you three, and Coach Adler. If you want to give up your seat, we would love to have our daughter sitting with us down by the field."

"Your daughter but not your daughter-in-law?" Ricky nods his head toward me. "What? Is she too good to sit out in the stadium with the fans now?"

"Jesus, Ricky!" I yell. "You complain that your girlfriend doesn't get one of the best seats, and then you complain that I don't want to sit in those very seats because they're not good enough. What the hell? Pick an argument. Your girlfriend and their wives are sitting with me in the suite. We'll have fun. Get over it and try to enjoy yourself or at least try not to ruin the mood for everyone else."

"What she said." Stone kicks Ricky's chair again. "Just chill out, man. Enjoy the moment."

Ricky smiles as he stretches out again. "Oh, I'm going to enjoy everything so much. And Sophie, thank you for letting our dates sit with you. I think you'll like meeting Kaitlyn—or Katie as Seb calls her. I'm sure he's told you about her. They dated most of high school."

"Shut up, Rick," Paul says. "You're so close to the edge. Just shut the fuck up."

"We didn't know he was bringing her, Soph," Stone says. "I swear. Until she boarded the plane with him this morning."

"It's fine. Really. And no, Ricky, Seb's never told me about her. We don't talk much about the past. We live in the present and keep our eyes focused on what's going to be a very happy future." I turn to Jack. "I need to get ready for tonight. I'm leaving you in charge."

Jack nods. "Since I'm in charge now, I think it's time for you three to leave."

"It definitely is," Stone says, jumping up. "Thanks for the hospitality, Sophie."

"Sure," I say, turning quickly toward the house before the frustration tears that are welling up in my eyes burst out.

Adie runs to catch up with me. "I'm calling Seb and telling him to send her home."

"Adie," I say, grabbing her arm, "don't call him. He needs to concentrate on playing. It's not a big deal. Ricky's just messing with me, as usual. Nothing or no one can get between Seb and me. All of this drama fades away when we're alone. Please don't call him."

"Okay." She nods as the guys walk past us into the house. "But I'm telling him everything after the series."

"Will we see you at the party tonight, Adie?" Ricky asks.

"No, we're hanging out with Sophie's parents here tonight," Adie says, glaring at him. "Alone. We'll see you at the game tomorrow night."

"You'll see us tomorrow afternoon," Ricky says, looking back at me. "We're coming over here to use the pool before the game."

"No, you're not," Jack says, pushing him toward the front door. "As long as I'm in charge, you're not setting one foot back in this house."

Chapter Six

SEB

October 29, 2022

When the elevator door opens, Butch saunters into the suite.

"Put me in, Coach," he says, mimicking a home run swing. "Just get me a uniform and a glove. I'm ready to play."

"No one wants to see your old ass trying to play baseball," I say as I walk over to shake his hand.

Nash, Mason, Millie, and Raine follow him into the suite with Joe pulling up the rear.

"Hey, man," Mason says. "You ready to go?"

"I would be more ready if they would let me stay with my wife the night before the game like I'm an adult."

"Yeah." Nash gives me a fist bump. "What's up with that? Sounds more like college than the pros."

"Our general manager is a micro-managing pain in the ass. He thinks this will help us focus."

"Damn," Butch says. "You had your best season ever. If you focus much more, there won't be a record in the books that you don't break."

"This suite is unbelievable," Raine says, spinning around to get a full view. "In fact, this entire hotel is amazing. Roman definitely knows how to do Art Deco. I love the black and gold with splashes of that rose color. It's the perfect combination of masculine and feminine, right?"

Everyone stares at her blankly. She sighs as she walks over to examine the wallpaper more closely.

"I have no idea what she's talking about, but we really appreciate the accommodations," Mason says. "We would like to pay you for the rooms. The front desk guy said we only had to pay for incidentals."

"You can't pay me for the rooms." I motion for them to sit in the living room area. "I didn't pay for any of it. The team bought out the entire hotel."

"Then we should pay the team back," Butch says. "Maybe that will make the little bald man with the wire-rimmed glasses settle down."

"That's our GM," I say. "Roman said he yelled at you. I apologize."

"Doesn't bother me," Butch says, shrugging. "I've been yelled at by bigger and better. I just don't want the little guy to have a stroke. The veins were bulging out of his forehead. I thought they were going to blow. We should probably at least offer to pay."

"Why? I thought you were playing for the team now," I say, laughing. "If that's the case, we owe you a salary, right?"

"You would be lucky to have me. I was king of the hot

corner in high school," Butch says, sitting down. He points to the snacks and drinks the hotel set out on the table.

"Yeah, help yourself," I say. "So you played third base, huh? It all makes sense now. I'm sure you got hit in the head with plenty of line drives."

Butch grabs a handful of pretzels. "Naw, I have quick reflexes. I'm like a ninja."

"A drunk ninja, maybe," I say, pointing at Nash. "If anyone from this group could still play, I'm guessing it's you. Did you play a little college ball?"

Nash shakes his head. "I went right into the Army, but I was a catcher like you all through high school. Well, I mean not like you in skill level, but I was okay. I couldn't even attempt it now. I messed up my knee in service."

"Mason," I say, pushing the ice bucket full of beer over to him, "how about it? You look like you would be a natural first baseman."

"Naw," he says, twisting the top off a bottle. "I was a football guy—quarterback."

"Of course you played quarterback," Butch says, rolling his eyes. "There's no way you could do anything without being the one in charge."

"Okay, are you guys done flexing?" Millie looks around at us. "Maybe we can talk about Sophie now."

"Right to business," Joe says from behind me. "All of this testosterone but no one can tell me she's not the one in charge."

"Smart man," Mason says, nodding at him. "Yeah, what's up with Sophie? Joe told us a little bit on the way up here. Is someone threatening her?"

"No one in particular," Joe says, taking a seat. "Just

some vague threats on social media. More trash talk than anything else, but it's making Seb uneasy."

"It's making me more than uneasy. It's pissing me the fuck off. And it's more than social media. Some guy followed her out of Target a couple weeks ago. She thought he was going to attack her. Turns out he wanted her to get my autograph and send it to him. Everyone knows who she is now. And with the World Series stuff and now this hotel isolation, I can't be there to protect her. I need someone to have her back. She won't let me hire a bodyguard because she doesn't want a stranger following her around, but she said she would be okay with you guys watching her."

"We're here for whatever you need," Mason says. "If you want us to stick close to her for the entire series, we're on it. No one will get to her."

"I appreciate that," I say, hesitating, "but Sophie and I feel a little weird asking you to do this because you're our friends and we want you to have a good time while you're here."

"You don't know us very well yet," Butch says, grabbing another handful of pretzels, "but believe me, protecting people is our idea of a good time. It makes us feel all manly and stuff. It's a done deal. Where is she now?"

"She's back at our house with my parents."

"Well if we're protecting her," Mason says, "either we need to stay there or she needs to stay at the hotel."

"She can stay here. I told her to pack."

Joe holds up his hand. "Seb, I think it might be easier if they stay at your house. Drew will lose his mind if Sophie stays here. No wives or girlfriends. No exceptions."

"Our house is full. Both of our families are staying there. She needs to stay here."

"There's no way Drew will approve it," Joe says, his face tightening. "He's already freaking out about these guys staying here."

"Then we'll have Dottie approve it. Drew works for her."

"Who's Dottie?" Millie asks.

"The team owner," I say. "She's awesome and she loves Sophie. In fact, Sophie's doing some work for her during the series. Technically, Sophie's a team employee again, so she could stay here under that premise."

Joe inhales through his teeth. "You're poking the beast. Drew's already pissed at you for being late."

"What's he going to do? Bench me?" I take a long drink of my beer. "I'll get Dottie to agree to it. She won't want anything to happen to Sophie."

"Okay," Joe says, the lines on his forehead deepening. "But Sophie's not staying in your room. Drew already thinks I give you special treatment. I told you he talked to me about that. I don't want to get fired because you can't go twenty-four hours without seeing Sophie."

"She can stay with me," Raine says. "I have an enormous king bed in my room. Plenty of space. It will be fun. We haven't had a sleepover since we were in grade school."

Joe points at her. "You're not sleeping with Alex either. I know you think you're sneaky, but I'm watching everyone like a hawk. This isn't some spring break movie. It's the World Series. Everyone needs to tighten up."

"Joe," Raine says, "it's cool. I'll make sure Sophie stays in my room all night. We're good."

"Yeah," Mason says, "if we're protecting her, Sophie doesn't need to be roaming the halls at night anyway."

"No one's roaming anywhere," Joe says, pointing around at the group. "But technically, she would be safe here. It's all team employees."

"How do you know the call isn't coming from inside the house?" Millie asks. "Most targeted threats come from someone the person knows."

"Like I said, most of the stuff is pretty vague," Joe says, "but there's one *Twitter* account that gets way too personal. She knows stuff that only a close friend or family member would know."

"What's the username?" Raine asks, pulling out her phone.

"Miamibballbabe," I say. "Stupid-ass name. Stupid-ass woman."

"Uh," Raine says as she starts scrolling through *Twitter*, "it might not be a woman. If this account is getting personal, they would want to stay as cloaked in mystery as possible. It might be a guy trying to throw people off by putting babe in the username. I'll check it out."

"You can't use any work resources for this," Millie says, pointing at Raine.

"I know," Raine says. "I won't need to. I'm guessing this is an amateur. I can figure out who the user is without bringing in the big guns."

"Speaking of resources," Mason says. "It would be nice to have a blacked-out SUV if we're transporting Sophie. Any ideas on where we can get one on short notice?"

"We're good," Butch says, tapping Mason's arm.

"Roman can help us with that and any other resources we need. He has connections."

I take a deep breath and exhale.

"Seb, it's fine," Millie says. "They know what they're doing."

"I know they do. It's just a lot to think about. And Butch, Alex told me Kit's pregnant. Congratulations, by the way. But if anything happened to you—"

"Nothing's going to happen to me or Sophie or anyone," Butch says. "And Kit's fine. We'll take shifts with Sophie. I'll be with Kit half the time and when I'm not, Elle won't leave her side."

"None of us will," Nash says. "In fact, I think you and Mason should cover Sophie. I'll be the constant with everyone else—Kit, Elle, Sam. Everyone's covered. No one gets to our group."

Mason nods. "That makes the most sense. Let's keep this group tight."

"Okay," I say, nodding. "This will make me feel better. Should I tell Sophie to head down here?"

"By herself?" Mason laughs as he stands up. He motions toward the door. Everyone jumps up. "That kind of defeats the purpose. We'll pick her up. Tell Sophie we're headed her way within the hour. Millie will text her when we leave. And get any permissions you need from the team's owner. I don't want to deal with the GM when we get back. And Joe, we're going to need security passes for the stadium."

"I've got you."

When the elevator door closes, I stretch out on the couch and call Dottie.

"Sebastian!" she screams into the phone. She's always too loud. "Are you at the hotel? I'm about ten minutes away. Did I tell you I'm staying there too? Drew's mad. He hates when I'm around. He thinks I'm spying on him."

"Hey, Dottie. No, I didn't know you were staying here, but I'm glad you are. Drew can f-f-f-f, uh, I mean he can get over it."

"Thank you for swallowing that word for me," she says, laughing. "You know how I feel about it."

"It's a bad habit. Sorry."

"Seb, what's wrong? You sound upset. Is everything okay?

"Yeah, I'm fine," I say slowly, "but I need a favor from you."

"Anything. You're like a son to me. Anything you need."

"It's nothing for you to worry about," I say, trying to keep the tension out of my voice. "But Sophie's been getting a lot of unwanted attention on social media and stuff. I'm worried about her being alone while we're locked down in the hotel. Some of my buddies are former military guys. They're staying at this hotel too. They said they would keep an eye on Sophie if she stays at the hotel but Drew probably won't let her."

"What kind of attention?" I've never heard her voice this quiet. "Are people threatening her?"

"It's probably nothing. I don't want you to worry, but it would make me feel better if she stayed here. I thought since she's helping you out and she's kind of a team employee again, you know, maybe we could make it work."

"Oh, it's going to work," she says, her voice back to its

normal decibel level. "We're just pulling up. I'll tell Drew she's staying here to be close to me. He can lump it if he doesn't like it."

"Thanks, Dottie. I really appreciate it. She'll stay in our friend's room so don't let Drew tell you there aren't rooms available."

"I have this handled, Seb. You concentrate on baseball. I'll see you tonight at the party. And to pay me back, promise you'll at least pretend to like the sponsors—if even just for a few minutes."

"I promise," I say, smiling, "but only for you."

Chapter Seven

SOPHIE

October 29, 2022

"Mom! Will you please stop?"

My parents arrived at the house twenty minutes ago. Adie and my mom are hanging out with me in the bedroom that I converted into an enormous walk-in closet. I moved some of the furniture from my old apartment into the room. It's bright and funky and extremely fluffy. It doesn't match the ultra-modern vibe of the house at all, but this room always makes me feel more grounded when things are spinning out of control.

Adie's sprawled out on the bright teal chaise lounge in the corner. She's sipping wine as she watches Mom swarm around me like a gnat.

"But why are you staying at the hotel, honey? I thought you were staying here with us." Mom holds up the dress I just put into my suitcase. "Too low cut, don't you think?"

"No, I don't think. That's why I'm packing it." I take it from her and throw it back into the suitcase.

"What do you think, Adie?" Mom picks it up again. "Seb won't like it if she's showing this much, right?"

"Sorry, Deb," Adie says, draining the rest of her wine. "I'm on Sophie's side. She's the only one who gets to decide what she wears. And believe me, Seb likes everything she wears and says and does. My boy's completely smitten with your daughter."

Mom sighs and drops it back into the suitcase. "You still haven't answered my question, Sophie. Why are you moving to the hotel?"

"The team owner, Dottie, needs me to stay close to her. I told you I'm helping her out with her interviews and speeches."

"Is everyone decent?" Jack's booming voice fills the hallway.

"Barely." Mom raises her eyebrows as she points to the dress.

"Yes, Jack," I yell. "Please come in here and get these two away from me."

Jack rounds the corner—his hand covering his eyes.

"Jack, she said we're decent," Adie says, laughing. "You can look."

"I feel weird coming into this room." Jack peeks through his fingers before dropping his hand completely. "It's like a lady place or something."

"It's not a lady place," I say, zipping up my suitcase. "Seb's always in here. He takes naps on that couch. He said the velvet's cozy."

"That's so cute," Adie says, pouting her lips. "Will you

please send me a picture of my sweet son napping on the cozy pink couch?"

"I will not," I say, pointing at her. "What happens in the lady place stays in the lady place."

"Your ride just got here, Soph," Jack says. "It's Butch and Raine."

"Raine's here?" Mom heads toward the door. "I haven't seen her since the wedding."

"I'll come with you," Adie says, bouncing off the chaise. "I like that Butch. He was a good time at the wedding."

Jack smiles as we watch them walk out of the room arm in arm. "I'm not sure who the happier couple is: you and Seb or Adie and Deb. Do you know they've starting meeting half way between Chicago and Grand Rapids for lunch once a month?"

"Mom told me. I think Adie's her BFF now."

"Yeah, they're pretty much connected at the hip." He pushes me back as I try to lift the suitcase. "I've got it. Your mom's been great for her. A bunch of Adie's friends stopped talking to her after the story broke about her jail time."

"Good riddance," I say, grabbing my phone and team security credentials off the makeup table. "If they drop her when she needs them most, they weren't very good friends in the first place."

"That's what I told her, but she was hurt." He motions me ahead of him out of the room. "Deb's really perked her up."

"It's been good for Mom too."

"It's been good for all of us. It's never too late to make

new friends. We love spending time with your parents. We invited them to the lake house this winter. I'm going to teach Bob how to ice fish."

"Did I hear my name mentioned with fishing?" Dad looks up at us from the foyer where he's chatting with Butch. "Jack, do you think we have time to catch a few tonight before we lose the light?"

"There's always time for fishing," Jack says.

"Amen, brother," Butch says, nodding. "And you can fish at night too. Just shine a light on the water's surface. They'll find you."

"Butch, you better catch a few with us before you leave," Dad says, pointing toward the back patio. "Seb left his equipment down on the dock."

"I would like nothing better than that, sir, but I need to get your daughter to the hotel. Raincheck?"

"Yep," Dad says. "I'm always down for fishing. Let's get at it, Jack. We'll see everyone tomorrow at the game. Butch, look after these ladies for us."

"Yes, sir," Butch says, turning to me. "Hey, Sophie. You ready to go?"

"Yes, but first, Seb told me the big news. Congratulations."

"Thank you," he says, a grin bursting onto his face. "We're really excited."

"What big news?" Adie asks from behind us.

"My girlfriend and I are expecting," Butch says, his face almost breaking as his smile somehow gets wider.

"Congratulations. Babies are such a blessing," Mom says, glancing at me with her eyebrows raised. "Is it the young lady you were with at the wedding? Ava?"

"No, ma'am," Butch says. "I met Kit this summer."

"Oh, that was quick. Was the baby planned?"

"Mom!"

Butch chuckles. "The baby was very planned. We both want kids and didn't see any need to wait once we found each other."

"That's so beautiful," Mom says. She points to Raine and me. "Maybe your girlfriend can talk to these two about the joys of bringing children into the world."

"Mom! Stop. It's none of your business, especially where Raine's concerned."

"It most certainly is my business," Mom says, crossing her arms. "For both of you. I've known Raine since she was born. I'll be a grandma to her kids just as much as yours."

Butch looks at Raine and me, narrowing his eyes. "I promise I'll work on them, Mrs. Banks."

Mom walks over and slides her arms around his waist. She lays her head on his chest. "Thank you, sweet Butch, and please call me Deb."

"Mom!" I pull her away. "Quit touching Butch. Adie control her."

Adie smiles. "Not a chance. I think she should touch him more. I'm actually a little jealous."

Butch flings his arms open wide. "Plenty of room for both."

Mom dives back into his chest as Adie skips over to join her. Butch wraps his enormous arms around them.

Adie makes an uncomfortable cooing sound. "Big chests were meant to rest on and yours is just the biggest."

"Adie! Oh my god." I point at Butch. "Release them and stop encouraging their drunken behavior."

"Spoil sport," Mom says as Butch squeezes them once more, and then releases them. "You probably just want him for yourself."

"Probably," Adie says, nodding. "Actually, I don't know if my son's going to like Sophie hanging out with someone so, uh, virile."

"Adie!" I throw up my arms. "Gross. Don't say virile. That's enough wine for both of you—for the rest of the trip. No more drinking. I apologize, Butch."

"It doesn't bother me. Moms love me and I love them right back." He winks at Mom and Adie. "And Mrs. Miller, your son's a very virile man. If I swung that way, I'd be after him myself."

Adie and Mom start giggling as they smile up at him.

"Butch!" I point at him again. "Stop encouraging. What is happening right now? We're leaving. And you two, stop drinking."

"Nope," Mom says, pulling Adie back toward the kitchen, "if I can't tell you what to wear, you can't tell me what to drink."

"Or how much to drink," Adie yells as they turn the corner. "See you tomorrow!"

"Ahh!" I put my face in my hands. "So embarrassing. Let's escape while we can."

When I start rolling my suitcase toward the front door, Butch grabs my arm and pulls me back.

"Lesson one," he says. "If I'm protecting you, I go through doors first. Always. No exceptions. You never know what's on the other side."

"I'm guessing not much," I say, laughing. "This island is so isolated from the real world."

"Lesson two," he says. "No guessing. We only move forward with certainty or if that's not possible, we move when I say we move. Do you understand me?"

"Butch, I don't know what Seb told you, but I think he's blowing this way out of proportion."

"Sophie." He puts his hand on my shoulder and leans down so he can look me directly in the eyes. "Seb asked us to protect you and that's what we're going to do. One more time. Do you understand me?"

"Yes. I understand. And thank you for doing this."

He nods, opens the door, and does a quick survey of our front entrance. "We're good. Let's go."

He opens the rear door of a huge black SUV. His head keeps swiveling back and forth surveying the front yard and the driveway as he helps us into the back.

"What happened to fun Butch?" I whisper to Raine as we crawl into the SUV. "He did a one-eighty in like ten seconds flat."

"You think he's bad?" Raine laughs. "Wait until Mason takes his shift covering you. He doesn't play when he's working. Neither of them do."

"They're not working. This is just silly stuff. No one's really after me."

"Maybe," she says as Butch climbs into the driver's seat. "I've done some research on the social media trolls who are after you. Most of them just seem stupid, but that miamibballbabe is a little too threatening. Plus the user seems to have some inside information. Do you have any idea who it could be?"

"None. I stopped looking at her stuff months ago. Is she still at it?"

"Yeah. I'm not convinced it's a woman, but I'm almost certain it's someone who knows you or who has at least met you or been around you. Do you know of anyone who doesn't like you?"

"Doesn't like me?" I roll my eyes. "Everyone *hates* me."

"What?" Raine scrunches up her face. "No one has ever hated you. You were universally loved when we were growing up."

"And then I married Seb, and all of a sudden, everyone hates me."

Butch glances back at us in the rearview mirror. "I'm guessing most of that is jealousy. You think this bballbabe lady just wants to get with Seb?"

"Maybe," Raine says. "Like I said, I'm not sure it's a woman. How about that Savannah maniac who was at your wedding? Or any of that mean girl group?"

"I haven't seen any of them since the wedding. I cut them out of my life after that week."

"I'm guessing that pissed them off," Raine says.

"At first," I say, "they texted me a bunch of shit, but then it faded away. Maisie still talks to them a little bit. I think everyone's moved on."

"How about Seb's friend Ricky?" Butch asks. "He didn't seem to like you much at the wedding."

"Yeah, he still doesn't." I lean my head back against the seat and close my eyes. "I saw him this afternoon. He's a passive aggressive piece of shit."

"Could be him," Raine says, scrolling through *Twitter*

again. "Most social media trolls are passive aggressive. They like to hide behind their keyboards."

"I don't know," I say, rubbing my temples. "It seems like a stretch that he would pose as a woman on *Twitter* to poke at me. He does a pretty good job of it out in the open."

"Raine," Butch says, "five minutes."

Raine dials her phone. "Hey. We're five minutes out. What's the situation there? Yeah? Still on the warpath, huh?"

"Little man?" Butch looks back at Raine who's nodding at him.

"He's not important to us," Raine says. "Are the police good? Yeah. Hold up. Sophie, do you know an Officer Dumar?"

"Yeah, Clyde. He works a lot of the games. He's cool."

"She knows him. Yep. See you in a few. Butch, ask for Officer Dumar at the entrance."

"Just pulling up now," Butch says as he rolls down the window. "Hey, man. I'm looking for Officer Dumar."

"You found him."

"Hey, Clyde," I say, trying to lean up into the front seat. Butch's hand flies up to block my face. "Butch, stop. Clyde, it's me, Sophie Miller."

"Oh. Hey, Sophie." His head pokes into the window. "Joe said you were coming in. Did Seb finally hire you a bodyguard? I gave him a few names."

"Uh, not really," I say, trying to see around Butch's hand. "These are our friends. They're going to have my back for the series."

"He picked the right guy to look after you," Clyde says, laughing. "I wouldn't fuck with you for a second with him at your side. You have a parking space right in front. Right next to that silver Jag. Head on in."

"Roger that," Butch says, rolling up the window. He maneuvers through the parking lot until he's parked in the spot. His head spins around when I try to open the locked door. "I always open car doors for you, and they'll always be locked from the inside and outside. Okay?"

"Okay." I sigh as he gets out of the SUV. I look at Raine. "I hate this so much. It's overkill."

"Just embrace it. Butch and Mason get off on this kind of stuff. If nothing else, think of it as you providing a fun game for them."

Butch opens the door and motions me out. His head's still swiveling all around.

"Incoming," he says. "Little man. The GM. Do you want me to stop him?"

"No, I'm good." I look around Butch to see Drew charging at us. "Hi, Drew. Everything good?"

"No, it's not good, Sophia," he hisses. "I'm in charge of this team. Everyone works for me including your husband. I know you have some kind of spell over Dottie. That's the only reason you're here but don't cross me. My rules are the law. Do you understand me?"

He spins back around and walks away before I can answer him.

Raine puts her arm around me. "I guess we can add him to the list of people who hate you."

"I think little man hates everyone," Butch says, pushing us toward the lobby. "I swear he's going to stroke out by the end of this."

***Twitter* @miamibballbabe**
(October 29, 2022)
I just saw #sopHOny arriving at the team hotel. She somehow weaseled her way in. Unbelievable! She doesn't trust @realsebmiller to be away from her for a second. She's probably afraid he'll find someone better. Everyone's better, Seb. Just look around.

Chapter Eight

SEB

October 29, 2022

"You ready for the party? Drew wants the team there in ten."

I glance over to the elevator as Joe walks into the suite.

"Yeah," I say, tucking in the shirt that Sophie packed for me. She said it's some special shade of blue. I can't remember what she called it, but she said it makes my eyes look dreamy. "Where's the party?"

"The rooftop deck. It's a pool party."

"Oh man. Are the sponsors wearing swimsuits? Talking to them is already uncomfortable enough."

Joe laughs. "I doubt anyone's going to swim, but someone might get thrown in at some point. Everyone's getting that crazy World Series energy."

I grunt. Sophie calls this reaction the "reluctant caveman." Basically I acknowledge what I heard but don't really like it, so now I would just like to move on.

"Sophie texted me about a half hour ago," I say. "She said she's at the hotel. Have you seen her?"

"Yeah, I witnessed her arrival. Drew's so pissed. He screamed at Max when he said hi to Sophie. All this stuff about team security not being responsible for Sophie. Max was like, "Damn Drew, I'm just saying hi to her." Then Drew ran over to me and told me Max was being insubordinate. Drew's gotten so insecure. He was never like that before this year."

"Because he had Gary Randall in his back pocket," I say, grabbing my phone and room key off the dresser. "Since Gary sold the team, Drew's been crazy as fuck. He thinks Dottie doesn't like him, and he's probably right. He's gotten all paranoid that she's going to fire him."

"He needs to chill. I'm sure Mrs. Morris loves the fact that he got her team to the World Series—"

"Drew didn't do shit," I say, pointing at him. "Bud and our coaches deserve the credit. Not him."

Joe holds the elevator door open. "Well, he got the right pieces in place. Drew's a dick, but he did a good job assembling this team. Maybe give him a little bit of a break."

I grunt again as the elevator opens on the rooftop level. Everyone turns to me when someone yells, "Seb's here!"

Joe puts his hand on my shoulder and starts pushing me through the crowd to where the rest of the team are standing.

"Hey, man," I say to Alex. "Have you seen Sophie? I just texted her, but she hasn't texted me back."

"Not yet. I'm sure she's fine, though. Raine said Mason and Butch haven't left her side since she got here."

"That makes me feel better." I pat him on the shoulder.

"How's this feeling for you? Your last year playing and all. It's got to be kind of bittersweet, right?"

"Honestly," he says, looking around the deck, "not really. I won't miss this stuff at all. You and the guys, yeah. Actually being on the field playing, yeah. But there's a lot I won't miss too. I'm looking forward to blending into the woodwork."

"You're not going to blend. Just because you're not playing doesn't mean people will leave you alone. They're still going to recognize you."

"Yeah," Alex says, nodding at Manny as he joins us, "but it's not going to be this intense, especially since I won't be living in Miami."

"Did you decide if you're selling your house here?" Manny asks.

"Not at first. Maybe not ever. I love Miami. But while I'm in school and Raine and I are deciding our future, I'll be in California more than here."

The team's head of sales, Evelyn, wedges her way into our group. "Gentlemen, you talk to each other enough. You need to mingle with our sponsors."

"Come on, Ev," I say, "you know how much I hate talking to strangers."

"I've worked with you for almost nine years. I know everything about you, but I also know you promised Dottie you would play nicely tonight."

I look at her and snarl. She crosses her arms as she smiles up at me. She's one of the only team employees who can get me to do sponsor stuff. It's been that way since I was a rookie.

"Fine, but only for you and Dottie." I whistle and motion to the rest of the players. "Time to mingle, boys."

As the team starts to filter through the crowd, I see my childhood friends waving at me from across the party. I give them a nod and head that way. As I get closer, a woman starts running toward me.

"Seb!"

I can't quite place her, but at the same time, I feel like I've know her all of my life. I pull Joe back as he tries to stop her.

"Eeeeeek!" she screams as she crashes into me and wraps her arms around my neck. "It's been almost ten years but this feels exactly the same."

"Yeah," I say, my mind spinning as it tries to connect the dots. I give her a hesitant hug, and then push her back.

She grins up at me. "Come on, Sebastian. I know you're all big time now, but how are you going to forget me of all people? It's Katie."

My mouth drops open. "Katie Barr? I'm sorry. Of course. It's just been so long."

"Yes, silly, Katie Barr. We dated for almost four years. And it's Houseman now, but I'm getting a divorce, so I might go back to Barr unless something else comes up."

"Oh, uh, I'm sorry to hear about the divorce." I shake my head to try to get the spinning to stop. "What are you doing here?"

"I'm here to watch you play." She hugs me again. This time, I don't return it. "You talked about playing in the World Series every day we were together. I'm so proud of you for getting here, Seb."

"Thanks, Katie." I push her back again. "But I mean what are you doing here—at this party?"

"I'm Ricky's plus one. Didn't he tell you he was bringing me? Or maybe I was supposed to be a surprise. Shoot. I should have jumped out of a cake or something."

The anger shoots through my body so quickly that it's almost painful. I try to smile, but I've never been very good at masking my emotions. "No, he definitely didn't tell me he was bringing you."

She tilts her head and laughs. "Well I hope I'm a welcome surprise."

"Are you going to say hi to your best friends?" Ricky yells as he walks toward us. "I mean, it's not like we've been with you since day one or anything."

"Rick," I say, shaking his outstretched hand.

"Damn, Seb. Shake it. Don't break it. Ease up on the grip, Hulk." He looks at Katie and smiles. "Katie was telling me it's been almost ten years since you've seen each other. Nice surprise, huh?"

"Yeah," I say, locking my eyes with his. "It's been a while."

Katie laughs again as she touches my arm. "I thought you forgot me there for a second."

"No way. Seb would never forget his first love." Ricky points his phone at us as Katie links her arm through mine. "Let me get a picture. You two are still a good-looking couple."

My other friends, Stone and Paul, make their way over to us with their wives.

"Fellas," I say, pushing Katie off me as I reach out to shake their hands. "Glad you made it in."

"Not as glad as we are," Paul says. "Can you believe it? Man, you've wanted to be in the World Series since we were playing tee ball."

"It's unreal, man. I just want to start playing."

"We're all so proud of you." Stone's wife, Anne, gives me a hug. "Where's Sophie? Stone said she would be here."

"Uh, yeah," I say, scanning the crowd for her again. "She's supposed to be here. I don't see her yet."

"Well, let's take advantage of our alone time," Ricky says, pushing Katie back toward me. "Honestly, it's nice to have the old gang back together. Just us. How many days and nights did we spend together growing up? Am I the only one who misses those days?"

Every muscle in my body tenses as I glare at him.

"Seb." Stone puts his hand on my arm. "I need to talk to you alone. Will you all excuse us for a second?"

He tries to pull me away from the group. I don't budge. I'm trying to decide if I should punch Ricky.

"Now," Stone whispers. "Not the time or place. Let's go."

I follow him over to the side of the deck. "What the fuck? Did you know he was bringing her?"

"Come on, man," he says. "You know I didn't. Neither did Paul. Ricky showed up at the airport with her this morning."

"Why didn't you text me and give me a little warning?" I glare down at him.

"Honestly, I was hoping you wouldn't even be around her. You said we were barely going to see you during the series."

"Keep them away from me," I say, growling. "Both of them. I gave Ricky his last warning at the wedding. The only reason he brought Katie here is to mess with Sophie."

"Yeah, I'm guessing that's right."

"No guessing about it. I don't have time to deal with it now but he's done."

Stone nods as the rest of the group head over to us. "You're going to do what you have to do."

"Stone," Katie says as she circles her arm around my waist, "you see Seb so much. I haven't seen him in ten years. You have to share."

"Seb!" Evelyn's power walking over to me. "I said mingle with the sponsors, not with your friends."

"Yeah, I really need to spend time with the sponsors." I'm suddenly unbelievably relieved to have a task—even one that I hate.

"What? You're leaving us?" Katie tries to keep her arm around me as I pull away.

"It was nice to see you again, Katie. Take care. Enjoy the games."

"I will." Her face melts into confusion. "But it's not like I'm not going to see you again. I'll see you at the game tomorrow."

"Let's go, Ev," I say, pulling her across the deck. "We have people to meet."

"Well she's in love with you," Evelyn says, looking back at Katie. "Old girlfriend?"

"She's not in love with me. We haven't seen each other in a decade, but yeah, we dated in high school."

"And she would definitely like to be dating you again.

Or strike that, she would like to be married to you. Sophie better watch out."

"Sophie doesn't have to watch out for anything," I snarl. "Speaking of Sophie, have you seen her?"

"No," Evelyn says. "You need to mingle with sponsors right now, not Sophie. Don't look at me like that. The team's only here for twenty more minutes. We need to make up for lost time."

"Alright, boss," I say, doing another quick eye sweep of the party to find Sophie. "I'm all yours. You know I only do this stuff for you. Well, I only do it cheerfully for you."

"This is cheerful?" She laughs. "It's the World Series. At least act like you're enjoying it."

"Okay," I say, plastering a fake smile on my face. "Is this better?"

"God, no." She covers her eyes. "It's somehow worse. Make it go away."

"Evelyn." A guy taps her shoulder. "You promised I could meet Seb at this party."

"And I'm delivering on that promise, Daniel." Her entire face lights up. It never ceases to amaze me how she can turn the charm on and off so easily. It's like she becomes a completely different person. "Daniel Crane, meet Seb Miller. Seb, Daniel represents our largest banking sponsor."

"And we've been trying like hell to get you to be our spokesman," Daniel says, shaking my hand for way too long. I finally pull it away. "We want Seb Miller as the face of our bank. What do you say?"

"Uh—"

"Daniel," Evelyn says, "come on. We're at a party. No

shop talk. And you should call Seb's agent if you're interested in an endorsement. Right, Seb?"

"Uh, yeah," I say. "You can talk to him, but I don't do a lot of endorsements."

"But everyone really appreciates your sponsorship of the team, Daniel." Ev looks up at me. "Don't we, Seb?"

"Yes. Thank you for your sponsorship of the team. It means a lot to everyone. You're the reason we're able to keep such good players around and make it into the World Series."

"Appreciate you recognizing that, Seb." He nods and pats my back. "Bring us home a winner."

"We'll see you later, Daniel. More people to meet." Evelyn pulls me away and whispers, "Damn, Seb. You nailed the script I wrote for you."

"Did I sound sincere?"

"Well, you were only a three on the sincerity scale at the last party. This time you were at least a five so nice improvement." She looks up at me. "Your eyes look amazing in that shirt, by the way."

"Thanks." I look away as my face starts to blush. "Sophie bought it for me. She said it's like sir million blue or something."

"Cerulean, dummy. Why would anyone name blue 'sir million'?"

"Why would anyone name blue period? It already has a name," I grumble as she grabs my arm and pulls me over to another sponsor.

"Jennifer, have you met Seb Miller? Seb, Jennifer represents the largest hospital group in Miami."

"Hi, Seb," she says, shaking my hand. "It's so nice to

finally meet you. My husband is your biggest fan. He watches every game. I love your shirt. That color blue is perfect on you."

"Thanks," I say, smiling. "It's cerulean."

Chapter Nine

SOPHIE

October 29, 2022

Even though Butch identified himself when he knocked, Raine still looks through the peephole of our hotel room door. Her extra caution is starting to freak me out a little bit. When she opens the door, Mason and Butch are standing outside.

Mason pushes past Raine. He looks mad. "Sophie, I would like to ask you again not to go to this party. Your arrival at the hotel this afternoon was a disaster. We underestimated the number of people that want to be near you."

"What? It was fine—"

"It wasn't fine," he says, hulking above me. "And this kind of party setting tonight is extremely dangerous—too many people in close quarters."

"I'm going to the party." I try to hold his stare, but quickly look down as his face somehow gets scarier. "I'm going. I want to see Seb. And anyway, I know most of these people. I'm around them all the time."

"It doesn't matter if you know them. That latest tweet was too personal. Not many people know you moved to the hotel." Mason walks over to the balcony, pushes the French doors closed, and locks them. "Raine, are you any closer to figuring out who owns that account?"

"No, the user's more sophisticated than I thought. I'm working on it. I'll figure it out."

Mason nods. "Until then, everyone's a suspect."

"Why is he so mad?" I whisper to Raine. "Did I do something wrong this afternoon?"

"You didn't do anything wrong. This afternoon was just surprising. Everyone wanted to be close to you. We don't like surprises."

"No more surprises," Mason snarls. "We're instigating a new system."

"A system? Do we really need that? I guarantee miamibballbabe won't be at the party tonight. She's not an insider. Did you see how many fans were outside the hotel when we arrived? They all saw me walk in. Any of them could have posted that tweet. It's not a big deal."

"It is a big deal," Butch says. "If we're protecting you, we need to be sure everyone approaching you is safe. Anyone could have a weapon. I mean, I just checked the venue. There are knives on the buffet table for fuck's sake."

"What? No one's going to stab me—"

"Sophie." Raine grabs me and pushes me into a chair. She gets down in my face. "Focus. This is an easy system that won't interrupt your fun but will keep you safe. I know you think this is all too much, but it's happening. Quit protesting."

She releases me after I nod. Mason stands over me.

"One, three, five," he says, showing me the numbers on his hand. His face looks a little more relaxed. "That's all you need to remember. When a person's approaching you, declare a number to us. One means: I know this person and he or she is of no threat to me. Three is: I don't know this person so I have no idea what his or her threat level is to me. Five is: I know this person and he or she is seconds away from attacking me. Are we clear?"

"Uh," I say, looking up at his unblinking eyes, "I guess."

Mason's face is back to terrifying. "No guessing. Do you need me to review the numbers with you again?"

"Kind of, but I'm really scared to say yes."

"Soph." Raine pushes Mason away from me and sits on the edge of my chair. "This is threat level only. One is no threat. Three is you don't know. Five is an immediate threat. You'll get the hang of it. It's just important to declare a number immediately when you're approached."

"What happens if I don't declare a number?" I look back at Mason.

"Then we," he says, pointing between himself and Butch, "make the call. You don't want us to make the call. Learn your numbers and react quickly. Are you clear?"

I nod. "I'm clear, but I want to go on the record again that I think you and Seb are elevating this way beyond where it needs to be."

"Soph, that doesn't matter. This is where we are now,"

Raine says. "Who's got first shift? We should probably let Sophie get to the party if she's going."

"Butch," Mason says, growling.

"On it," Butch says. "Just do your thing, Sophie. I'm on your back. You won't even notice me unless you need me."

I look up at him and smile, but honestly, I'm not sure how anyone's going to miss this enormous man following me around the party.

When the elevator door opens on the rooftop level, Butch walks out, looks around, and then motions me to follow. We've barely cleared the door when I see one of the team's sponsors hurrying toward me. I met him last year, but I'm forgetting his name.

"Sophia Banks! You're looking gorgeous as usual."

I look up at Butch who's suddenly stuck to my side.

"Speak, Sophie," Butch says, putting his hand on my shoulder and pulling me back a little. "Or I make the call."

"One," I whisper, "or maybe a three, but also kind of a five."

Butch pulls me behind him just as the sponsor opens his arms to hug me.

"No." Butch pushes him back.

"What?" He looks up at Butch. "Who the hell are you?"

"I know we've met," I say, moving as far around Butch as he'll let me, "but I'm not remembering your name."

"That hurts my feelings," he says, winking at me. "I'm Matt Lowry. We met at the end of last season when you were doing some work for Gary Randall."

"Right," I say, giving him my best fake smile. "I remember now."

Matt looks at Butch again. "Did Seb hire a bodyguard

for you? I can't say I blame him. You have quite the body to guard."

"Wow," Butch says, shaking his head. "If you're trying to hit on a married woman, you're going to have to bring more game than that."

"I'm not trying to hit on anyone." Matt glares at Butch. "Sophia and I are old friends. She was going to do some work for me before she latched onto Seb. I don't think my bankroll was big enough for her."

"I'm guessing there's a lot about you that isn't big enough for her," Butch says, putting his arm around my shoulders. "We're done here."

I look back at Matt as Butch pulls me away. His mouth is hanging open. "Butch, I'm not saying I didn't enjoy that, but you were maybe a little bit harsh."

"Mason warned you that you don't want us to make the call." Butch looks down at me. "Do you need to review the numbers again? That was unacceptable."

"I was confused because I forgot his name, so he's a three, but I remembered that he's a total creeper, so he might be a five. Your system is flawed, not me."

"You recognized him but couldn't place him. He's a three. If he's not going to attack you at this very moment, he's not a five."

"Sophie!"

I turn around to see the team's clubhouse guard, Chick, walking toward me with his wife.

"One, one, one," I whisper. "Zero. Darling people."

"Chick," I say, diving into him for a hug. "I'm so glad you're here. And you got Joni to leave the house. It's a miracle."

"Sweet Sophie," Joni says, her raspy voice rumbling in my ears as she hugs me. "For all these years, I told Chick I would only come to baseball things if it was for the World Series. And here your husband has to go and make that a reality. You tell Seb I'm mad at him for that."

"I'll tell him, but he won't like you being mad at him. I know he wants to be invited over for dinner again."

"You both are always welcome at our house," she says. "I'll have to teach you how to make my macaroni and cheese. I thought Seb was going to eat the entire pan."

"He still talks about it," I say, laughing. "We'll have you over to our house when the season's over."

"You don't have to pay me back. I like cooking and entertaining." She pats my stomach. "Or maybe just name your first little one after me. Do you have one in there yet?"

"Jon," Chick says, pulling her hand away, "that's not appropriate."

She puts her hands on her hips. "I know you're not trying to tell me what's appropriate, Cornelius."

"Cornelius?" I smile at Chick. "I didn't know that was your first name."

"For a reason. I don't want anyone calling me that."

"After fifty-two years of marriage," Joni says, shooing him away as he tries to put his arm around her, "you're lucky that's the worst thing I call you. Sophie, sweetie, who's this man hovering behind you?"

"I'm sorry," I say, grabbing Butch's arm. "This is our friend Butch. Butch, this is Chick and Joni. Chick's the clubhouse guard at the stadium."

"Sir," Butch says, shaking his hand. "And ma'am. It's nice to meet you both."

"I like this one," Joni says, looking up at Butch. "He's polite and very handsome. Are you single? I have a granddaughter who's looking."

"No, ma'am," Butch says, smiling. "I have a girlfriend and we have a baby on the way."

"Girlfriend? And when are you going to marry this young lady?"

"Jon!" Chick puts his hands over his face and sighs. "I apologize—"

"No need." Butch laughs. "She sounds like my mom. And I would marry Kit in a second if that's what she wanted. She says she's not the marrying type."

Joni looks around. "Is she here? I want to talk to her."

"No, ma'am. She's sleeping in our room right now."

"Well," Joni says, patting Butch's arm, "pregnancy makes most women very tired. You treat her like a queen and pamper her. Do you understand me, uh, I already forgot your name?"

"My name's Butch, but my given name is Gabriel. No one calls me that except my mom, but you can call me that if you want."

"Thank you." She smiles up at him. "And Chick's been in security long enough for me to recognize a bodyguard when I see one. You take extra good care of our precious Sophie, Gabriel."

"I promise, ma'am." Butch shakes Chick's hand again before they walk away. "It was good to meet you both."

I get on my tiptoes. "Do you see Seb? He texted me that he was here."

"Yeah," Butch says, tapping me and pointing across the deck. "He's over there—by the purple palm tree. I'll get you through the crowd. Remember one, three, five if someone tries to stop us."

Butch puts his arm around my shoulders again and pretty much lifts me across the deck. Several people try to say hi, but he doesn't stop. He releases me when we get to Seb.

"Seb," I say, reaching up to touch the ends of his hair that always curl up at the nape of his neck after he showers. He spins around. His entire face lights up when he sees me. "Soph, I was looking for you. Where have you been?"

"Sorry, babe," I say, burying my face into his chest. "A few people stopped me when I got here."

"It's fine," he says, kissing the top of my head as he wraps his arms around me. "I'm just glad you're here now."

I look up at him. His eyes are so sparkly. "That shirt really does make your eyes look pretty."

"You said they looked dreamy last time. Why the downgrade?"

"Do you like dreamy better?"

"Kind of," he whispers as he nuzzles into my neck. "Dreamy seems better than pretty."

"Then your eyes are the dreamiest." I giggle when he starts nibbling. "Stop. The last thing I need to be right now is horny."

"Hey Sophie," the VP of sales for the team, Evelyn, says as she walks over to us.

"Hey, Ev." I push Seb back. "Is Seb behaving for you?"

"He's doing great. Have you been working with him?"

"Nope, it's all you, sister. You know he would do anything for you."

"Yeah." She smiles up at Seb. "Actually, we're not done and we only have a few more minutes. I want him to meet one more person."

"Naw, Ev," Seb says, pulling me back against his chest. "I'm done. I haven't seen Sophie all afternoon. I want a few minutes alone with her."

"Seb." Evelyn's face tightens. "This is a sponsor party. It's not a family thing. Sorry, Sophie."

"Go, Seb," I say, reaching up to kiss him. "Help Evelyn do her job. I need to check on Dottie anyway."

Evelyn grabs his arm, but he yanks it away. "The sponsors can wait. I want to talk to my wife."

He pushes me over to the corner of the deck and spins me around so I have my back to his Michigan friends. The woman in the group who I don't know hasn't taken her eyes off me since I walked up to Seb.

"Are you trying to hide your high school girlfriend from me?" I tilt my head up and smile at him.

A deep line forms above his eyes. "No, I'm not, but how do you know who she is?"

"The boys stopped by the house this afternoon. Ricky told me all about her."

He snaps his gaze over to them, his jaw tightening. "I told them the house was family only. Was she there?"

"No, I haven't met her yet." I start grinding against him. "I'm so looking forward to it."

His hands settle on my butt as I continue to press into him. He shakes his head as he smiles down at me. "Are you marking your territory right now?"

"Yep," I say, pulling his face down for a long kiss. "Does it bother you?"

"Oh yeah." He pulls me closer as he runs his lips over mine. "I really hate when my hot-ass wife grinds her body into mine. Please stop."

"Never. I want to make sure everyone's clear who you belong to—"

"Right back at you," he says, squeezing my butt. "Hey. You said a couple people stopped you coming into the party. Has anyone tried anything?"

"Do you think anyone's going to try anything with Butch lurking around me? I think he scares most people into not even saying hi."

"He's a good man. That entire Blitzen Bay group is solid, right?"

"Yeah." I circle my arms around his waist again as I lay my head on his chest. "I feel so comfortable around them. And speaking of Butch, I think our moms want to have a three way with him."

"Wow, wow, wow," he says, letting out a slow whistle. "I could have gone the rest of my life without hearing those words."

"You didn't have to see them flirting their asses off with him. It was awful. I can't get the picture out of my head."

"Again, that is information I never needed to know."

"We're married now. We share everything, including disturbing mental images. For better or worse, remember?"

"Yep," he says, turning around as Evelyn grabs his arm again, "and I'm finally understanding what the worse part means."

"Go," I say, pointing to Evelyn, "before she has a breakdown."

He growls and hugs me tighter.

"She's just doing her job, babe. Help her out, okay?"

"Okay. Only for you," he whispers as he leans down to kiss me again. "Just two more weeks until we're alone at the lake house."

"Just you and me," I whisper. "I can't wait. Now, go. I'll call you when I get back to my room."

Chapter Ten

SEB

October 30, 2022

After the party last night, I talked to Sophie on the phone for almost an hour, and then tried to get some sleep. I was very unsuccessful. I tossed and turned most of the night thinking about ways to sneak her into my room. In the little more than a year we've been married, we've only spent a handful of nights apart. She's my security blanket. I get edgy when she's not around.

As we pull up to the stadium for the first game of the series, I'm a weird mixture of exhausted and hyper. I feel like I have no energy and way too much energy at the same time. The adrenaline keeps bursting through my body in uncomfortable jolts. I'm usually pretty even. It feels weird to be this jumpy.

"Damn," I say as our bus pulls into the underground parking. "First the crazy crowd around the hotel and now at the stadium. There have to be a couple thousand people out there. The game doesn't even start for seven hours."

Joe laughs. "I already told you just because this isn't a big deal for you doesn't mean it's not a big deal for the rest of the city. Miami's crazy right now. Everything is about this team."

As we get off the bus, a group of people start walking toward us down the concourse. They're all dressed in team jerseys. Dottie's leading the way. They form a two-sided receiving line that leads from the bus to our clubhouse.

"Welcome, team!" Dottie yells. She starts a clap that ripples through the rest of the line. "Good luck tonight!"

She gives us high fives as we start down the line. The other people mimic her and offer us fist bumps and words of encouragement as we funnel through their human tunnel. Evelyn's at the end of the line. She's has her hand over her mouth trying to hold in a laugh.

"Was this your idea?" I ask, pointing at her.

"It wasn't," she says, finally letting the laugh come out, "but seeing that awkward, pained look on your face has made it all worthwhile. This was actually Ken's idea."

"Hey!" Ken shoves her as she continues to laugh. "Don't try to get me into trouble with him. This was entirely Dottie's idea. And since she signs our paychecks, we can all act like we're enjoying this little pep rally. Seb, pregame presser in ten. MLB is running it. Let's try to be on time."

I nod as I walk into the clubhouse.

Bud walks over and pats my back. "Exciting, right? You ready?"

"Just any other game," I say as I throw my bag at the foot of my locker. "Once we get on the field, anyway."

"Seb," Ken says from the door. "Let's go. Alex, Manny, you're with us too."

As we start walking down the concourse to the interview room, I spot Sophie standing with Dottie. My body relaxes instantly when I see her.

"Soph!" I jog over to her.

"Hey!" She runs over and flings her body into mine. "I'm so glad I got to see you before the game. I missed you last night. Did you sleep okay?"

"Not at all." I pull her to me. "I think I've forgotten how to sleep without you curled up next to me."

"Same. I'm sure I kept Raine up most of the night."

Mason's standing a few feet away. His face is drawn. It makes my body tense up again. "Did something happen this morning? Mason looks like he's about to kill someone."

"Nope. All good." Her voice is fake cheerful.

"Soph," I say, tilting up her chin, "you know I get crazier when you hide stuff from me. What happened?"

"Nothing important." She puts her hands on my chest. "When we left the hotel, a bunch of fans were yelling stuff at me, but they didn't get close. Butch and Mason have been stuck to my side."

"Seb." Ken's waving me toward the interview room.

"Hold up!" I yell at him. "I'll be there in a second. What were they yelling?"

"The normal stuff—how I'm a distraction to you. It's no big deal."

"You're not a distraction."

"I certainly don't mean to be." She looks over at Ken

who's yelling my name again. "Ken needs you. Go. It will make me feel better. I'm fine."

I hug her one more time, and then back up toward the interview room. I motion between us. "This—you and me—is the only thing that matters. Everything else is the distraction. Okay?"

"I know." She nods and smiles. "Good luck tonight. I'm so proud of you."

I blow her a kiss before I turn around and walk into the room. It's packed. I've never seen this many reporters anywhere. And they're all staring at me. The MLB woman who's running the media room is frowning. She points to a chair on the podium between Alex and Manny.

"Sorry we're starting a few minutes late everyone," she says, looking at me again. "When I call on you, please say your name and media outlet and who your question is for. At the dais, we have Manny Roja who's pitching for Miami tonight. Alex Molina who's playing in his last season in the league. And Seb Miller who's—well, he's Seb Miller."

Everyone laughs as she points to the first reporter. He mumbles his name and outlet. I'm not really paying attention until he says my name.

"Seb, your ninth season in the league and your first World Series. How are you feeling?"

"Uh." A bunch of cameras flash as I look up. "Pretty much the same as every other game. You know, once we get on the field, it's just baseball."

"I'm sure you're telling yourself that," he says. The reporters laugh again. "You split your games against L.A. this season. Do you think you can turn it around for the series?"

"We only played two games against them, so I think a split is pretty decent."

The reporter stands up. "A split's not going to get the job done in the series though."

"The series is seven games, man," I say, shaking my head. "How are we going to split that? You know the difference between odd and even numbers, right?"

"Okay." The MLB woman walks in front of me. "Let's have a question for Alex about playing in his first World Series in his last season in the league."

I look at Alex and mumble, "I hate this shit."

"Couldn't tell, man. You cover it so well." He looks across me to Manny. "Right, Manny?"

Manny laughs. "So well. Seriously, Seb. Maybe after you retire, you can go into some kind of undercover work. No one can ever tell what you're thinking."

The MLB woman gives us a stern look. "Alex, do you need me to repeat the question?"

"I'm good. No, I don't regret my decision to retire, and no, I won't change my mind if we lose the World Series. And the thing I'll miss most is my teammates." Alex whacks my arm. "Even Mr. Personality here."

We're coming off the field after warm-ups. I flat out sucked. Nothing felt right. My energy level is still crazy. I've been trying to burn off the extra steam since I arrived at the stadium. Nothing's calming me down.

"What's wrong with you?" Bud follows me off the

field. "Your throws were all over the place, and you were swinging way too early during batting practice."

"I'm fine." I walk past him into the dugout. "Just a little keyed up."

"Well get it under control. You know the team follows your energy."

"You good?" Alex pats my shoulder as we head down the tunnel to the clubhouse. "Your throws to second were high."

"I know what they were," I snarl. "Just worry about yourself."

"Hey!" He steps in front of me and shoves my chest. "Not with me. Either tell me what's wrong or get it under control, but keep the bullshit attitude to yourself."

Alex is the only person who can get away with talking to me like that. I've known him my entire time in the league. We've played together since day one.

"Sorry, man," I say. "I didn't get much sleep last night. I have a lot on my mind."

He nods. "Game related or Sophie related?"

"Sophie."

"She's fine. You know Mason and Butch will take care of her."

"I know."

"Deal with your business for the next few hours, and then you can see her after the game."

"I don't know what I'm going to do without you next year," I say. "You always say the right thing."

"I'll only be a phone call away," he says as he follows me into the clubhouse.

"Seb." Our head trainer, Carl, hustles toward me.

"Seems like you're still too wired. You want to get on the bike again?"

I clip off my chest protector and throw it onto the chair at my locker. "It couldn't hurt."

Carl watches me from a distance for about ten minutes as I tear up the stationary bike in the training room. He finally walks over.

"Your energy level is normally high, but this is crazy." He gets closer and whispers, "Did you take something before you got here?"

I stop pedaling and glare at him. "Are you being serious right now? What do you think, Carl?"

"I think you didn't," he says, taking a step back, "but I've never seen you like this. I guess it's just extra World Series energy."

Joe walks over. "You feeling better?"

"Not really." I climb off the bike. "I don't know what's wrong."

"I do." He follows me back to the clubhouse. "You're an extreme introvert. All of this extra stuff—the World Series hype, the media, the family and friends in town—is triggering you."

"Maybe." I collapse into my chair. "And I just feel like everyone's coming at Sophie and me right now. All I want to do is play baseball, and then go home to my wife. That doesn't seem to be too much to ask."

"It's not," he says, looking around the clubhouse to make sure no one's listening, "but sometimes the people in power make the stupidest decisions and they double down on the stupid when they think they're losing power. That's what Drew's doing right now."

"It's not only Drew," I say, wiping the sweat off my face. "My friends are being assholes too. I don't know who to trust anymore. And I haven't had nearly enough Sophie time. She keeps me even."

"Hey," Joe says, lowering his voice as he looks around the room again. "Why don't I have Max sneak you into your office right now? I'll get Sophie and you two can get a little alone time before the game."

"What do you mean by 'alone time'?" I look up at him —my eyebrows raised.

"Do I look like a fucking pimp to you? I thought maybe you could talk. Get your mind out of the gutter."

"My bad," I say, smiling as I think about spending even a few minutes with Sophie. "And yeah, that would actually be nice. Do you think you can get her down here without anyone seeing?"

"How are you asking me that?" He backs up toward the door. "You already know I can pull off anything. They used to call me NoJoe in the Marines because no one could see me coming."

I roll my eyes. "No one called you that."

"You don't know what they called me. I was the shit in the Corp." He points at me. "And by the way, only one of your friends is being an asshole. I hate to say it but I don't think he's going to stop coming after Sophie. He's obsessed with bringing her down. It's probably time for him to go."

"Way past time, man," I say, sighing. "That's the first thing I'm dealing with when this series is over."

Chapter Eleven

SOPHIE

October 30, 2022

"Everyone in here is a one," I say to Butch as we walk into the private suite at the stadium. "All friends and family. Why don't you guys just enjoy the game?"

"We'll enjoy the game," Butch says, looking around the room, "but one of us is going to stay next to you. Do your thing and ignore us."

He pulls me away from the door as it opens. It's Ricky with Seb's old girlfriend.

Although I'm tempted to yell five to watch Butch tear Ricky apart, I whisper, "One."

"What does 'one' mean?" Ricky smirks at me and then turns to Butch. "Hey, Butch. I didn't know you were in town."

Butch nods at him.

"What are you doing up here?" I ask. "If you're not using the field seat, someone else will want it."

"I'm using it," he says. "I just wanted to introduce you to someone first. This is Kaitlyn Barr. She's known Seb for twenty plus years."

I turn to her and smile. "It's so nice to meet Ricky's girlfriend. I wasn't sure he was ever going to settle down."

"His what?" Kaitlyn laughs as she looks over at Ricky. "I'm Ricky's plus one for the series, but we're not dating. Seb knows that better than anyone."

"My mistake. I must have misunderstood you yesterday, Ricky." I lock my eyes with his for a second, and then look back at Kaitlyn. "Kaitlyn, I'm so glad you made it in. Seb loves when his friends from Michigan visit."

"We were more than friends. We dated for almost four years. I've known him since third grade—before he was rich and famous. I went to all of his high school baseball games. The only thing that's different now is that I won't be holding his wallet and car keys while he plays." She stops and laughs. "I guess you do that now. Make sure you hold it close. His wallet's a lot bigger now."

"I don't hold his wallet during games. He has an entire clubhouse for that now."

"You might not hold it," Ricky says, glaring at me, "but you certainly have no problem getting into it."

I take a step toward him. "Seb pays for your flights, hotels, and tickets every time you see him play. You don't seem to have much problem getting into his wallet either."

"My relationship with Seb is none of your business," he hisses.

I close the rest of the distance between us. "Right back at you, Ricky."

Butch grabs my shoulder and pulls me back. "Rick, I

think it's time for you to find your seat."

"Come on, friend," Ricky says, chucking him on the shoulder. "Lighten up."

"Naw, Rick," Butch says, "we're not friends. You're a dick. As I said, I think it's time for you to find your seat. Don't make me say it again."

Ricky looks from him to me, his face starting to flush.

"Fine," Ricky says, spitting out the words. "This suite life isn't for me anyway. I like to be down with the real fans."

I roll my eyes as he spins on a heel and walks out. Kaitlyn's staring at us—her mouth gaping.

"Kaitlyn," I say, smiling, "you better grab a seat before they all fill up."

I walk over to the bar, pour myself a generous serving of wine, and chug until Butch pulls the glass away from me.

I growl up at him. "What number do I declare if I want you to punch someone?"

"We don't really have a number for that," Butch says, laughing, "but from the look on your face, I'm guessing we probably should."

"Sophie." I look over to see Joe walking through the door. I think this is the first time I've ever seen him on the suite level. He's usually glued to the players, especially right before a game.

"What's up, Joe? Is everything okay?"

"Everything's fine," Joe whispers, "but Seb wants to see you."

"Now? It's only an hour before they take the field. He never wants to see anyone before a game. Is he okay?"

"Uh, he seems a little off. He's in his office. He almost seems nervous."

I pull my head back. "Are you sure? He's never nervous."

"Come on." He motions me to the suite door. "He won't talk to me. Maybe he'll tell you what's going on. Butch, we're moving."

"Yep," Butch says, falling in behind us.

When we get off the elevator at field level, Joe and Butch sneak me into the hallway that goes behind the clubhouse. That's where Seb has a private office.

I head down the hallway and knock softly on the door. "Seb, it's me."

The door flies open. He pulls me in and slams it.

"Seb," I say, grabbing his arm, "what's wrong?"

"I have too much energy." He starts pacing. "You know how I get when I don't work out for a while—edgy and stuff."

"Yeah," I say, trying to get him to stand still. "Did you work out today?"

"Everything. I did everything the same. I jogged and rode the stationary bike. I even did some wind sprints on the field. The energy goes down a little, but then it surges back up. I'm way too amped."

"Well, babe, it's the World Series. You've never been here before. I think this is normal. Once you get on the field, you'll be fine. The nervousness will disappear."

He grabs my shoulders. "Soph, I'm not nervous. I never get nervous before playing—even on this stage. I just have too much energy. I make mistakes when I'm this keyed up. And nothing's helping."

"Okay." I slide my arms around his waist and lay my head on his chest. His heart's beating so fast. "You still have a little time before you take the field. You can fit in more cardio."

"It's not helping," he says, wrapping his arms around me. "I almost broke the bike a few minutes ago. I was going so fast. I have way too much adrenaline."

"You know there's something we can do to help you burn off a lot of energy very quickly," I say, laughing as I run my hands down his body. "We only needed a few minutes yesterday."

"I didn't ask you to come in here so we could have sex."

"Fine." I push him away and back up against the door. "If you're not in the mood, maybe I can find someone else—"

"You know I'm always in the mood." He points at me. "And don't even tease me about finding someone else."

"Okay." I pull up my dress, shimmy out of my panties, and kick them over to him. "How would you like me to tease you?"

He snags them out of midair—the pink silk quickly disappearing into his hand.

"Soph." His neck muscles begin to bulge like they always do when he feels he's losing control of a situation. "Put them back on. I don't need you to do this."

"Well, babe, this relationship isn't only about what you need. Maybe I need you to service me right now."

"*Service* you?" He tries unsuccessfully to keep a smile from coming to his face. "What are you? A car?"

"If that's how you want to role play, it's fine with me.

You're the mechanic. I'm the car. Bring your tools over here and start fixing me."

"Stop it," he says, holding the panties out to me as he starts to laugh. "Please put these back on."

"Wow, okay." I duck under his arm and spin away from him. "The first time we were together you ripped the undies right off my body. Now you're telling me to put them back on. I guess the honeymoon really is over. How disappoi—"

Before I can finish the sentence, he grabs me and backs me up against the wall.

"Soph," he says, looking down at me with the wide eyes he only gets when someone has hurt his feelings. "Please don't ever say I'm disappointing you. All I ever want to do is make you happy. You know that."

"Oh, baby." I wrap my arms around him again. "I'm just trying to get your mind off everything. You could never do anything to disappoint me."

"You're everything to me." He squeezes me so tightly that I almost can't breathe. "None of this crap matters without you. You understand that, right?"

"You know I do. You're my world. It's you and me first. Always."

He lays his head on top of mine and lets out a long breath. "I think I want this season to be my last. I haven't told anyone yet, but I've been thinking about it for months. Is that okay?"

I look up at him. "Of course it's okay. Anything you want. It's your career—"

"It's my career, but it's our life." His face is more earnest than I've ever seen it. "It's just, you know, with everything that I've brought down on you—all the unwanted attention. It might be better for you if I'm not playing."

"Seb," I say, rubbing his back. "Baby, none of that is your fault. I don't want you to quit until you're ready. I'm tough. I can deal with it."

"I don't want you to have to deal with it. Please tell me when it gets to be too much. I'll quit that second. Just don't leave me."

"Leave you? What are you talking about? I'm never leaving you." I look up at him again. His eyes are watery. "Seb, I'm never leaving you. Let the trolls bring their best stuff. I won't let it get between us. In two weeks, we'll be at the lake house and all of this craziness will fade away."

"That sounds so good." He hugs me to him again. "I can't wait to be there—just us."

"Just us," I whisper into his chest. His heart rate is almost back to normal.

There's a light tapping on the door.

"Seb," Joe says. "It's time. Bud wants to address the team."

Seb takes a long breath and blows it out slowly. "Will you come down here right after the game?"

"Right after."

"Promise?" He smiles down at me. His face looks relaxed for the first time since I came in here.

"Promise," I say, as I start backing toward the door.

He holds up my panties. "Aren't you forgetting something?"

"Nope." I open the door. "I'll get them from you tonight after the game."

Seb whips the panties behind his back as Joe walks into

the room.

"Have a good game, babe," I say as I start walking down the hallway.

"Sophie! Get back here."

I twirl around, causing my dress to rise up a little bit. "You can't make me."

"Joe, can you see, I mean, uh, Sophie's dress, can you —" Seb says, sputtering as he points at me.

"I'm wearing a dark dress that goes below my knees. No one will see anything—unless I want them to."

"Sophia, get back here," Seb says, a smile spreading over his face.

"Nope. Maybe you can wear them during the game like that guy did in that movie—"

"*Bull Durham*," Joe says, exhaling loudly as he looks at the ceiling. "The name of the movie is *Bull Durham*."

"Yes, thank you, Joe. *Bull Durham*." I blow Seb a kiss. "See you after the game. It's up to you how long that is."

"This is going to be the shortest fucking game of my life," Seb says, pointing at me. "I want you to be the first person I see when I come off the field."

"The very first. I promise." I give him another smile before I spin around again.

"Less spinning, please," he yells as I continue down the hall.

"Y'all give me a headache." Joe snarls from behind me. "Are you good now? Can we concentrate on the game?"

"I'm all good," Seb says. "Let's get on the field already. I've got a game to win."

Chapter Twelve

SEB

October 30, 2022

We won the first game of the series 4-0. I went three for four with two RBIs. Manny pitched a three-hitter. Alex went two for four, scored two runs, and made a few highlight-reel plays at short stop.

As we come out of the dugout tunnel, I immediately see Sophie. She's standing just to the left of the other wives. Her eyes are glued to the tunnel exit. When she sees me, an enormous grin breaks out over her face. She sprints over, leaps into my body, and starts placing little kisses all over my face.

"You played great, baby. I'm so proud of you."

"I played great because I knew I got to see you immediately after the game. You're my motivation."

"Was I the first person you saw?" She beams up at me as I lower her to the floor. "I tried to separate myself from the group a little so you would have an unobstructed sight line. Maybe I should start wearing neon colors or something."

"You glow just fine without them," I say, leaning down for a kiss.

"Hey," she says when I finally stop trying to inhale her. "We're out in the open. I thought you didn't like everyone getting pictures of our intimate time."

I brush my lips over hers again. "I don't care what they get pictures of. I just want to kiss you."

She pushes the sweaty hair off my face. "God, you look so sexy right now."

"Right back at you," I whisper. "Maybe we can sneak some alone time when we get back to the hotel."

"I don't know." She peeks under my arm. "Drew's glaring at us right now. He'll probably post his minions outside your room tonight."

I glance over my shoulder. Drew's standing at the entrance to the clubhouse—shifting from foot to foot. His eyes are fixed on me.

"Drew can fuck off," I say, turning back to her. "I swear I think he's losing it."

"Right? His control issues are almost getting creepy. I went into the press box with Dottie during the game. She had an interview with the local radio. When she was in the booth, he pulled me aside and told me that I needed to stay in my lane."

"What does that mean?" I glare back at Drew. This time he looks away.

"I don't know—like maybe he didn't want me in the

press box or something. He's so wound up. He should be basking in the glow of the World Series. Dottie barely talks to him. She called him an 'a-hole' tonight. You know how much she must hate him if she even uses a hybrid cuss word."

"I think that's why he's wound up. He thinks he's going to lose his job. Has Dottie said anything about firing him?"

"No," she says, shaking her head—her long blonde ponytail whipping back and forth. "We don't talk about team stuff except what's pertinent to her interviews."

Joe walks over and taps my shoulder. "Seb, almost everyone's off the field. You need to get into the clubhouse."

"Okay." I kiss the top of Sophie's head and inhale slowly. Her hair always smells so good—like a mix of flowers and oranges. It's like scent therapy for me. "Don't worry about Drew. I'll take care of him. I'll text you when we're headed back to the hotel."

"Can you join us for a drink when you get back?"

"Who's 'us'?" I ask as I back up toward the clubhouse.

"Our families and the Blitzen crew. Roman reserved the private dining room for a postgame party. Will you stop by?"

"I'd prefer to be alone with you, but yeah, I'll be there. Save me a seat by you, okay?"

"Always." She tilts her head and smiles—the green flecks in her light brown eyes shimmering.

"You know what that look does to me. I won't be able to concentrate on anything the media says in the post press conference." I raise my eyebrows. "And speaking of things that distract me, I still have something that belongs to you."

"Yeah, I'll have to get those back from you sometime." She smiles and blows me a kiss.

When I turn around, Drew's lurking right behind me. I have to take a quick sidestep to avoid knocking him over. He follows me toward the clubhouse.

"You played great tonight, Seb," he says, patting my back.

"Thanks," I grumble, not turning around. I give Chick a fist bump. "What'd you think, Chick? Give me my game notes."

"Stellar play, Seb." Chick stretches back in his chair. "I already told Alex but you might want to watch their left fielder. His lead at first base in the sixth was insulting."

"Yeah," I say, leaning against the wall next to him. "We haven't seen him yet this season. He came up from the minors after we had already played them. He was definitely trying to distract me. I think he's a little too nervous to run, though."

"That's what I told Alex. The way he was jumping around, he looked like he had firecrackers in his pants. Maybe pick him off first if you get the chance. I'm not sure he could get back."

"Chick, I'm sure Seb doesn't need you to tell him how to play," Drew says, trying to guide me into the clubhouse. "He has a manager and coaches for that."

"What did you say to him?" I push Drew's arm off me. "What Chick and I talk about is none of your business. Or do you want to try to regulate that too?"

"We're all good, Seb." Chick taps my leg. "No need to get upset. Leave it on the field."

I glare at Drew for another few seconds and then give

Chick a nod. "I'll watch for the pickoff at first, Chick. Appreciate the heads-up. I'll see you tomorrow."

Drew follows me into the clubhouse. I wait for the door to close, then whip my finger into his face.

"Never talk to Chick like that again. Do you understand me? That man has worked for this organization for forty years. Show him some respect."

Everyone in the clubhouse turns to look at us. Drew puts his hand on my shoulder.

"Seb," he whispers, "I think we need to do a reset. I know you're upset about staying at the hotel, but you have to admit the isolation produced a good result tonight."

"No, Drew," I say, settling into the chair in front of my locker. "Manny's three-hitter produced the good result tonight. It had nothing to do with him being isolated in a hotel room. He's just a great fucking pitcher."

I lean over to snap off my leg guards. Drew crouches down beside me.

"Seb." He looks over his shoulder to make sure no one's eavesdropping. "I heard you snuck Sophie into your office before the game. That's not even close to being appropriate. We'll have to take the office away if you're using it for uh, personal reasons."

I put my elbows on my knees so my face is just a few inches from his. "I'm only going to say this one time so pay close attention. You do whatever you want with team rules—make me stay in a hotel, take my office away, trade me, bench me, whatever—but if you comment again about what's appropriate for my wife and me, there aren't enough cops in this stadium to pull me off you."

Joe tries to subtly wedge his leg between our faces. "Everyone's watching, gentlemen."

"And let me add," I say, pushing Joe's leg out of the way. Drew's bald head is now covered with sweat. "Don't talk to my wife again. Don't look at her. Forget you ever knew her name. Are we clear?"

"Ray Franklin's looking right at you." Joe puts his hand on my shoulder. "The front-page story should be about the win and not whatever this is, don't you think?"

"Nice game, Seb," Drew yells as he bounces up. He looks around to make sure everyone's watching. "Keep up the great play, man."

Joe looks down at me after Drew walks away. "What's wrong with you? Can you get through one day without picking a fight with someone?"

"I don't pick fights."

Joe collapses against my locker, grabs his gut, and lets out an exaggerated laugh. "You don't pick fights? Seriously? Are there people who you haven't threatened? I mean, just let me know who and I can get them over here. How about that batboy who put your bat in the wrong cubby tonight? What's his name? Billy? I can get him over here if you want to take a swing. He's only like thirteen but never too young to learn a lesson. Maybe don't hit him in the face though because he has braces and that's going to cut up his lips. Hey, Billy. Come over here. Seb wants to talk to you."

Billy looks up from the corner of the clubhouse where he's sitting with our other batboys, shoving in some leftover cupcakes from the pregame catering.

"Stay where you are, Billy," I say as he starts wiping

the frosting from his hand onto his jersey. "And good job tonight—all of you."

"Okay, well Billy's safe for now. So, uh, let's see, how about Miss Frieda? You know the lady who caters the team's pregame meal room. She's the one who makes the little fried peach pies just for you. I had one tonight. I think she used too much butter. Maybe rough her up a little. She's like Chick's age, but if she can't make your damn pies right, she probably deserves a good whooping."

"Okay, Joe. You made your point."

"Did I?" He looks down at me. "Are you sure there's not anyone else you want to fight?"

"Actually, I'd kind of like to take a swing at you right now."

"Pshhh. Son, you couldn't come close to taking me down. You wouldn't even get a swing in. Especially now. You've gotten soft since you met Sophie."

I raise my eyebrows. "Okay, NoJoe. Be here when I get back and we'll see who's soft."

"I'm not going anywhere," he says, puffing out his barrel chest. "I'm always here."

"No truer words have ever been spoken," I say, sighing.

I grab my toiletry bag out of the locker to see what Sophie packed. Before every game, she stuffs it full of little bottles of shampoo, conditioner, and lotion, and the soap I like that smells like coconuts. And she always includes a note.

Only two more weeks until we're at the lake house! I

promise I'll try to bait my own hook this time. But can I use gummy worms instead of the real ones? I think the fish will like them. xxxxoooo

---

"What did Sophie pack for you tonight, sweetie?" Dane looks over from his locker. "Some pretty perfumes? Or maybe a sweater in case it gets cold later."

Manny walks by and tries to grab the note. I stiff arm him.

"Ooo, Seb, use the little soapies I pack for you," he says, ducking under my arm. "You smell so good, baby."

"Fuck you," I say. "Just because you pitched a three-hitter doesn't mean I won't come after you."

"I thought you didn't pick fights," Joe says. "And I told you I'm right here if you want to fight someone."

"Take him down, Joe," Manny says. "I'll pay to see it."

"How much?" Joe asks. "Maybe we should get pay-per-view involved."

When I get out of the shower, Ray Franklin, our beat reporter from the Miami newspaper, is sitting next to my locker.

"Good game, Seb."

"Thanks, Ray. Isn't the media supposed to catch us in the interview room during the post season?"

"Yeah, mostly. Ken always sneaks me in here since I'm with you guys every day of the season." He pauses for a second. "So what was that tense conversation with Drew about before you went into the showers?"

I pull on a clean t-shirt. "It wasn't tense. Just a conversation."

"Was he talking to you about putting some more years on your contract? You've only got one left—well two if you count your player option year."

"No, he wasn't talking about my contract." I rake a dab of the cream stuff Sophie gave me through my hair. She said it defines my waves.

"Has he talked to you about extending your contract? You're turning twenty-nine this year but you're playing at the absolute top of your game. You probably have five, even ten years, left in you. Do you want to keep playing?"

"Seriously, Ray, I'm not even thinking about my contract. We're in the World Series. We just won the first game. I'm trying to take everything one day at a time." I grab my shoes out of the locker and hold them up to him. "Sophie bought me these shoes. She said they're boat shoes or something. What do you think? They're not really my style."

Ray watches me pull them on. "My wife has dressed me for thirty years. I think it's best not to ask questions. They usually get it right."

"Yeah, I guess. She hasn't missed yet. People always say how they like the things she picks out for me."

He laughs. "I think Joe's right. You are getting soft—but in a nice way. Sophie's good for you. And I'm not talking about the shoes. You seem happier now."

"I am. So much happier. Sophie's changed everything.

People talk about her being a distraction when she's really the only thing that keeps me sane."

He looks up from his notebook. "Can I quote you on that? I know you don't like talking about your family to the media."

"Yeah, you can use it. And make sure you put it in all capital letters. I want everyone to know she's not a distraction. She's my world now and it's a pretty fucking amazing world."

Chapter Thirteen

SOPHIE

October 30, 2022

"I just want to lick you. Settle down."

"Oh my god," I say, shoving Kit away from me. "Butch! Control your woman. She's trying to lick me."

"Pass," he says, leaning back on a bar stool. "I like my woman wild. You go ahead and lick her, baby. Let Daddy watch."

"Eww! Stop referring to yourself as Daddy." I try to whack him across the chest.

He grabs my hand and curls it into a fist. "I see you subscribe to the Raine style of fighting. The fist is your friend. Use it. Open-hand is for babies."

"Really?" I ask. "Do you know babies who are using open-hand slapping as a defensive technique?"

"Some," he says, rolling a toothpick around in his mouth. "Mine's going to be hitting with a fist from day one, though."

"Speaking of," I say, hip bumping Kit away from me as she tries to lick me again, "you're going to be real parents soon. You'll have to learn how to behave in public."

"Naw, that's not true at all," Butch says. "Some of the wildest people I know are parents."

"Are you talking about me again, honey?" Millie walks up behind him and circles her arms around his neck.

"You know I am, sugar," he says, kissing her cheek.

"I still don't understand this group's free-loving-on-Butch policy." I look at Kit. "Millie and Raine are always hugging on him. Doesn't that bother you?"

"Not at all," she says, smiling as Millie squeezes him even tighter. "He can hug on whoever he wants as long as he's only sticking it in me."

"Oh my god!" I choke on my drink and spit half of it out.

"Soph," Millie says, handing me a napkin, "if you're going to hang with us, you have to learn the rules. First rule, Butch and Sam are free game for all the hugs you can give them. Second, we say what we mean. You need to toughen up."

Maisie pounds on my back a few times as I continue to cough. "Toughen up, Soph. This group is amazing. You have to be part of it, so I can be part of it by association."

"Agree, we need both of you in the group," Kit says as she backs up in between Butch's legs. He gives her butt a squeeze then circles his arms around her waist. "Okay, Soph, if you won't let me lick your perfume, at least tell me what it is so I can start wearing it for my man."

"Oh, baby, you don't need to do anything else to turn me on." Butch buries his head in her neck. "And if you like it enough to want to lick it off Sophie, it sounds like I should be wearing it. I'll start taking baths in it if necessary."

"It's not, baby." She spins around in his arms and licks his lips. "You know I like to lick you anyway."

"Stop!" I put my hands over my eyes. "The PDA in this group is just—"

"Shut up!" Maisie pulls my hands down. "What are you even talking about? You and Seb are always on each other."

"Not like that!" I point at Butch and Kit.

Kit turns back around and smiles. "Watch, learn, and then try it on your own. What's the name of the perfume?"

"Salt Air." I grab the bottle out of my bag and spray it at her. She starts licking the air. "It's supposed to smell like the beach. I'm never wearing it around you again."

"Do I want to know why Kit's licking at the air?" Nash asks as he walks over to us. He holds up his hand. "Nope. Wait. I definitely don't want to know. I withdraw the question. Butch, poker game starting over in the corner. You up?"

"Yep," Butch says, giving Kit another kiss before he stands up. "Millie, you want in?"

"No, sweetie," she says, smiling. "I'll let you keep your money tonight. I think I'm going to hang with my ladies."

"Thank God," Butch grumbles as he walks away with Nash.

We got back from the stadium a little more than an hour ago. We're hanging out in the private cigar bar at Roman's hotel. He reserves it for family, friends, and celebrities. It's the hottest ticket in Miami. Everyone wants in, but very few are invited.

Roman styled it after his grandfather's house in Havana. There are deep red, plush couches accented with bright yellow pillows scattered throughout the room. The only lighting comes from chandeliers that were handcrafted out of old hubcaps from classic Chevy Bel Airs—the car that his grandfather drove. The hand carved bar is made from deep mahogany that Roman imported—probably illegally—directly from Cuba.

Roman emerges from behind the bar, circling us with a fresh pitcher of his signature cocktail—Paloma's Punch. He named it after his mother because just like her, it kicks your ass every time you get near it. I have no idea what's in it, but it's the most potent, delightful thing I've ever tasted. My head's already spinning after the first glass.

"Ladies," Roman says, a wicked grin covering his face. "Time for refills."

Elle holds up her glass for more. "This stuff is delicious. It tastes like birthday cake mixed with sunshine. Will you teach me how to make it? I want to serve it at my wedding."

"Invite me to your wedding." Roman tops off her glass. "I'll make it for you."

"You're absolutely invited. Would you really come?"

"Definitely. My husband, Michael, and I want to open a hotel out west. Maybe we'll open something in Blitzy Bay."

"*Blitzen*, like the reindeer." I drain my glass and hold it up for a refill. He pushes it back down. I hold it up again. He pushes it down again. "Why though? Roman, more drinky, please."

He ignores me. "This recipe is a well-protected family

secret, but I promise I'll make sure all of you are swimming in it every time you visit me in Miami."

"Are we invited back?" Millie asks, tilting her head and smiling. "Or maybe we'll never leave."

"Nothing would make me happier," he says, lifting her hand and kissing it. "Sophie didn't tell me how delightful her new lady friends are."

"I didn't tell you because they're taken, you're taken," I say, holding my glass up again, "and, oh yeah, you're gay."

"I appreciate beauty in every gender." He pushes my glass back down. "No more for you, lightweight. I promised Seb after the last time."

"Booooo. Boooooooooooo." I try to grab the pitcher from him.

"Stop," he says, pulling it away from me. "You already have the Sloppy Sophie look in your eyes."

"Just halvsies then. Please." I bat my eyelashes at him. "Pretty please."

"Half," he says as he pours. "Drink it slowly. And eat something. We're not repeating the pool party incident."

"What pool party incident?" Elle asks.

"Michael and Sophie were trying to *Riverdance* after being over served. It took a bad turn—into the pool to be exact. Seb had to go in fully clothed and pull Sophie out." He points at me. "And stay away from Michael tonight. He's a Sloppy Sophie enabler."

"Honestly, Sloppy Sophie sounds amazing," Kit says. "What's it going to take to get her there?"

"Believe me, she's already there." Roman points at Raine. "Come on, Raine. Don't try to hide. I know you can hold your liquor."

"What are you putting in this punch?" Raine peeks around Millie's body. "It tastes so good, and it makes me feel all yummy inside."

"You say that like it's a bad thing." Roman laughs as he grabs her glass and tops it off. "Let loose, Raine. Nothing but love here tonight."

Raine looks at her phone. "Speaking of love, Alex just texted me. The team bus is almost back. Come on, Soph. I want to make out with him for a few minutes before his curfew."

I slam the half glass of Paloma. "Do you want me to watch or something?"

"Oh god, yes. Do that," Kit says, whistling. "Super hot. Can we all watch?"

"No one's watching anything," Raine say, pointing around the group. "Soph, I want you to come with me because that means your husband will be back too. You remember him, right?"

"Oh yeah," I say, nodding as the liquor takes control of yet another section of my brain. "They play for the same team, don't they? I forgot that for a second."

"Good Lord," Raine says as she starts pulling me across the bar.

"Stop." Mason jumps up from the poker table and blocks us. "No leaving the bar without an escort, especially with the way you're both swaying right now."

"We're fine, Mason. Go back to your poker game." I look around the room. "Wait, am I yelling? Why am I yelling?"

"Mason," Roman says from behind the bar. "Go back to your game. Enjoy. My brother can watch them. Los!"

"What's up?" Carlos asks from the corner table where he's huddled with their other brothers—smoking cigars and observing the scene.

"Sophie and Raine are meeting the team bus," Roman says, not looking up from the drink he's mixing. "Make sure no one touches them except Seb and Alex."

"On it." He saunters over to us and puts his hand out to Mason. "I'm Los. You one of the SEALs?"

"Yep," Mason says as they size each other up.

"I'll take care of the ladies," Los says, cracking his neck. "No one will get near them. Believe me."

Millie walks over and grabs Mason's arm. "I'll go with them in case he needs backup. I want to call Dad anyway to see how Mo's doing."

"Mo!" I throw myself into Millie and Mason and wrap my arms around them. "Please tell me your sweet son is coming to a game in L.A. I need to see him again so badly."

Millie laughs. "I'll have Dad bring him up to L.A. if you can get them tickets."

"Mo can have anything he wants," I say. "He can have a million tickets. I love him so much."

"Come on, Soph. The bus is pulling in." Raine grabs me and pulls me toward the lobby. "And quit yelling, you freak."

Chapter Fourteen

SEB

October 30, 2022

When I walk off the bus in front of the hotel, I literally run into Evelyn. When I reach out to steady her, she mistakes it as an invitation for a hug. She dives into me.

"Hey! Good game tonight," she says as I give her an awkward squeeze and then push her back. "Are you headed up to the roof for the party? I'll ride up on the elevator with you."

"Uh, yeah." I look over to Alex. "Is our party on the roof?"

"I don't think so," he says, throwing his bag over his shoulder. "Raine said it's in that swanky private cigar bar."

"Oh, sorry, Ev. What party's on the roof?"

Her forehead wrinkles up. "The team party. I didn't know there was another one. You should go to the team thing."

"I might stop by before I call it a night," I say, nodding

to Stone and Paul who are walking across the hotel parking lot with their wives. "What's up, fellas?"

"Good game tonight." Stone gives me a fist bump. "Manny was throwing bullets. Do you still have use of your hand?"

I hold up my catching hand. "Yeah, but barely. I'm sure I'm going to have a few bruises in the morning. His fast ball was definitely popping."

"Hey," Paul says, nodding his head backward. "Our names were on the clearance list, but Ricky's wasn't. He's standing out there with Kaitlyn."

"And he can continue to stand out there with Kaitlyn." I motion them toward the lobby. "You can come in or go back out there with him. Your choice."

"Oh, we're coming in," Paul says. "He has to learn that his actions have consequences. You want to let him know or should I?"

"I'm not saying anything to him," I say, turning toward the lobby. "He can stand out there all night for all I care."

"Seb," Evelyn says, pulling on my arm. "Will you sign autographs for me? A few of my clients are in the lobby."

"Uh, yeah but fast. I want to see Sophie."

She pulls me over to a few people who are standing by the registration desk. As I sign a few autographs, Millie walks over to us.

"Hey, Millie," I say. "Is the party started?"

"More than started. It's at full tilt. You better get back there." She holds her hand out to Evelyn who's following me for some reason.

"Hi," Millie says. "I'm Millie Davis. I'm a friend of Seb's."

Evelyn shakes her hand. "You must be new. I've been around since Seb was a rookie. I thought I had met all of his friends."

"Brand new." Millie smiles. "And who are you?"

"I'm Evelyn. Seb and I have been friends for almost a decade. Right, Seb?"

"Uh, yeah."

"It's nice to meet you, Evelyn," Millie says, linking her arm through mine. "Seb, I'll show you where our party is."

"I know where it is," I say, narrowing my eyebrows as I look down at Millie. She holds my arm tighter when I try to pull it away.

"When should I tell everyone you'll be at the team party?" Evelyn asks as she glares at Millie.

"He won't have time to come to that party." Millie lays her head against my arm. "We're going to take up all of his time tonight. Bye, Ellen. It was nice meeting you."

"Millie, what's wrong with you?" I laugh as she pulls me away. "Are you drunk?"

She glances over her shoulder, and then smiles up at me. "Just doing a little experiment."

"What experiment?"

She releases my arm. "Did you ever have a thing with Evelyn?"

"Evelyn Marks? That Evelyn?"

"Yes, Seb. That Evelyn."

"No. God no. Never. We just work together."

"Hmm." Millie starts walking again.

"What? What does 'hmm' mean? You don't believe me?"

She stops again. "I believe you, but I think Evelyn might be interested in you."

"Not a chance." I do a quick eye sweep of the lobby to try to find Sophie. "You're wrong."

"Sometimes, but not very often," Millie says, pointing to the group of ceiling-high palm plants across the room. "Incoming."

"Seb!"

I look up to see Sophie coming around the palms at full speed. She jumps into my body and wraps her arms and legs around me.

"Hey," I say, circling my arms under her butt. She dives into my lips for a very drunken kiss. "Wow. Okay. Have you had a few already? Maybe three or four?"

"No, I've only had one glass of liquor." She puts one finger in my face to accentuate her point. And then mouths, "One."

"One glass, huh?" I lick her finger sending giggles rippling through her body. "How big was the glass? And what kind of liquor are we talking?"

She looks around the lobby like she's about to reveal classified information.

"Paloma," she mouths as she looks back at me.

"Oh, okay," I say, whistling. "Now I understand. I thought Roman agreed not to serve you Paloma after his last pool party."

"He gave me one Paloma," she whispers as her forehead leans against mine. "He said he wouldn't give me any more, but I talked him into another half glass. Don't tell anyone. Our secret."

"Of course you talked him into it. He's never been able

to say no to you. I guess that's something we have in common." I kiss her nose. "Where are Butch and Mason? They're supposed to be watching you."

"Playing poker." She arches her back until she's basically doing a backbend and points to Roman's brother, Carlos, who's about ten feet behind her. "Hi, Carlos!"

"Hey, Soph," Carlos says. "You're yelling again. Inside voice, remember?"

"Wait," Sophie says. "Why am I upside down?"

Carlos walks over and pushes her back up. "We're good, Seb. I'm keeping an eye on her."

"Appreciate it, Los."

"Carlos is covering me," she whispers as he goes back to his watch position. "He said he would whip anyone who got near me. Whip-p-p. That's fun to say. Whip-p-p-p. Seb, say it."

I shake my head. "Whip."

She laughs to herself as she pinches my lips together. "It makes your lips pucker. Say it again."

"Tequila makes you so crazy," I say, biting at her fingers. It makes her giggle again. "Cute crazy, but still crazy."

"No," she says slowly. "I drank Paloma, not tequila."

"Baby," I say, heading back toward the cigar bar with her still attached to my chest. "Paloma has tequila in it."

She gasps and pulls her head back. "No, it doesn't."

"Yes, it does."

Her mouth drops open. "It doesn't taste like tequila at all."

"That's because Roman puts about a hundred different things in it to mask the taste."

"Did I hear my name?" Roman looks over to us as we walk into the bar.

"Are you responsible for this?" I ask as I lower Sophie onto a couch.

"I swear, man," Roman says, "I only gave her one glass."

"And a half," Sophie says, pointing at him.

"Quiet, drunkie," he says, looking down at her. "I'm getting you food right now."

"I want tacos. And doughnuts."

"You're getting rice and plantains," he says. "Those are the only things that soak up Paloma."

I sit down on the couch next to her and pull her onto my lap. "Promise me you won't get near a pool tonight."

"I promise," she says, putting her hands around my face and pulling me in for kiss.

"Your breath smells like cherry Jolly Ranchers."

"Sorry." She covers her mouth with her hand.

"I didn't say it was a bad thing." I kiss her again and let my tongue explore a little bit. "I think I might get drunk just from the leftover in your mouth."

"Good game, Seb." Butch walks over and hands me a beer. "Soph, what were you saying about PDA?"

Sophie curls up her fist and punches his stomach in slow motion. "Butch is teaching me how to fight."

"The fist is better," he says, laughing, "but we're going to need to get you on the speed bag."

I look up as Roman puts a bowl of rice and plantains on the table in front of us.

"Eat up, Soph," he says. "No more liquor until you make a happy plate."

She sticks her tongue out at him as he walks away. "You're not the boss of me!"

"Inside voice, baby," I say, shifting her onto the couch beside me. I dish out a large portion of rice. "Let's get something in your stomach before I have to go up to my room. From the looks of this party, I'm guessing you're not done drinking for the night."

Chapter Fifteen

SOPHIE

October 31, 2022

Seb and I spent about twenty minutes together when he got back from the stadium last night. He stopped by our party at the hotel, had a beer, and then went up to his room to get some sleep in preparation for game two tonight.

I wish I had gone to my room early. Our families and the Blitzen Bay crew partied well into the early hours of the morning. It was such a nice release at the time, but this morning, I'm tired, hungover, and struggling to make an early meeting with Dottie.

Raine takes the pillow off her head and tries to focus on me—her eyes barely open. "Dottie won't care how you look. She was at the party pretty late too."

"I'm trying to at least look good since I smell straight up like a liquor bottle."

"Didn't you take a shower?" She pulls the blankets over

her face. "I remember hearing running water. Or was that in my dream?"

"I took a shower, but I still smell like booze." I pull down the blanket and hold my arm out to her. "Smell me."

"Ooo," she says, pushing my arm away. "I don't want to smell you. I already feel like I'm going to puke. I swear that stuff Roman was making last night had some kind of opiate in it. What did he call it? Paloma's Punch? Who the fuck is Paloma? I hate her."

I grab a water bottle out of the mini fridge and hand it to her. "Paloma is Roman's mother. She's eighty-three and could still kick both of our asses."

"Her stupid punch already did that. I should have stopped way earlier." She pushes herself up on an elbow and takes a few sips of the water. "Why did we drink so much?"

"Because Millie and Maisie are really bad influences." I pull on the dress that Mom didn't want me to pack. "I swear those two could drink most men under the table."

"Could? They pretty much did last night. We never should have introduced them. They're really dangerous together." She takes another sip, then sinks back into the pillows. "I like that dress."

"Mom thinks it shows too much boob."

She twirls her finger to get me to spin around. "No, it's perfect. Deb can get over it."

"Okay, big talker. Say that to Deb's face. I dare you."

"Not a chance." She holds up her hand as she pauses to retch. "Your mom has always scared the bejeezle out of me."

Raine sniffs a few times as I spritz my perfume and run through it. "Is that the stuff you were wearing last night? Kit wanted to lick it off you."

"She literally tried to lick me several times. She's a trip—the perfect match for Butch." I hand her the rest of the crackers that I've been munching on since I woke up. "These help to soak up Paloma."

She stuffs a handful into her mouth and mutters. "Fuck Paloma."

"I had so much fun last night," I say, crawling back under the covers with her. "It was the perfect mix of people. I felt so comfortable—like I didn't have to watch everything I said and did. That doesn't happen much these days."

"Yeah, that was a good group. I even enjoyed talking to Stone and Paul and their wives. They're cool when they're separated from Rick the Dick." She grabs her phone and looks at a text that just came in. "Do we know why he and the high school girlfriend weren't there?"

"No idea. Don't care. It was just nice not feel under attack for once." I lay my head on her shoulder to try to see her phone screen. "Who's texting?"

"Alex," she says, pulling it away from me. "He wants to make sure I'm okay. Paloma talked me into texting him some pretty filthy stuff last night."

I groan when I hear a knock on the door. "Please don't make me leave this bed."

"Go, before they break down the door." Raine shoves me as a louder knock vibrates through the room. "SEALs don't like to be kept waiting."

I groan again and roll off the bed. "Do you know who my bodyguard is this morning?"

"I'm guessing Mason. Butch and Kit were still going strong when we left last night."

"Can you imagine what Kit's like when she's not pregnant?" I ask as I trudge to the door. "She was the life of the party without an ounce of liquor."

"I've witnessed drunk Kit. Honestly, there's not much of a difference. I'm not sure she has any inhibitions, regardless of alcohol consumption."

I look through the peephole. Butch is standing in the hallway.

"How?" I ask as I open the door. "How do you look this refreshed when you drank double what I did and went to bed after me?"

He shrugs as he walks in and closes the door. "SEAL training and about a decade more drinking experience than you. There's no way you can compete."

I point to Raine who's peeking out of the blankets. "Are we the only ones who are this hungover?"

"Naw, I just left Mason's room. Millie's pretty bad. We told y'all not to drink that fruity crap. Roman looked like a mad scientist when he was mixing it," he says. "By the way, Mills wants the women to meet in her room in about an hour for girl talk. She said it's something about Sam."

"What about Sam?" I ask, pouting my lips. "Is he okay?"

Seb and I met Sam this summer when we bought Blitzen Bay from him. He's an adorable seventy-eight-year-old widower. Although he gives me absolutely no reason to worry about him, for some reason, I always do.

"I'm sure he's fine," Butch says. "Millie's just obsessed with him. She never knew either of her grandpas. I think she's adopted him."

"We all have," I say, frowning. "Now I'm worried."

"I'm pretty sure I know what it is." Raine's eyes get wide as she throws her hands over her mouth.

"You have a secret!" I hop back on the bed and pull her hands down. "What? You have to tell me."

She lets out a little squeal. "Okay. Brace yourself. Our precious Sam . . . left the party last night . . . with Dottie. I think there might have even been a sleepover."

I push her shoulders back. "You put those words back in your mouth right now! They're both in their seventies."

She looks up at Butch. "You saw them, right? Over in the corner of the room, whispering to each other all night."

"I saw." Butch nods. "And I think you both need to mind your business. Let my guy live."

I look back and forth between them. "How did I miss this? Someone fill in the details."

"Quit being nosy." Butch nods to the door. "It's five minutes before seven. We need to leave. I hate being late even when it's not my thing."

I point at Raine. "I'll meet you in Millie's room when I'm done. No gossip until I get there. Promise?"

"Promise. And pump Dottie for information." Raine sinks back into the bed. "If I can't have sex with my boyfriend until this stupid series is done, I might have to live vicariously through a seventy-year-old."

Butch surveys the hallway, and then points me out of the room. As we start down the hall, Sam comes out of his room. I stop so suddenly that Butch crashes into me.

"Well, good morning," Sam says, a warm smile spreading over his face. "Careful where you're walking, Butch. You almost killed our sweet Sophie. Are you okay, dear?"

"I'm fine," I say, throwing my arms open to give him a hug, "but a hug will make me feel even better."

"I'm always up for hugs." He squeezes me tightly. "Why are you up so early? Frankly, I wasn't sure any of you would be alive this morning after last night's party."

"I'm barely alive, but I promised the team owner I would help her with a few interviews this morning." I tilt my head and smile at him. "Her name's Dottie. I think you met her last night."

"I did. She's a lovely woman."

I look up at Butch and smile. He shakes his head and points toward the elevator.

"Where are you off to, Sam?" Butch asks.

"I thought I would get a walk in on the beach before things get too crazy."

"That sounds good," Butch says. "Remember to get a security card from the police before you leave so they'll let you back into the hotel. Do you have your phone? Call me if you have any problems."

"I'll be fine," Sam says. "You just take good care of Sophie. She looks a little pale this morning."

"I'm extremely hungover." I pat my face a few times to try to get some color running through it. "I hope you didn't drink as much as I did, Sam."

"I had three beers. That's one more than I usually have," he says, laughing. It causes his entire body to shake.

It's so adorable that I throw myself into him for another hug.

"Sophie," Butch says, pulling me back, "it's seven. What floor is Dottie on?"

"Um." I act like I'm looking for her room number on my phone. "I know I wrote it down somewhere, but I can't find it."

"She's in room 212." Sam pats my shoulder as he walks by us. "I'm going to take the stairs to get a few extra steps in. Have a good morning. I'll see you at the game later."

Butch looks at me and rolls his eyes as we watch Sam walk through the stairwell door. "Subtle. You should go into some kind of spy work."

"He knows her room number!" I push at his chest with all of my strength. He doesn't budge. "Butch! Did he sleep there last night?"

"He probably walked her to her room, nosy." He holds the elevator door open for me. "But if he made it inside, more power to him. There's no age limit on sex. I might have to buy him a beer later."

When the elevator stops on the second floor, Butch does an eye sweep of the hallway, and then motions me ahead of him. I barely get a knock in on Dottie's door before she flings it open.

"Good morning!" She waves us inside. "Come in. Come in. Butch, you're invited in too. I have breakfast and lots of coffee."

"Thank you, ma'am, but I already ate. If you don't mind, I'm going to hit the gym while Sophie's with you."

"Oh, yes, please do," Dottie says. "There's no better

way to start the day. I did a little exercise myself this morning."

"I bet you did," Butch says under his breath.

I push him out the door and whisper, "I hate you."

"Yep," he says, laughing as I slam the door in his face, "that's usually the way the Butch friendship begins."

Chapter Sixteen

SEB

October 31, 2022

We leave for the stadium in about an hour for the second game of the series. I haven't seen Sophie all day. She took the Blitzen crew over to our house to nurse their hangovers at the pool before they head to the game tonight. I just called her to make sure she's coming to my office again before the game. I barely got a word out before she told me about Sam and Dottie.

"Soph, there's no way—"

"Seb! He knew her room number," she says as her eyebrows shoot up. "There's every way."

"Well," I say as I crawl off the couch to get some water. "Good for them, I guess."

"That's what Butch said," she says, giggling. "He wants to buy Sam a beer."

I haven't heard her sound this happy in a long time.

"I'm going to buy them both a beer," I say, plopping

back down on the couch. "Still hooking up in their seventies. I'm happy for them."

"Do you think we'll still be having as much sex in our seventies?" She walks away from where her phone's propped up on our kitchen island.

"Definitely," I say, flipping on the TV. "But honestly, I'm just concentrated on now. I feel like I haven't touched you in a year."

"I know, baby," she says, setting half of a watermelon in front of her as she slides back onto the bar stool. "I miss our morning routine."

I smile. "The sex or the smoothie I make you afterward?"

"All of the above," she says, scooping a big chunk of watermelon right out of the rind and shoving it into her mouth. Some of the juice runs down her chin.

"You look happy, babe."

"I am happy," she says as she wipes the juice off with her hand. "The party last night was so fun, and today, the same group is over here. They're so easy to be around. I wish you were here, though. Everyone misses you."

"Yeah, I wish I was there too."

"Do you want me to come back to the hotel?" She picks up the phone and looks more closely at me. "We could maybe hang out for a few minutes before you leave for the stadium."

"No," I say, yawning. "Just stay and have fun. It makes me happy when you're happy."

"Are you sure?" Her voice gets softer. "I'm worried about you. You have your sad puppy eyes going."

"I'm fine. I just miss you." I look back at the TV. "Should I watch *Moana* or ESPN?"

"*Moana*. Duh." She spins her finger around. "Turn me to the TV. I'll watch it with you."

"Baby, you don't need to do that. Go back to the party." I smooch her a kiss. "I'll see you in a few hours. You're still coming to my office before the game, right?"

"Definitely," she says, smooching me back. "If Joe can get me down there. You said Drew lectured you about it last night. You know he's going to be watching, especially after he caught Roman trying to sneak me into your room last night."

I shake my head. "Yeah, I'm never trusting Roman with a covert operation again. I definitely should have asked Mason or Butch to do it."

"Sophie." I hear my dad's voice in the background. "Is that Seb?"

"Yeah," Sophie says, turning the phone to Dad. "What's wrong?"

"Nothing you have to worry about. Hey, Seb."

"Hey, Dad. What's up?"

"Uh," he says, taking the phone from Sophie. His face is tight. "Ricky's at security. He wants to be cleared."

"No." I sit up and glare into the phone. "Not going to happen."

"The guard said he's alone—no Katie," Dad says, glancing up at Sophie. "And Stone and Paul are here with their wives."

"Don't let him in Dad," I say, growling. "He makes Sophie uncomfortable. She's having a good time. He'll ruin everything."

"Seb." Sophie peeks around Dad's body. "It's okay. I don't want to cause tension between everyone."

"You're not causing anything. He's the one being a dick." I pause for second. "Look, he still has tickets to the game, and Katie has a pass to the suite, but I don't want them at our house. Don't let him in."

"Soph!" I hear Maisie scream. "Kit's telling the story of how she and Butch met. It apparently involves a raccoon. I told her to pause until you get out here. Is that Seb? Hey, Seb! Good win last night. We miss you!"

"Hey, Mae. I miss you guys too." I smile at her as she waves in the background. "Soph, go out and hear the raccoon story so you can tell me later. If it involves Butch and Kit, you know it has to be good. Dad and I will handle this. Okay?"

"Okay," she says, smooching another kiss at me. "I'll hopefully see you before the game. I love you."

"I love you, baby. Have fun."

The elevator beeps to alert me that someone's on their way up to the suite. It has to be Joe since he has the only other elevator pass key.

"Hey, Dad," I say, "Joe's on his way up. I have to go. Don't let Ricky in. He's done this to himself."

"I won't," Dad says. "Don't even think about it anymore. I have it handled. Have a good game. We're so proud of you, Seb."

"Thanks, Dad," I say, hanging up as the elevator door opens.

"I have another thirty minutes, Joe."

"You have another twenty-two minutes," he says. "And bring your bags. We're not staying here tonight."

"What?" I raise up a little bit and look at him over the back of the couch. "Are we headed to L.A. after the game? I thought we were leaving tomorrow morning."

"We are leaving tomorrow morning. Drew decided to let the team stay at their homes tonight."

I jump up. "Seriously? Please tell me you're not fucking with me."

"I would never kid about something as important to you as spending the night with Sophie. I would like to keep living beyond today."

"Damn!" I jog into my bedroom and start throwing my stuff into the suitcase. "I can't wait to tell Sophie. Are you sure about this?"

"Yeah. Drew just texted everyone."

I grab my phone and read the text. "Amazing. Why did he change his mind? Is he trying to ease up on the reins a little bit?"

"I doubt that's the case. I think he's just pissed at Roman. They apparently got into it last night about something. Max heard Roman calling Drew a 'controlling little fuck.'"

"Uh, that was probably me. I asked Roman to sneak Sophie up to my room. It didn't exactly go as planned."

Joe shakes his head. "All of you are behaving like sixteen-year-olds at summer camp."

"I can't help it. I'm having serious Sophie withdrawal symptoms. I feel like my dick is about to explode."

He spits out a little of the water he's drinking. "What the fuck, Seb? That's a textbook example of TMI. Keep that shit to yourself."

"Sorry, man. All this excitement must have temporarily

disabled my filter." I take a deep breath and smile. "God, I can't believe I get to spend the entire night with her."

"You are the most whipped man I've ever met." Joe throws some socks from the floor into my bag. "Does Sophie give you treats when you walk this nicely on your leash?"

"Oh yeah," I say, nodding, "she definitely gives me treats."

"Damn. I walked right into that one."

"Yup." I grab my suitcase and head out into the living room. "Can you bring Sophie to my office before the game again?"

"Why? You can't wait a few more hours until you get home?"

"I can wait. I just want some alone time with her."

"I'll try," he says, punching the elevator button. "But Drew's probably going to be on high alert."

"We won last night after she came to the office," I say, walking onto the elevator. "We probably don't want to screw up that mojo."

He cocks his head. "You aren't at all superstitious. Don't give me that shit."

"I'm not, but you're superstitious as fuck. If you want us to lose because I'm not following the exact same pregame ritual, I guess that's up to you."

Joe hisses. "If I get her in there, you better fucking win."

"Get who in where?" Roman asks as we walk out into the lobby.

"Joe sneaks Sophie into my private office at the stadium before games sometimes. She helps me focus."

"Man, we should have had him in on the mission last night," Roman says. "I thought for sure I could get Sophie up to your room. Maybe I'm not as sneaky as I thought I was."

"Man, you're not sneaky at all. You have the subtlety of a sledgehammer. I don't know why I even asked you."

"Desperate times call for desperate measures." Roman lowers his voice and continues, "You should have asked Alex's girlfriend, Raine, to sneak Sophie up there. I think she's CIA. She's barely five feet tall, but she still scares the fuck out of me."

"Wait until you meet her friend Millie," I say, whistling. "She's the one who scares me."

"I met Millie last night." He pauses and takes a slow breath. "And I *highly* approve. I already told Michael if he divorces me, I'll switch teams immediately and go hard after her. She's one hundred percent my type—besides the fact that she's not a man, of course."

"Don't let Mason hear you say that. He's not going to like that talk even from a gay man," I say, walking toward the doors as the bus pulls up.

"I'm way more scared of Millie than Mason," Roman says, closing his eyes and smiling. "And I mean scared in the absolute best way."

"Man, keep your fantasies to yourself. We're not friends like that." I look over my shoulder. "Thanks again for the hospitality. No offense, but I hope we don't have to stay here when we get back from L.A."

He points at me. "Win two in L.A. and you won't have to stay anywhere except your house until next season."

Leave it on the Field

Chapter Seventeen

SOPHIE

October 31, 2022

Seb has texted me three times in the last five minutes. He's waiting for me in his office.

"Drew saw you go in there last night," Joe says as we're getting off the elevator on the field level. "He mentioned it to Seb after the game, and then he balled me out for sneaking you in."

"Joe, I don't want you to get fired." I pull back on his arm. "Seb will survive without me. Let's just go back up to the suite."

"I'll get you into the office undetected," Butch says from behind us. "I'm pretty good at the sneaking stuff."

"Fuck." Joe stops as we get closer to the clubhouse. "Drew's standing right there. This isn't going to happen."

"What's not going to happen?" Evelyn walks up behind us. "You three look like you're on a super-secret mission or something."

"Hey, Ev," I say. "Seb's back in his office. He wants to chat with me before the game. I went in there before last night's game, and since they won, I'm sure he's just trying to repeat everything. You know how superstitious athletes are."

"Sophie!" Joe spins around. "No one's supposed to know about this."

"It's just Evelyn," I say. "She's not going to tell anyone. She loves Seb."

"I do love Seb. And I love winning even more. If this is what it's going to take, let's get it done." She looks around until her eyes land on Drew. "What's the problem? Is Drew trying to keep you from getting back there?"

"Kind of." I barely get it out before she starts in Drew's direction.

"I'll distract him," she says, looking over her shoulder. "Give me a minute."

"Evelyn!" Joe tries to grab her, but she's already headed across the concourse.

She glides up to Drew and puts her hand on his shoulder. She leans into him and whispers something. He smiles. She turns and walks away. He waits for a minute, and then follows her.

"Well, they're definitely fucking," Butch says.

"Ooo!" I backhand him across the stomach. "Don't say things like that. She's not having sex with Drew."

Butch whistles. "I'm not the best at reading body language, but she was definitely putting out some strong fuck-me vibes. What do you think, Joe?"

"I think we need to move while we have the opportunity." Joe pushes me toward Seb's office. "You have twenty minutes."

I hustle down the hall and knock on the office door. When Seb opens it, I jump into his arms.

"Hey, baby," he says, hugging me to him. "I thought you were standing me up."

"Never. Drew was posted outside the hallway like we knew he would be."

"You would think he'd have more important things to do before a game."

"He probably thinks the same thing about you."

"Nothing's more important than seeing you." He sits on the bed and pats his lap. "How did you get past him?"

"Evelyn distracted him," I say, hiking up my dress and straddling him. "Butch thinks they might be having sex."

"Who?"

"Evelyn and Drew," I say, crinkling up my nose.

"Oh, yeah, they're definitely having sex. Have been for years."

"What?" I lurch back and almost fall off his legs. "You knew they were having sex and you didn't tell me?"

"Why would you want to know? No one needs to think about that."

"Gross." I stick out my tongue. "Why would she have sex with him?"

"I don't know, babe," he says, rubbing my back. "I guess power is attractive to some women."

"Not when it comes wrapped in that ugly package." I bury my face into his neck. "And I'm not talking physically. He has such an ugly little soul."

"So, you're saying he's okay physically?"

"There's nothing okay about him." I melt into his body as he starts stroking my hair. "Yuck. I'll never be able to get this out of my head. What if they're having sex right now?"

"Whatever. I guess, everyone has to find someone."

"Does she know that you know?" I sit back up. "Have you talked about it?"

"Soph," he says, running his index finger down my face until in lands on my lips. "I don't want to talk to anyone about their sex life, especially not when it involves Drew."

"But you and Evelyn are friends. How have you not talked about who she's dating?"

"First, I'm not sure they're dating. They're having sex, but it doesn't seem to be a public relationship." He pulls me back against him and nuzzles his face into my hair. "And second, Evelyn and I aren't friends."

"What? How? You've worked together for nine years." I start wiggling on his lap as his lips make it to my neck. "Of course, you're friends—at least work friends. You've never talked to her about who's she dating?"

"Soph." He flips me down on the bed and stretches out beside me. "I've never talked to her about anything except work. She doesn't know anything about me personally and vice versa."

"Huh. That surprises me." He starts to run his fingers down my body. "I think she thinks you're friends."

"I don't know what she thinks. And I don't really care." His hand stops on my belly. "Can we please talk about something else? Or maybe not talk at all."

He rolls on top of me and quickly separates my lips with his tongue.

"Seb, stop," I say, pushing on his chest. "What if there are cameras in here?"

"Then, the world will see me lying on a bed, kissing my wife."

"Yeah, and then they'll add their own smutty details about what happened next—even though nothing happened."

I try to get away from him, but he throws his leg over me to stop my escape.

"Seb, seriously. Not the time or the place. Everyone's already calling me a whore. I don't need them having video evidence of it."

"Video evidence of what? Kissing your husband? I'm not sure how that makes you a whore."

"You know how it is." I push his leg off me and sit up. "You're the golden boy who can do no wrong, so any time something goes wrong, everyone blames me."

"Nothing is ever your fault," he says, running his hand down my arm. "Absolutely nothing."

"But I still get blamed for everything. Speaking of, have you heard from Ricky after we didn't let him into the house this afternoon? I'm sure he's blaming that on me. The security guy said he threw such a fit that they almost had to call the police."

He closes his eyes. "He's texted me almost nonstop over the last few days. I haven't read any of them or answered them. I don't want to get into it with him now, but I'm cutting him loose after the series."

"Seb, you don't have to do that. I just won't be around when he is."

His eyes pop open. "I'm not limiting my time with you because he's an asshole."

"But—"

"Soph, it's my decision," he says, squeezing my arm. "You would do the same thing if Maisie was coming after me."

"I guess," I whisper. "But I'd tell her to knock it off first."

"I told Ricky to knock it off. I've talked to him again and again. He's not stopping."

I shake my head. "God, it would kill me to cut Maisie out of my life."

"It is killing me," he says, pulling me back down on top of him. "Ricky and I have been friends since kindergarten, but I've given him so many chances. He can't keep doing this. You're everything to me. He knows that."

"Why do you think he hates me so much?" I rest my head on his chest. "I was so nice to him when we first met."

"You haven't done anything to make him hate you. It's not about you." He pauses for a second. "Have I told you about the classes the league made us take as rookies?"

"Yeah. The ones where they told you to always wear condoms and to never fall asleep around a woman you just met because they would probably take pictures of you in bed and post them to social."

"Yeah," he says, "some of the stuff like that was pretty basic, but I really liked one lecture from a psychologist. He was talking about what he called the Fame Quotient. Basically, that when you become famous, everyone wants a part of you, so you start dividing yourself into little pieces to accommodate the new people in your life: agents, publicists, team people, new friends. In making room for the new people, you have to shrink the pieces of you that the people who have always been in your life have—like your family, your childhood friends. They don't have as much of your time anymore."

I raise my head to look at him. "I think that kind of happens anyway as we get older, right? I mean, since we got married, I don't spend nearly as much time with Maisie or any of my friends. I think that's pretty natural even without the fame."

"It is, but multiply that times a million when you get famous. Everyone wants a piece of you, and the pieces that everyone gets become microscopic."

"So Ricky's mad because his piece keeps getting smaller?"

"I guess. And when you came into my life, it shrunk a whole lot more."

I roll off him and stare up at the ceiling. "Paul and Stone don't seem to care. They're really cool with me. They always have been."

"Yeah, they have wives and kids, though." He props himself up on an elbow and kisses my forehead. "They have their own lives. Since Ricky got divorced, he's counted on me for entertainment. I think he thought we were going to ride the bachelor thing into the retirement home."

"You've never told me why he got a divorce. He said his ex is psycho."

"No, his ex is cool. Penny transferred into our high school sophomore year. They started dating immediately and got married while they were still in college."

"So what happened?"

"He cheated on her." He looks up when Joe knocks.

"Two minutes," Joe says through the door.

"Who did he cheat with?" I ask as he pulls me off the bed. "It wasn't Katie, was it?"

"No. I mean, he might have cheated with her, too. But the one Penny found out about was a woman Ricky hooked up with when he was here visiting me."

"Who?" I ask, falling into him for one last hug. "Someone we know?"

"He's never said and I don't really care. I think it was just a fangirl he met one night."

"Time," Joe says, knocking on the door.

Seb leans down and gives me a soft kiss. "I can't believe we get to spend the entire night together. I can't wait to get home."

"Are you positive you get to stay at the house tonight?"

"Yeah. We've already checked out of the hotel and we're not flying to L.A. until tomorrow morning." He opens the door. "I'm feeling another very fast game tonight. Make sure you're the first person I see when I come off the field."

"Always," I say, blowing him a kiss. "Seb, you're going to win tonight. I can feel it."

"Oh, baby," he says, smiling. "I already won the day I met you."

Chapter Eighteen

SEB

October 31, 2022

We won the second game of the series 9-7. I had a three-run homer—five RBIs total. Alex continued his unbelievable play in the field. Dane pitched. It wasn't his best outing, but he still got the W.

Sophie was the first person I saw when I came out of the dugout after the game. She was standing in the exact same place as last night. All I could think about when I saw her is how we get to spend the night together for the first time in two days. I can't wait to get home.

"You seem like you found your groove," Alex says as we walk toward the interview room after the game. "You're killing it on the field."

"Yeah, I feel better. Sophie's safe. Mason and Butch have her covered. No one's even attempted to get at her. And there haven't been any more of those stupid tweets since the series started."

"That's great," he says. "Raine's still trying to find out who's posting those. She said the user must have some computer or IT background. They've done a pretty good job of hiding their identity."

"I don't care who they are," I say, following him onto the podium, "as long as they quit talking about her, I'm good."

Twitter @**miamibballbabe**
(October 31, 2022)

2-0 and @realsebmiller is killing it. Probably because team security's sneaking #sopHOHOHOny to his private office for pregame conjugal visits. Don't believe me? Why do you think there's a bed in there?

I take a seat between Alex and Dane. Everyone's still getting settled. I exhale and relax back into the chair. I feel so good that I almost don't mind being here.

The MLB woman starts the press conference. Some guy has a question for Alex about the possibility of him being the MVP for the series. He gives the perfect answer—humble as usual.

"Can I jump in here?" I ask when he finishes. "The way Alex is playing, he deserves the MVP and a lot more. He's the heart of this team. It's not going to be the same playing without him next year."

"Thanks, man." Alex nods. "I'm going to miss playing

with you—with all the guys."

"Seb, you seem almost emotional," the reporter says. "Are you thinking about retiring too?"

"Not right now, but we all have to retire sometime. I'm just glad I have the opportunity to play in the series with Alex before he's done. We've been through a lot together. This is a great way to end it."

The MLB woman looks at me and smiles. I think I might have won her over. She points at a reporter I've never seen. He stands up.

"Hey, Seb. Fred Marshall, *TMZ Sports*. Someone just tweeted that you have a private office in the stadium equipped with a bed and that before the games your wife joins you there for, uh, conjugal visits. Can you confirm first that the office exists? And then confirm that your wife is there before the games? And how often does that happen? I mean before games."

The minute he mentions Sophie the painful energy bursts through my body again. I can feel the veins in my neck popping out. My teeth are clenched so tight that I'm not even sure I can unlock them to answer.

Ken rushes over to stand in front of us. The MLB woman scowls at him. He ignores her.

"Fred," Ken says, "that's not even close to being an appropriate question. Not to mention that everyone knows Seb doesn't talk about his family to the media."

"Can you confirm the room exists?" Fred looks from me back to Ken.

"Yes. As part of Seb's five-year deal, he received a

small office off the clubhouse to take care of business dealings. As I'm sure you can guess, Seb's the most sought after player on our team. He spends extra hours in his private office answering fan mail and taking meetings with staff and sponsors."

"Is there a bed in the office?" Fred looks back at me with a wry smile on his face. I want to punch it off so badly. "And if so, why?"

"Because sometimes I take naps during rain delays," I say, glaring down at him. "I like to sleep. The team was nice enough to provide a place for me to do that. It's not there for any other reason. The bed's no bigger than this table. I can barely get my body on it, much less someone else's."

"Alex," Fred says, the stupid smile still on his face. "How do you feel about Seb having a private space when you and the other players don't?"

"I'm in favor of it, Fred," Alex says, leaning forward on the podium. "If you had to deal with Seb's impatience and grumpiness during a rain delay, you would be glad he has a timeout room too. Right, Dane?"

Dane slaps my arm. "One hundred percent. I'm thinking Seb could use a timeout in his room right now."

Everyone starts laughing.

Fred points at me. "You still didn't answer my question about your wife before the game today. I have a source who saw her go in there."

When I leap to my feet, the media jolts backward in their chairs like they were all just hit with a tidal wave. Alex grabs my arm.

"As Ken said," I snarl at Fred, "I don't talk about my family to the media. Don't mention my wife again."

"Okay," the MLB woman says, locking her eyes with mine and nodding to my chair. "That's plenty on that subject. How about a question for Alex or Dane?"

I sit back down slowly. Everyone in the room is staring at me.

"Does anyone have questions about the game?" Ken asks. "Like maybe ask Alex about how high he got off the ground to catch that liner in the eighth. That was the play of the game."

Ray Franklin stands up. "That was the play of the game. They would have tied it up if you hadn't caught that. You're having the best year of your career. Are you sure you want to retire?"

"Why? Are you going to miss me, Ray?"

Everyone starts laughing again. Fred finally sits down. I'm still glaring at him when I see someone waving from the back of the room. I look up to see Evelyn. She points to her face and smiles. I nod and try to smile back. I somehow make it through the rest of the press conference. As I come off the podium, Evelyn catches up with me.

"Thanks for the save, Ev."

"No worries. Your head was getting close to blowing. It was a nice win. Concentrate on that."

"Yeah, I'll try."

She pulls my arm. "Hey, can I talk to you for a second?"

"Do you need me to sign an autograph for one of your clients or something?" I look around. "I can do it quickly, but I need to get into the shower."

"No," she says, looking over her shoulder. She lowers her voice to a whisper. "You know I don't usually gossip, and I don't want to get in trouble. Will you vault this? Or at least not tell anyone you got it from me?"

"Yeah, I've got you," I say, shifting impatiently. "What's up?"

She looks around the hallway one more time, and then whispers, "I saw your buddy Ricky talking to that *TMZ* reporter after the game. The reporter was waiting for him right outside the club entrance. You know the one where the people with VIP seats enter the stadium?"

"Yeah." My teeth clench up again. "Did you hear what they were saying?"

"No," she says, leaning closer to me, "but the reporter was scrolling through his phone while they were talking—like he was looking at *Twitter* or something."

"Okay. Thanks for telling me. I have to go. All I want to do right now is get home to Sophie."

"Get home?" She tilts her head. "I thought the team was leaving tonight."

"We're leaving tomorrow morning," I say as Joe steps in front of me.

He puts his hand on my chest and tries to move me toward the clubhouse. I don't move. "We're leaving tomorrow morning. Right, Joe?"

"In the clubhouse," he says, pushing me a little harder. "We can talk about it there."

I look up at the ceiling and shake my head. "We're leaving tonight, aren't we?"

"Drew changed his mind," he says as we walk toward the clubhouse. "We're wheels up to L.A. tonight."

I squeeze my water bottle so hard that the top flies off, sending the remainder of the water shooting out. I slam the bottle against the wall and walk into the clubhouse. Drew's waiting by my locker.

"I warned you, Seb," he says. "We can't have this kind of press during the series. If you can't control yourself, then you force me to control you."

I collapse into my chair. "Are you the one tweeting this bullshit out?"

"What? Come on, Seb," he says, a deep crease covering his forehead. "I don't even have a *Twitter* account."

"Maybe not a public one." I nod as I rub the scruff on my chin. "Don't I remember that you started working in baseball after leaving a job in the tech field?"

"What does that have to do with anything?" He looks around the room. "Any idiot can post to social media."

"Yep. They definitely can," I say as my brain tries to process the new information. "Hey, do you still have my friend Ricky's phone number? Remember when you called him while you were trying to get me to sign my five-year deal? Do you two still talk?"

"I have no idea what you're talking about," he says, spinning around and walking away from me. "Get in the shower. We're wheels up in an hour."

***Twitter* @miamibballbabe**
(October 31, 2022)

Damn! @realsebmiller was so mad that the media asked

him about his #sopHOny sex room. He completely lost it. He said she's the only thing that keeps him sane. Keeps him insane is more like it. Come back from the dark side, Seb. It's time.

Chapter Nineteen

SOPHIE

November 1, 2022

"I'm sure your dad wants to kill me."

The morning news is full of stories about me sneaking into Seb's office. Most of them at least suggest the possibility of us having sex before games. The *TMZ Sports* story pretty much just says it outright.

"I haven't seen him this morning," I say, looking back at my phone that's propped up against my suitcase. Seb's stretched out on the couch in his L.A. hotel room. "I've been hiding in our bedroom until we leave for the airport."

"That's probably a good idea." He scrunches up his face and turns his head like he's preparing to take a punch. "Have you seen your mom? I'm sure she's pissed."

"Oh, she definitely is. She woke me up at six to show me the stories."

He exhales slowly. "Is she mad at me? You? The situation in general?"

"Believe me, she has plenty of anger to go around." I grab my suitcase and phone and head toward the door.

"Did you tell her we didn't have sex?" He pauses to yawn. It goes on forever. "I mean, we barely kissed."

"It's none of her business what we did or didn't do. It's nobody's business except ours."

"But she was just starting to like me—"

"Seb," I say, looking at the phone as a text comes in. It's Raine saying they're five minutes out. "She's always liked you."

He raises his eyebrows. "Really? She told you not to marry me."

"She did not. She just outlined what she thought being married to a famous man would be like. And honestly, she wasn't far off."

"So, what?" His face tenses up. "You're saying she was right? You shouldn't have married me?"

"I'm saying she was right about the fame part." I kiss his face through the phone. "You know I had no choice but to marry you when I'm this stupid crazy in love with you."

He smiles. "Back at you. I'll apologize to your parents when I see them tonight. I thought about calling them, but it's probably best to do it in person. Shouldn't you be headed to the airport? I thought the plane was leaving at two."

"It is. Butch and Raine are picking me up in a few minutes. Our parents left a couple of hours ago. I think they were having lunch first to talk about *the incident*."

"Man," he says, gritting his teeth, "that just sounds horrible."

The security alarm goes off. "Hold up. They're here. This is Sophie."

"Hi, Mrs. Miller. It's Steve. Butch Harrison is at the gate for you."

"Yep, let him through."

Seb yawns again—louder and even longer this time.

"Seb, you need to get some sleep."

"I can't sleep. I'm too pissed."

I head down the stairs, pulling my suitcase behind me. It clunks on each step. I'm way too exhausted to lift it. "Let it go. The story will die out. They always do."

"I don't want to let it go. People are saying awful things about you. Have you seen the stuff on *Twitter*?"

"No, and I don't want to. I'm sure it's no different than what's been said all season." There's a knock at the front door. "I have to go. I'll text you when we get to L.A."

"Okay," he says. "Hey, I told Dad to juggle the flight manifest around so Butch and Raine could fly with you. Did he tell you?"

"I haven't seen your dad this morning either. I've been in hiding, remember?"

He grunts. "Yeah. Make sure at least Butch gets on the plane with you. God knows what kind of attention you'll get in L.A."

"I'll make sure. Babe, I swear this will fade away like every other media story. Just try to get some sleep, okay? You sound horrible."

"I'll try," he says. "I love you, Soph. I'm sorry you're getting slammed. I told you before, whenever it gets to be too much, just tell me and I'll quit that second. I'm not just saying that. I'm serious. That very second."

"It's not too much and I don't want you to quit." I look through the peephole and see Butch standing on the driveway. "We'll figure it all out. I have to go. I love you."

When I open the door, Butch grabs my bag. "You ready?"

"Yeah. Hold up. I need to call Seb's dad to make sure he has open seats for you on the plane."

"Already done," Butch says, herding me toward the car. "He texted me this morning. I guess he bumped two people off."

"Who?"

He shrugs. "No idea. Let's get going. You already know how much I hate to be late."

Raine pulls me into the back of the SUV with her. "Are you doing okay?"

"Yeah. I don't want to talk about it—to anyone. Will you run interference for me on the plane? If not, it's going to be the longest five hours of my life."

Raine puts her arm around my shoulders. "We've got you. Did you hear that, Butch? No one talks about the sex room."

I swat her leg. "Not helpful."

Butch laughs as he looks at me in the rearview mirror. "I didn't tell anyone. I swear on my grandma's grave."

"Wait. You knew?" Raine kicks his seat. "How are you not sharing that juicy information with me?"

"You know how I am—when I promise to vault, it's locked down."

Raine hisses at him, and then turns back to me. "So, was it full-on sex? Or just a little foreplay?"

"It wasn't anything. We just talked." I put my head in my hands and groan. "This day is going to be from hell."

"I'm just teasing. We'll shut down anyone who starts in on you," Raine says, rubbing my back. "I promise."

I put my head on Raine's shoulder and close my eyes. I'm almost asleep in the ten minutes it takes us to get to the airfield.

"We're here," Raine says, shaking my arm. "And it looks like we have a situation."

Jack and Ricky are standing by the boarding stairs of the plane. Kaitlyn is off to the side of them. Ricky's yelling and pointing at the plane. He tries to get around Jack to board the plane. Jack pushes him back.

"Eek!" I bury my head back into Raine's shoulder. "I think Jack bumped Ricky and Kaitlyn off the plane."

Raine cracks her window just in time to hear Ricky yell, "What are you talking about? I always have a seat!"

"Stay in the car," Butch says, opening his door. "Let me see what's going on first."

Jack steps in front of Ricky again. "Rick, you need to leave."

"Mr. Miller," Butch says as he heads over to them. "Everything good?"

Ricky spins around and charges at Butch. He puffs out his chest. "This is none of your goddamn business, Butch. We don't need input from Princess Sophie's bodyguards."

"Ricky, I'm not telling you again," Jack says, "your name's not on the manifest. You're not boarding this plane."

"Are Stone and Paul on the plane?" Ricky tries to walk

around Jack to get to the airport coordinator who's holding the boarding list.

"It doesn't matter who's on the plane." Jack pushes him back again. "You're not. If you're going to L.A., you need to fly commercial."

"Stone and Paul aren't answering my texts." Ricky gets on tiptoe to try to see into the plane's windows that are at least ten feet above his head. "What's going on? Is Sophie trying to freeze me out?"

"This doesn't have anything to do with Sophie," Jack says. "Seb decides who gets seats—on planes and at games."

"What?" Ricky takes a step back and puts his hand over his chest like he's having a heart attack. "Do I not have a seat at the games anymore?"

"We already discussed that. You have two tickets at Will Call for every remaining World Series game."

"Will Call? Since when do we have to go to Will Call to pick up our tickets? Seb always gives us our tickets before the games so we don't have to wait in line."

"I don't know what to tell you. You made your own bed here, Rick." Jack shakes his head. "Seb's given you more chances than any other person in his life."

"What are you talking about? There's no way Seb's cutting me loose. I'm his best friend!"

"Like I said, you have two tickets to every game for the rest of the series, but if you're going to L.A., you'll need to get out there by yourself." Jack turns to Butch. "Do you have Sophie? We need to get in the air."

"I'm not taking her out of the car until he leaves or I

frisk him." Butch nods at Ricky. "He's a little too unstable for me."

"Who the fuck are you to talk to me like that?" Ricky tries to push Butch in the chest.

Butch reacts so quickly that I don't even register what's happening until Ricky's face down on the tarmac with both arms pinned behind his back. Butch is holding him there with one hand while he frisks him with the other.

"Holy crap!" I scoot away from the car window and crash into Raine's body.

She wraps her arms around my shoulders. "It's fine. Butch won't hurt him."

Butch whistles without taking his eyes off Ricky.

"That's our cue," Raine says. "Let's go. We need to get you on the plane."

She opens the door, pulls me out, and starts pushing me toward the boarding stairs.

"I need to get my bags," I say, trying to turn around.

She keeps pushing. "Butch will get them. You're getting on the plane. Now."

Ricky's still face down—his cheek pressed against the concrete.

"Get off me!" He's trying very unsuccessfully to get out of Butch's hold.

"Butch," I say as we walk by them, "let him up."

"I will," Butch says, "after you're on the plane."

Ricky's gaze shoots up to me. "You fucking bitch! Are you trying to get rid of me? Seb and I have been best friends for twenty five years."

"Hell no!" I look up to see my mom charging out of the plane. "You do not talk to my daughter like that."

Butch springs to his feet, picks me up around the waist, carries me to the boarding stairs, and turns Mom back around. "Everyone on this plane. Now!"

Butch turns to face Ricky who has made it to his feet. "I don't want to hurt you, Ricky, but if you make another attempt to board this plane, all bets are off."

Ricky brushes the dirt off his shirt, then looks up at me. "I'm calling Seb right now to tell him you had his best friend kicked off *his* plane. You think he's going to pick you over me? You're just some whore he picked up at a bar so he would have someone to fuck before his games."

I fall back against the stair railing. I feel like someone just punched me in the gut. I can't move. I try to catch my breath, but the air's not making it in.

Jack leaps up a few stairs and puts his arm around me. "Breathe, Sophie. Don't listen to him. Listen to me, you're the best thing that's ever happened to my son. Seb knows it. I know it. Everyone who matters knows it."

I take a shaky breath and try to nod. Jack pushes me up the stairs. Mom's waiting for me at the top. She puts her arm around my shoulders.

"Everything will be okay. I promise," she whispers, kissing the side of my head.

When I hear the concern in her voice, the frustration tears that I've been holding in for days start pouring down my face.

Adie jumps up from her seat on the plane and throws her arms around both of us. "Come on, sweetie. You're sitting with Deb and me. Just the girls."

I let them guide me to the back of the plane. Mom pulls me down on a couch and holds my head to her chest.

"It's okay, honey," she says, stroking my hair. "You've been through so much. Let it all out. It doesn't matter what anyone says. I'll never leave you. No matter what. I'm always on your side."

"Why does everyone hate me?" I get out between my gasps for air as I start to sob.

"This has nothing to do with you," she says, pausing for second. "This is all because of who Seb is. I'm sorry, Adie, but it is."

I lift my head. "Mom, it's not Seb's fault."

I look back at Adie. She's slumped into the couch. Her face has lost all of its color.

"I know it's not his fault," Mom says, pulling on my chin until I'm looking at her again, "but this all started when you met him. You're the sweetest person I know. Everyone knew that before you became Seb Miller's wife."

"Adie," I say, grabbing her hand as she starts to stand up, "she didn't mean it like that."

She squeezes my hand. "I'm not mad at her, Sophie. Just promise me you'll give Seb a chance to make this right. He loves you so much."

She kisses the top of my head, and then walks back to her seat at the front of the plane. I turn back around to Mom.

"Mom," I say, wiping the tears that are now dripping from my chin. "That wasn't necessary. We're all family now."

"I've been protecting you since before you were born," she says, holding my face in her hands. "I'm not going to stop now. This has gotten out of hand. It needs to end."

"I know, but you don't have to protect me from Seb." I

lay my head down on the pillow she just put on her lap. "You know how much he loves me. He'll do anything for me."

She starts stroking my hair again as I close my eyes. "Then it's about time for him to prove it."

After about ten minutes, I hear the boarding door slam shut. I peek through the strands of hair that have fallen over my face to see Butch and Raine taking the seats right in front of us.

"He called her Princess Sophie and a whore. Both words from the *Twitter* stuff," Butch says to Raine. "Ricky has to be posting it, right?"

"It's not him. He's too stupid and volatile to be the user. He might be feeding information to the person, though. There's been some pretty detailed stuff that only Seb's friends and family would know."

"How about that little side piece who follows him around?" Butch asks. "The high school girlfriend. She could be posting the stuff."

"I don't think so," Raine says, peeking back at me. "I think the user is probably someone we haven't even thought of yet. I'm guessing it's someone Seb and Sophie trust."

Butch shakes his head. "Why would anyone close to them be posting that stuff about her?"

"That's what we need to figure out," Raine says.

Chapter Twenty

SEB

November 1, 2022

***Twitter* @miamibballbabe
(November 1, 2022)**
OMG. #sopHOny flew to L.A. today on the private plane @realsebmiller provides for her. I guess Princess Sophie can't fly commercial. Anyway, his best friend tried to board the plane and she wouldn't let him on!!

Her bodyguard kept him pinned to the ground while she boarded the plane. And then she left Seb's BEST FRIEND standing on the tarmac as she flew away. Come on, Seb. Open your eyes. She loves your money, not you.

Dad called me from the plane to tell me what happened with Ricky. I've been trying to get ahold of Sophie ever since. She isn't answering her phone.

I try again as we get back to our hotel after our off-day workout at the stadium. Her phone goes directly to voicemail.

"Dad said they're at the hotel." I turn to Joe who's just getting off a call with Butch. "Does Butch know what room she's in?"

"Yeah. 1102. He and Raine just left her. Butch said we should meet them up there."

As we walk onto the eleventh floor, Butch whistles from where he and Raine are sitting in the lounge area next to the elevator.

"Hey," I say, walking over to them. "I need to get to Sophie. 1102?"

"No need to rush. She's sleeping." Raine motions to the chair across from her. "Before you go to the room, we have some questions for you. Joe, do you mind if we talk to him privately?"

Joe looks up from his phone. "That's up to Seb."

When I nod at Joe, he walks to the other side of the elevators.

Raine looks up at me and motions to the chair again. "Did you see the latest tweets?"

"Yeah," I say, not sitting down. "I read them on the way over here."

"There are only a handful of people who saw that exchange at the airfield," she says, glancing over at Joe.

"It's Ricky. He must be the one posting." I look up at the ceiling. "He's lost his fucking mind."

"It's not him," she says, "but I think he's an informant to the user. Who does he talk to that's maybe just one or two places removed from your inner circle?"

"Someone saw Ricky talking to the *TMZ* reporter after the game yesterday," I say, finally sitting down. "Drew's the only one who knew Sophie was in the office with me. He must have told Ricky and Ricky told the reporter."

"Well, Drew *and Joe* both knew Sophie was in the office, right?"

I narrow my eyes. "Joe hasn't told anyone anything. And he's not one or two places removed from the inner circle. He is the inner circle."

"Joe knows everything about you," Butch says, "including the private stuff this user has been posting all season."

"Ricky knows all of that too." I motion Joe back over. "Joe is not the informant or the user or anything."

"It's cool, Seb. They're just being thorough." Joe holds his phone out to Raine. "Check my messages. Check anything you want."

She stares at him for a second, but then shakes her head. "I'm good. Seb, who told you they saw Ricky talking to the *TMZ* reporter?"

"Someone who works for the team."

"Who?" Raine asks.

"I promised her I would vault it," I say, standing up. "There's no way she's coming after Sophie."

"She, huh?" Raine shakes her head as she turns to Butch. "Damn it. How is Millie always right? Her ability to read people is so freaky."

Butch shrugs. "I've always told you I think Millie's part witch."

I look between them. "Who are you talking about?"

"Never mind," Raine says, pulling a room key out of her pocket. "This is the spare key to 1102. I swiped it for you before I left because God knows Deb won't let you into that room. I've never seen her this mad."

"Deb's in Sophie's room?" I ask as I start backing down the hall.

"Yep," Raine says, nodding, "and she's got full mama-bear mode activated. You might want to put your cup back on before you go in there."

I stop in front of the room to try to steel myself for Deb. She's gotten used to me in the past few years, but she was never a fan of Sophie marrying me. She was worried Sophie was too sensitive to deal with the attention that comes with my fame. I told her I could protect Sophie from it. It kills me that I was wrong.

As I walk into the room, I see Sophie sleeping on the couch with her head in her mom's lap. I think Deb was half-asleep before she heard the door open. Her head bobs back up.

"Don't wake her up," she whispers, not returning my smile. "She just fell asleep. I'll tell her you were here."

"I don't need to be anywhere right now." I squat down in front of Sophie, push a strand of hair out of her face, and kiss her forehead. "I'm not leaving until she wakes up."

I look up at Deb. She holds my stare for a second, and then looks away.

"Deb, I'm sorry about all of this—"

"Stop," she says without looking back at me. "I don't want to hear it."

"Deb." She finally looks at me. I nod my head toward the door. "Can we talk outside for a second?"

"No." She doesn't move.

"Please, Deb," I say, looking down at Sophie. "We don't want to wake her up, remember?"

Deb continues to glare at me but finally lifts Sophie's head onto the couch, stands up, and walks toward the door. I follow her and close the door behind us.

"Deb, I know you're pissed—"

"Yes, I'm mad, Seb. Really mad. My daughter is getting attacked—verbally and physically—because of you." She holds up her hand to stop me from saying anything more. "I know you love her, but I'm her mother. I won't stand by and let this smear campaign happen. She's the sweetest person in the world, and she's being made out to be some kind of wicked creature because of you and what you do for a living."

I close my eyes. "I know, and I feel awful about it."

"That's not enough, Seb." She's pacing when I open my eyes. She finally stops and looks over at me. "Maybe you two need a little time off from each other."

"What?" I fall back like she just shoved me. "That's not happening. I'll quit baseball today before I'm separated from Sophie."

"Will you? You've said that before, but you're still playing." She looks down when her eyes start getting watery. "I don't care what you do. I just want my daughter to be happy and safe."

I try to put my hand on her shoulder, but she moves away. "Deb, you know that's all I want too."

"I don't want to talk about it anymore. Like I said, I'll let her know you were here when she wakes up."

"Deb." I lunge between her and the door. "Sophie's my wife. I'm going to be with her right now."

She narrows her eyes into tiny slits. "What if she doesn't want to be with you?"

"Then she can tell me that herself." I open the door and block her from coming in. "I'm sorry I've brought this down on her and your family. I really am, but this is between Sophie and me. You need to leave."

She tries to stop the door with her hand, but I press it shut. Sophie's sitting up when I turn around. She looks confused.

"What time is it?" She rubs her eyes. "And what day? I feel like I just woke up from a coma."

"Shh," I say, rushing over to her. "I think your mom will literally break down the door and kill me if she thinks I woke you up."

"Was she here? Is it morning?"

I sit down beside her on the couch and take her face into my hands. "She just left. It's Tuesday, six p.m. You got into L.A. a few hours ago. Are you okay? You look like you're going to pass out."

She tries to get up. "I'm fine. I just need some water. I'm really dehydrated."

"Stay. I'll get it for you. I just got back from practice. I've been trying to call you."

"Oh, sorry," she says, squinting at me. She still looks

really out of it. "I turned off my phone. I was getting crazy messages about the incident."

"Which incident? The "conjugal visit" incident or the Ricky-at-the-plane incident?"

She tilts her head. "Who told you about the Ricky thing?"

"Dad." I sit down and take her hand. "I'm so sorry for what he said to you, baby. You know none of it's true."

"I know." She chugs half the bottle of water. "Why didn't you tell me you kicked them off the plane? I could have at least been prepared."

"I didn't think he would come to the airfield after Dad texted him that he didn't have a seat."

"You should have told me, though," she says. "I hate when I don't have all of the information."

"You've been so happy. I didn't want to ruin it."

"Well, you did." She straddles me and loops her arms around my neck. She looks directly into my eyes. "Seb, we're supposed to tell each other everything. Remember? We promised after all that miscommunication kept us apart after we met. Everything. The minute it happens."

"Yeah, I remember," I say, leaning my forehead against hers. "I messed up. I'm sorry."

"It's fine," she says, running her hands through my hair. "Just don't do it again. Tell me everything. Always."

"I promise."

"Thank you. Now can we stop talking and maybe make better use of our first alone time in three days?"

"My thoughts exactly. What did you say the other day? That you wanted me to service you?" I pull out the collar of her shirt and peek inside. "Let me look under your hood. I think it's time for your annual inspection."

"Oh my god," she says, giggling as I flip her onto her back. "You're the worst at role play."

"Then I promise," I say, letting my hand slowly move down her body, "I'll be very good at everything else."

Chapter Twenty-One

SOPHIE

November 2, 2022

"Are you sure you want to do this?"

Maisie crawls up on a chair to peer out of the stadium window again. We're in the L.A. baseball offices, getting ready to go to our seats for game three.

"Yeah, I mean, that's where our seats are. We have to go out there if we want to watch the game." I get on my tiptoes and look out with her. "I don't think anyone will say anything to me."

"Soph," Maisie says, hopping down from the chair. "At least a dozen people yelled stuff at you on our way into the stadium."

"She's right," Mason says from behind me. "I hate that we don't have a suite here. You'll be out in the open. Maybe we should go back to the hotel and watch from there."

"No one's tried to touch me yet, and I can take the

verbal abuse." I look back at him. "Besides, your adorable son is waiting for us, right? Millie said her dad was bringing him tonight."

"Yeah, he's here," Mason says, smiling. "I saw them before we left the hotel. Millie has him wearing the Seb jersey you gave her. He looks so cute."

"I will not be denied his cuteness because of some drunk, mouthy idiots." I take a deep breath and point toward the door that goes into the stadium. "Let's do this."

"Alright," Mason says, heading toward the door. "I'm on your back, but the first indication I get that it's too hot, I'm pulling you out."

The second we walk out onto the concourse, heads start turning, fingers start pointing, and phones start snapping pictures. Mason puts his arms around Maisie and me and starts pushing us toward our section. As we walk down the stairs to our seats, the smack talk starts.

"Hey, Sophie! Seb doesn't look too happy tonight. What's up? Doesn't he have a private office here?"

"I'm available for a conjugal visit if Seb isn't."

"Holy crap," I say as Maisie wraps her arm around my shoulders. "How do people think this is appropriate?"

"Just concentrate on our seats," she says, nodding to where Jack and my dad are standing.

"Dottie put us in the middle of the team employees," Jack says, motioning us into our row. "Five rows of buffer on both sides."

I sink into my seat. "That's not even close to being enough."

Raine leans down from where she's sitting in the row

behind me and whispers, "Ignore them. They'll settle in. Distract yourself with Mo."

I look to where she's pointing. Millie's two rows up, holding her son.

"Eek!" I lean over Raine's legs to get closer. "How did I miss the most handsome man in the stadium? Look how cute that little jersey is on him."

"Mo," Millie says, turning him around on her lap so he's facing me. "This is your Aunt Sophie. Can you say, 'Hi, Sophie'?"

"Hi, Pophie," he says, his chubby little arm waving at me.

"Hi, sweet baby." I wave back to him. "Millie, he looks just like you."

"No," she says, nudging the man next to her. "He looks just like Grandpa. Sophie, this is my dad, Mack."

"Nice to meet you," Mack says, reaching his hand out to me. "I've heard a lot about you."

"Likewise," I say, grabbing Raine's leg. "Most of it from Raine's adoring mouth."

"Stop," Raine says, shoving me. "Mack already knows I have a crush on him. But look at him, can you blame me?"

"I definitely cannot." I look from Mack to Mo. "But I have a bigger crush on you."

Mo giggles as I shake his little sneakered feet. He immediately reaches for me.

"Wow, he usually doesn't go this quickly to anyone except Dad or Butch," Millie says. "Do you want to hold him?"

"So much that it's almost physically painful. I need

baby therapy so badly right now." I sigh. "But his precious face will be splashed all over social media if he gets anywhere near me."

"It's fine. He hangs out with Butch all the time. His reputation is already shot." Millie holds him out to me. "He's really tired. He might be a little crabby."

As I stand up to take him, there's another round of "Sophie!" screams as phones shoot into the air. I pull Mo against my chest and start placing kisses all over his sweaty strawberry blond curls.

"Poph," he says, looking up at me. He's trying so hard to keep his eyes open.

"Go to sleep, baby Mo," I whisper, rubbing his back. "Everything will be better when you wake up."

When his forehead nods against my chest, I take a long whiff of his head. He smells like straight up baby heaven. I think I can literally feel my ovaries starting to dance.

"Uh oh," I hear from behind me. "Sophie has baby fever. Seb better watch out."

I turn to see Evelyn staring at me from about four rows back. She's smiling, but her eyes are oddly intense.

"Oh, believe me," I say, laughing. "Seb wants one as badly as I do."

"Really?" Her voice is almost squeaky. "He's never told me that."

Before I can reply, Adie and Mom start working their way down the row in front of us.

"Oh my gosh!" Adie says, her hand flying to her chest. "Who is this beautiful baby?"

Maisie leans in and whispers, "In three, two, one—"

"That looks so good on you, Sophie. You're a natural. I

think it's time for one of your own." Adie nudges Mom. "Don't you think so, Deb?"

"There it is," Maisie says. "The baby bomb. Right on time."

Mom's nodding, but barely smiling. She locks her eyes with mine. "There's plenty of time for kids later if . . . Well, there's no rush."

"What?" Adie whacks Mom's arm. "I thought we were on the same page about grandchildren."

I watch them walk to their seats. The muscles in Mom's neck are popping out. I can tell she's clenching her teeth.

"Well Deb's still pissed," Raine whispers as she leans down between Maisie and me.

Maisie whistles. "Oh yeah. She's at the highest level on the Deb anger scale. Is it just about the sex room or did something else happen?"

"Well," I say, leaning closer to them. "Did I mention that Seb kicked her out of my room and basically told her to mind her own business?"

They both lurch away from me.

"Holy shit." Maisie's mouth is hanging open. "How's Seb still walking today?"

"Don't know," I say. "Mom hasn't said a word to me about it."

"I'm guessing that will change," Raine says. "That's not something Deb's going to brush off."

"She'll get over it," I say, kissing Mo's head.

"You sure about that?" Raine sits back in her seat. "I've never known her to get over anything."

We lost tonight. 4-1. Seb went 0 for 3. None of our players could hit L.A.'s pitcher. He was throwing smoke all night.

I'm waiting for him to come off the field. Mason, Millie, Mack, and Mo are with me.

"He hasn't stopped clinging to you for hours," Mack says as he looks at Mo still fast asleep on my shoulder.

"I think he senses my emotional neediness right now." I hug Mo tighter. "He's trying to love the stress out of me, and I think it's working."

"Yeah, he's a sensitive little guy. He picks up on stuff like that," Mack says. "I'm sorry you're going through all of this. I seriously don't know what's wrong with some people. I'm a big baseball fan, but I could give a crap about the players' personal lives, and that goes double for their families."

"I don't understand it either. The amount of hate I get is almost stunning."

"Speaking of hate," Mason says, nodding his head to Drew who's charging toward us. "Little man is on the war path again."

"Sophia!"

"What now, Drew?" I turn my body to block him from Mo. "What else have I done wrong? Maybe call Ricky so he can get it up on *Twitter*."

"I don't know what you're talking about," he hisses, "but I do know you have too many people in your group. Each family only gets four after-game passes, *even* the Seb Miller family."

"One, two," I say, pointing at Millie and Mason then to Mack and me, "three, four."

Drew swats Mo's back. "Five."

Mack grabs Drew's wrist and bends it back until Drew yelps and falls to his knees.

"Dad, stop," Millie says. "He's Miami's GM."

"I don't care who he is," Mack says, giving Drew's wrist a twist before he releases it. "Touch my grandson again and you're going to lose that hand."

"Dad!" Millie steps between Mack and Drew. "Please take Mo and meet us back at the hotel."

Mack glares at Drew for another second, and then lifts Mo off me. Mo wakes up and starts crying.

"Don't cry," I say, kissing his silky cheek. "I'll see you back at the hotel."

"Don't worry, little man. I have the same reaction when I have to leave her." Seb comes up behind us and stands right in front of Drew, blocking him from our group. "Is this the famous Mo? Nice jersey, little man. Do you want me to sign it for you?"

Joe walks over and hands Seb a Sharpie. Mo immediately grabs it and starts sucking on it.

Mack laughs. "I think he wants to eat the pen more than get an autograph."

"Seb," Millie says, "this is my dad, Mack."

"Nice to finally meet you," Seb says as Mack shifts Mo to his other arm so he can shake Seb's hand. "I've heard a lot about you."

"Most of it good I hope," Mack says. "Nice to meet you too. I'm a big fan."

"Appreciate it. Sorry you had to see such a crappy game."

"Not much you can do when you run into a buzzsaw like that." Mack shakes his head. "His sinker is crazy."

"Yeah, it moves like there's a magic spell on it or something," Seb says.

"Seb," Joe says, handing him a baseball and another Sharpie, "it's time to go. Why don't you sign this? I don't think the little bruiser is going to let you sign his jersey."

Seb scrawls a quick autograph on the ball and hands it to Mo. Mo tries to take a bite of it.

Mason grabs it from him. "No, buddy. This one's too valuable for you to smear. We have to protect it."

"Ball!" Mo reaches for it, his face flooding with determination. "Ball!"

"You like baseballs as much as I do," Seb says, rustling his hair.

"Ball was the third word he learned after Mom and drink," Mason says, laughing.

"Glad to see he has his priorities straight," Seb says. "Let him have it. He can get another one whenever he wants it."

Mason hands it back to Mo. "Maybe Uncle Seb will give you a baseball lesson some day."

"I'll definitely do that. As many as he wants." Seb leans down to kiss me. "I'll see you back at the hotel, baby. Did everything go okay during the game?"

"A little smack talk," I say, smiling, "but Mo protected me."

"Good man. High five." Mo swings his little hand into Seb's with all his might. "Nice swing, buddy. You're going to take my spot in the lineup any day now."

Chapter Twenty-Two

SEB

November 3, 2022

After the game last night, Sophie spent the night in my room. Our L.A. hotel is huge. There's no way Drew and his staff can monitor all of our rooms. And I'm not sure he's even trying anymore. He's pretty much steered clear of me since I accused him of feeding information to Ricky.

This morning, Sophie and the California crew headed up to Blitzen Bay for lunch. It's about an hour outside of L.A. She just texted me a picture of them having drinks on Nash's back deck that overlooks the lake and mountains. I want to be with them so badly that I almost can't look at the picture.

I'm in my hotel room, stretched out on the couch in my underwear, watching *Aladdin*. We leave for the stadium in a couple hours. Hopefully, we'll get a better outcome than we had last night. At least we won't have to face that same pitcher again.

I hear my door beep as someone swipes a room key.

"We don't have to leave for two more hours, Joe," I say without looking over there.

"Two hours is plenty of time, but please don't call me Joe again if you want me to enjoy myself."

I leap up from the couch when I hear a woman's voice. Kaitlyn Barr is standing in my room.

"What the hell?" I look around quickly for my pants. "How did you get in here?"

She winks as she walks over to me. "I have my ways, but you already know that. You remember how I could talk anyone into anything. I haven't lost that skill."

"What are you doing here, Katie?" I point at the door. "You need to leave."

"Don't worry," she says as she puts her hands on my bare chest. "No one saw me come in here, and no one will see me leave. Your reputation is safe."

I take a step away from her. "You need to go. Now."

She walks to the other side of the suite toward the bedroom. She stops and leans against the door. "Ricky said you had massive trust issues now. I get it, but you know you can trust me. I won't tell anyone."

She smiles, spins around, and disappears into the bedroom. I text Joe.

911. Unwelcome in my room.

I think about staying in the living room until Joe gets here, but I really want to put on pants, and unfortunately, all of my clothes are in the bedroom. I peek around the corner.

Katie's lying on my bed. Her shoes are off, but thankfully, everything else is still on.

"I was going to wait until tonight to sneak in here," she says, patting the bed, "but after last night's loss, I thought you could use a little stress release before the game."

"Get off my bed," I say, pulling her up as I grab my jeans off the chair. "And get out of my room."

"Ow!" She pulls her arm away. "Seb, stop. You're hurting me."

I release her and point toward the door again. "Leave."

Her forehead wrinkles up. "I don't understand. Ricky said you were expecting me."

"He said what?" I ask, zipping up my jeans.

"Why are you putting your pants back on? Are you going to make me work for it?" She tries to cup my crotch with her hand. I jerk back away from her.

"Don't fucking touch me," I snarl. "And tell me everything Ricky told you right now."

Her face melts into confusion. "He said your marriage was on the rocks, and that you were reminiscing with him about how great our relationship used to be. That's why he brought me to the games. He knew I was getting a divorce, so he thought it might be good timing for us to rekindle. I mean if you need a little more time, I get it. I can wait."

"Katie." I collapse into a chair. "I'm sorry you got pulled into the middle of whatever this is, but Ricky's wrong. My marriage is perfect. Sophie's perfect. I don't even think about other women."

"He said you would say that," she says, smiling as she walks over to me. "I know you hate the media talking about you, and the divorce will be a lot, but this doesn't have to hit the media. It's just between us. You know you can trust me."

I jump up as she tries to sit on my lap. "Katie, I want to make something perfectly clear, so listen closely. I haven't thought about you for more than a few minutes since I left Grand Rapids ten years ago. Even if there was something wrong with my marriage—which there definitely is not—you would not be my choice to replace my wife."

"Wow." Her mouth drops open. "That's a little harsh, don't you think? I'm just trying to be nice."

"No, Katie, you're not just trying to be nice. You—and Ricky—are trying to start some bullshit." I look over my shoulder as the door beeps and then look back at her. "Are you the one coming after Sophie on *Twitter*?"

"What are you talking about?" she asks as Joe charges into the room.

"How the fuck did you get in here?" He grabs Katie's arm. "You're leaving."

"Don't touch me!" Katie screams.

"I'm going to do a lot more than touch you if you don't move toward that fucking door."

"Katie," I say, pulling Joe away from her. "Go home. Go back to Michigan. You no longer have tickets to the games. And if you ever show up at my hotel or any other place I am, I'll have you arrested as a stalker."

"A stalker?" She looks up at me—her eyes wide. "How are you saying that to one of your oldest friends?"

"We're not friends. We're not anything. We haven't been for a decade. This isn't a fucking high school reunion. Stay away from me. Stay away from Sophie. And if you're the one posting that crap on *Twitter*, I suggest you delete the account before I find out for sure because I'll have no mercy for that person—no matter how long I've known them."

She shakes her head as she passes me. "Ricky's right. She's changed you, and definitely not for the better."

Joe steps between us and points to the door. "Now."

"I'm going," she says, glaring at him. "I don't need an escort."

When the door clicks behind her, Joe turns back to me. "How did she get in here? Did you lose your key?"

I point to my key on the table.

"I'll talk to security. She must have bribed someone on the hotel staff." He points at my phone. "Call Sophie right now and tell her about this. If that woman is the *Twitter* person, this is about to be splashed all over the media. Did she get any pictures?"

"I don't know. I was just wearing underwear when she came in."

"Call Sophie right now."

I look at my phone and shake my head. "No. She's up in Blitzen enjoying herself. I'll tell her after the game tonight."

"Seb," he says, pointing at my phone again. "Do it now. It's better if she hears it from you."

"Hears what? Nothing happened."

"I know nothing happened. And Sophie will know that too. But you need to tell her before she sees it on *Twitter*. Do it. Now."

I watch Joe charge out of the room and then collapse back down on the couch. I stare at my phone for a few seconds and finally call Sophie.

"Hey!" She sounds so happy. It makes me feel even worse. "Why didn't you FaceTime me? I want to take you on a tour of Nash's place. It's so warm and cozy. You would love it."

"Am I on speaker?"

"Yeah," she says, her voice getting softer when she hears the tension in my voice. "You're not now. What's wrong?"

"Will you go some place private?"

"Seb," she whispers, "what's wrong? You're scaring me. Are you hurt?"

"I'm not hurt." I pause to try to summon the strength to say the next part. "I need to tell you something. It's not good."

"Okay." I can barely hear her. "Tell me. I'm alone now."

I take a deep breath and let the words explode out of my mouth. "Katie was in my hotel room. She just left."

"Katie who? Like Katie, the ex-girlfriend Katie?"

"Yeah."

She's quiet for a few seconds. "What was she doing in your room?"

"Nothing happened. She somehow got a key. Joe's talking to hotel security right now. She let herself into the room. I told her to leave immediately. And she did, but she got into my bed before I could stop her. She might have taken a picture of me. I don't know. I was so confused."

"A picture of what?"

"I don't know—like of my bed or me. I was just wearing underwear when she broke in. Nothing happened. I swear, Sophie. Nothing happened."

"I know nothing happened, Seb." Her voice has recovered. It's getting louder with every word. "But how did she get in? And what did she think was going to happen? And why did she think that? Have you been talking to her?"

"Not at all. Soph, I swear. I haven't seen her since that party the first night, and I said like twenty words to her there. I think Ricky's feeding her some bullshit about how our marriage isn't working. He's done, Soph. I was going to wait until after the series, but I'm telling him today. Okay?"

There's complete silence on the other end of the phone. I don't even hear any background noise.

"Sophie? Say something." Still nothing. "Sophie!"

"Say what, Seb?" She finally gets out. "What do you want me to say? If Ricky's the *Twitter* person or if Katie is, this is going to be all over the media by game time."

"Maybe not—"

"Seb, this person hasn't held back on anything for almost a year now. It's not like they'll hold back now."

I close my eyes. "Nothing happened—"

"I know nothing happened!" Her voice is so loud that it makes me drop my phone. "I know you didn't cheat on me. I know you don't want to cheat on me. But it will still be awful. God! It won't stop. We're just getting through one fake scandal and now another one pops up. I can't take it anymore. I'm so fucking tired."

"I'll quit," I whisper. "I'll come up to Blitzen right now."

"You're not quitting!" This is the first time I've heard her really scream. "Because God knows everyone's going to blame me for that too. I don't need any more hate right

Leave it on the Field

now. You're finishing this series. Do what you want after that, but you're finishing this fucking World Series."

"Okay. I'll finish," I whisper. "I'm so sorry, baby."

"I know you are, and it's not your fault, but the apology doesn't help right now." She pauses and inhales loudly. "Thank you for telling me so I can at least try to prepare myself."

"Everything. Right when it happens. That's what we said, right?"

"Yeah."

No one says anything for a strong three minutes. It feels like three years.

"Are you coming to the game tonight?" I finally ask.

"I don't know." Her volume level's back to normal, but her voice is cold. I've never heard her sound like this. "Let's see what shows up on *Twitter*."

"Okay."

"I have to go. I'll text you when we're on our way back to L.A."

"Okay. I love you, Sophie. More than anything."

"I know."

When she clicks off the phone without saying it back, it feels like someone just plunged a knife into my chest. I throw the TV remote across the room. It hits the lamp and knocks it off the table.

I text Ricky.

You're done. Stay away from me for your own good because if I see you, I'll fucking kill you.

Chapter Twenty-Three

SOPHIE

November 3, 2022

Raine and I monitored *Twitter* all day waiting for the post about Kaitlyn visiting Seb's room. It never came. I decided to go to the stadium when there still wasn't anything an hour before the game. A few fans heckled me when I walked to the seats, but nothing about the room visit.

"I thought you weren't looking at *Twitter* anymore," Dad says, nudging my shoulder. "Are you just trying to avoid watching this game? Frankly, I wish I didn't have to watch it either."

It's the top of the ninth. We're losing 8-1. Seb has played horribly, including making an error for the first time all season. He made a wild throw to second on a steal attempt. I've never seen him make even a slightly bad throw. It's been spot-on perfect every time until tonight.

"Is something wrong between you and Seb?" Dad asks. "He's been looking down here all night. Either he's looking at you or he finds his third baseman really interesting for some reason."

"There's nothing wrong. Everything's fine."

"Nice try," he says, patting my leg. "You only use the word 'fine' when things are definitely not fine."

Twitter @**miamibballbabe**
(November 3, 2022)

We're going to lose again tonight! @realsebmiller has played horribly. He keeps looking over here to where #sopHOny is sitting. He's so distracted. Could someone please take her out? It's the only way he'll finally move on.

I jump as the tweet posts. I scan it. Nothing about Katie. I turn to Raine to see if she saw it.

"*Here*," Raine says, handing her phone to Butch and tapping her finger on the screen. "Over *here* to where she's sitting."

"Let's go," Butch says, putting his hand on my shoulder. "We're leaving."

"What? The game's not over. I never leave early—even if we're losing."

"You're leaving early tonight." He does a quick eye sweep of our section as he stands up.

"Come on, Soph," Raine says. "This game's over for all practical purposes. Let's get back to the hotel."

Raine hands her phone to Millie. "Will you take care of this?"

Millie scans the phone, and then hands it back to her. "I'm on it. Take Mason with you to help protect Sophie. I'll use Nash to distract her."

"Distract who?" I look back and forth between Raine and Millie. "What's going on?"

They ignore me.

Millie laces her fingers, stretches out her arms, and cracks her knuckles like she's preparing for a street fight. "Nash, I need you to create a distraction for me."

"On it," Nash says, leaping up. He's standing so straight that I'm half expecting him to salute Millie. "Just tell me where and how big."

Millie nods toward the concourse. "Bring your beer. I think we can use it as a prop."

"Prop?" I scrunch up my face as she and Nash take off up the stairs. "What's happening right now?"

"Don't worry about it," Butch says, pulling me out of my seat. "We're moving."

Dad stands up. "What's going on?"

"We want to get Sophie out of here before the game ends," Raine says, her face melting into a reassuring smile. "Nothing to worry about. You can come with us if you want."

Dad nods and turns to Mom. "Deb, quit typing on your phone. Let's go."

"What?" Mom looks up, her face displaying the confusion that I'm feeling.

"We're leaving," Mason says. "Now. Anyone who's coming with us needs to move."

"What am I missing in that tweet?" I look over my shoulder at Raine.

"Walk, Sophie," she says, pushing me from behind.

"Is it the 'take her out' part? It's a figure of speech. No one's going to literally take me out."

"Keep moving," Mason says, grabbing my arm as he starts to pull me up the stairs.

"Have you seen enough, Sophie?" A guy stands up and points at me.

"Sit," Mason commands, throwing a finger in the guy's face.

The guy thuds back down into his chair like he's suddenly lost all control of his legs.

"Who else has something to say?" Mason looks around to see if anyone else wants to challenge him. Everyone looks down quickly.

As we continue toward the concourse, Millie and Nash are coming back down the stairs. When they get to us, Nash trips and spills his beer—its contents flying all over our section.

"I'm so sorry," Nash says from behind me as Mason continues to pull me up the stairs. "Let me dry you off."

As we step onto the concourse, a guy in an L.A. jersey points at me. "Princess Sophie! Look, it's Seb Miller's wife."

A bunch of fans stop to look at me.

"Keep distracting, Seb!" Another L.A. fan holds up her beer cup to toast me. "He's playing like shit. You're our secret weapon."

"Walk, Sophie," Raine says. "Put your eyes down and walk. We need to get out of here."

The crowd starts to follow us. Raine loops her arm through mine. Butch gets in front of us and starts plowing through the crowd like an angry bulldozer. Mason has his arms wrapped around us from behind.

As we start moving faster, the crowd keeps following, pressing closer into us.

Someone yells from behind us. "Did you not get to have sex with Seb before the game tonight? I've never seen him look this bad."

As Butch breaks into a trot, I trip and one of my flip flops flies off.

"Stop! I lost my shoe."

Raine scurries over to grab it. Just as she's coming back, a man wearing Seb's jersey walks by and throws his beer at me. I scream as the cold liquid hits my face.

"You're the reason we're losing!" he screams. "You're killing Seb!"

Butch pushes him against a wall. "Go! I'll hold him, and then get the car."

Before I can even wipe the beer out of my eyes, Mason wraps his arm around my waist and lifts me off the ground. He starts running. Raine's in front of us, trying to clear traffic.

When a few cops join us, the crowd quickly dissipates. The yelling fades into the background as we finally get to the entrance to the L.A. team offices. When we clear the doors, Mason puts me down into a chair in the corner of the room. He squats down in front of me.

"Are you hurt?"

I shake my head as I try to wipe the beer off my face. I

look down at my dress. It's soaked. "Where are my parents?"

"We're right here, honey," Mom says, pulling tissues out of her purse. "It's okay. You're fine. Let's just get out of here."

"Butch is bringing the car around," Raine says. "He'll be here in eight minutes."

A few L.A. employees start pulling out their phones as they look over at me. Mason stands in front of me to block their view.

Mom kneels in front of me. She dabs the last of the beer off my face as she forces out a laugh. "I got wet too. We don't even like beer. They should have at least thrown wine."

"You don't have to try to make me feel better, Mom," I say, sniffing as I feel the tears coming again. "I don't even think that's possible right now."

"I'm just trying to distract you so you won't break down in front of everyone," she says, a tense smile forming. "I think it's time to leave, Sophie."

"Butch isn't here yet," I say as she blots the beer off my dress.

"No, sweetie," she says. Her voice is so tight. I can tell she's about to scream. "I mean leave L.A. We need to get you out of here—away from all of this—before something really bad happens."

"Maybe you're right," I whisper. "I'm so tired, Mom."

"I know, honey." She looks up at me, nodding. "Dad and I will take you home tonight. We can leave this behind. Just breathe right now. Nice deep breaths."

I close my eyes and try to just concentrate on breathing.

"Did Millie get the clone?" Mason says from above me.

"Yeah," Raine whispers. "Apparently Nash took off his t-shirt to cause the distraction."

"Whatever it takes," Mason says.

I want to ask them what they're talking about, but I'm too tired to even open my mouth.

Raine taps my arm. "Butch is out front. Are you ready?"

Mom grabs my hand. "You're fine, honey. All of this will be over soon."

Twitter @miamibballbabe
(November 3, 2022)

A fan threw a beer in #sopHOny's face as she was leaving the stadium. I mean, I get it. She's the reason we're losing. She's distracting @realsebmiller. When he plays bad, the team plays bad and he sucked tonight. Time for her to go.

Coincidentally a man spilled a beer on me too. BUT he immediately pulled off his shirt and started drying me off with it. DID I MENTION HE WAS HOT?! Like burly mountain man hot. I almost passed out. He can spill a beer on me anytime he wants.

Chapter Twenty-Four

SEB

November 3, 2022

When I walk out of the dugout after the game, I don't see Sophie. I take a few steps toward where the other wives are standing. They're staring at me but look down quickly when they see me heading over to them.

"Hey," I say, waving to try to get their attention. "Where's Sophie?"

Paige finally looks up and nods her head across the concourse to where my dad's standing.

"Dad. What? What happened? Is she hurt?"

"She's not hurt," he says, his face drawn. "A fan threw a beer in her face after the game."

"Fuck!" I yank off my mask and throw it against the wall.

Everyone outside our clubhouse freezes. The hallway's suddenly so quiet that I can hear Dad's phone vibrating in his hand.

"Where is she?"

"She's not hurt—just a little shaken up. Bob and Deb are with her. They're headed back to the hotel." Dad looks at his phone. "This is from Butch. They just arrived. She's headed up to her room."

I put my hands over my face and scream out the frustration that's been building up inside me for days.

"She's fine." Dad puts his hand on my shoulder. "Just do your postgame stuff. We'll see you back at the hotel."

I take a deep breath as I lower my hands. "No. Give me five minutes. I'm going with you to the hotel right now."

"Seb," Joe says from behind me.

I ignore him. "Five minutes, Dad. Be here when I get back."

"I'm not going anywhere."

I push past Joe into the clubhouse. I head directly to my locker and throw on my clothes.

"Are you going to take a shower?" Dane asks from the locker next to mine. "No one wants to ride back on the bus with you smelling like that."

"Seb," Joe says from behind me, "you can't leave."

I grab my bag. "I'm going to my wife. You can come with me if you want. That's your choice, but I'm leaving."

I head toward the door. Bud and Ken follow me.

"Seb, what's up?" Bud tries to block my way. I push him aside. "What happened?"

I turn back around. Everyone's staring at me.

"Someone threw a beer in Sophie's face after the game," I say loud enough so everyone can hear me. "I've had enough. I'm leaving to find her. Do what you're going to do. Fine me. Bench me. Whatever. I need to be with my wife right now."

Joe follows me and points at one of the LAPD officers guarding the clubhouse. "Hey. Seb needs to get back to the hotel in a hurry. Family emergency. Can you give us a lift?"

"Yeah," the officer says, clicking the speaker on his radio, "give me two minutes."

I head over to Dad. "Did they get the person who threw the beer?"

"Yeah, they got him. The cops said he was drunk out of his mind. I think it was just some random fan."

"Seb, let's go," Joe says, motioning me over to where a squadron of police are now standing.

"Ride back with us," I say to Dad.

"Your mom's waiting for me upstairs. Just get to Sophie. We'll see you back at the hotel."

When I walk into Sophie's suite, her parents are sitting on the couch in the living room surrounded by suitcases.

"Hey," I say, eyeing the suitcases. One of them is the bright pink hardshell case I bought Sophie for her birthday. "What's going on? Where's Sophie?"

Bob nods toward the closed bedroom door but doesn't say anything.

"Is she okay? Dad said they just threw a beer on her."

"Just?" Deb asks, jumping up. Bob grabs her arm. "One of your fans threw a beer in my daughter's face and you're saying 'just'?"

"No, not just," I say, stuttering. "Not like that. But she's not hurt, right?"

"Not physically." Bob stands up and pulls Deb toward the door. "Tell Sophie we'll be right outside when she's ready to leave."

"What do you mean 'leave'?"

Deb starts to say something, but Bob puts his hand up. "No more, Deb. This is between them."

When they leave, I walk over to the bedroom and crack the door open. The room is pitch black.

"Soph?"

No reply. I flip on the lights. She's lying on the bed—fully dressed—staring at the ceiling.

I walk over and grab her hand. "Baby, are you okay? Are you hurt?"

She shifts her eyes to me but doesn't move any other part of her body. "I'm not hurt."

I sit on the bed next to her and put my hand on her forehead. "Are you sick? Do you have a migraine?"

"I'm not sick. I'm just . . . I'm . . ." She sits up so quickly that it makes me jump. "God, Seb, I'm fucking exhausted. By all of this. People yelling at me, grabbing me, throwing things on me. The media saying I'm the reason you aren't playing well. It's too much. I can't deal with it anymore. I'm going back to Miami tonight."

"Okay," I say, stroking her arm. She pulls it away from me. "Baby, let's go home. I'm coming with you."

"You're not leaving." She crawls off the bed and walks into the bathroom to get her purse. "Just me. I'm going back with my parents. I need some time alone. I can't do it anymore, Seb. I'm going home."

"What can't you do?" I jump off the bed and grab her shoulders. "Sophie. Answer me. What can't you do? Watch my games? Be married to me? What?"

She shakes her head and tries to get around me.

"Sophie," I say, hugging her to me. "Stop. Answer me."

"Let me go." She pushes at my chest.

I release her just enough so she can look up at me. "Not yet. Answer my question."

She takes a deep breath. "I love you, Seb, but I need to take care of myself right now. It's too much. I'm so stressed out. I'll see you on Saturday when you get back and we can talk some more."

I take in a sharp breath and hold it. I'm almost afraid to let it out.

"Talk about what?" I finally whisper as the air seeps out of my mouth.

She maneuvers around me to the door. "We need to leave if we're going to catch our flight."

I reach over her and hold the bedroom door shut. "Talk about what, Sophie?"

"We can't miss our flight. It's the last one out tonight."

"What?" I turn her around and put my arms on either side of her—my hands pressing against the door. "The plane leaves when you get there."

She won't look up at me. "We're flying commercial. I'm not taking your private plane."

"*Our* private plane, Sophie." I tilt her chin up and look directly into her eyes. "*Ours.*"

"Let me go," she says, trying to duck under my arm. I stop her. "Seb, get out of my way."

"Is Butch flying back with you? Or Mason?"

"I don't want them to. All of this is too much. The bodyguards, everything. I'm turning into someone I don't even know. I just want to be Sophie again."

I lean down until our eyes are even. "You are Sophie. You're *my* Sophie. Nothing changes that. Just me and you, remember?"

She turns her head as I try to kiss her. "Seb, I can't think straight anymore. I need to get out of here. Please."

I put my forehead against hers for a second, and then roll off her until my back is pressed against the wall.

"Please don't leave me," I whisper as I start to sink down the wall. "Please."

"I'm not leaving you," she says from above me, "but I have to leave here. I'll see you on Saturday."

I grab her leg. "Soph, just stay with me tonight. You can fly out in the morning."

"I need to get out of here now. I have to find my center back."

She pulls my hand off her leg, kisses the top of my head, and then walks out of the room.

"Please, don't leave me," I whisper as I hear the door to the room shut behind her.

I put my head between my legs and close my eyes. Joe walks into the room. He slides down the wall until he's sitting next to me.

"If you want to follow her back to Miami, I'm with you. Just tell me when you want to leave."

"She doesn't want me to follow her. She said she needs time."

"Then give her time." He puts his hand on my shoulder. "She's not going anywhere."

"She already went somewhere, man."

"She's not leaving you. She'll be at the house when we get back to Miami."

"Will she?" I slowly raise my head. "I don't even know anymore."

"She'll be there. She loves you. She knows you love her." He pushes himself off the floor, and then pulls me up. "The only thing you can do right now to make it better is to honor her wishes."

Chapter Twenty-Five

SOPHIE

November 3, 2022

When I walk out of the room, Maisie's standing in the hallway talking to my parents.

"Hey," she says. "We just got back from the game. I was coming to see you, but your parents said you're headed back to Miami. Do you want me to come with you?"

"I told you, Maisie," Mom says, taking my hand and pulling me toward the elevators. "Just our family right now. We'll see you when you get back."

Maisie runs in front of me and pushes on my shoulders to get me to stop. "Stop, Soph. Hold on. Are you sure you want to go home? Maybe chill out for a few hours with Raine and me, and then talk to Seb about all of this."

"I just talked to him." I nod my head back toward the room. "I don't have anything more to say about it to anyone. I just need space to think."

"No you don't. Too much thinking is dangerous," Maisie says. "You need to fight back."

"Who should I fight?" I look at her as my eyes start to well up again. "I don't even know who most of the trolls are who are coming after me."

Dad punches the elevator button. "She can't fight who she can't see."

"Yes, you can, Sophie," Maisie says. "I know you're tired, but you can't run away. You need to talk to Seb and fight this together."

Mom points at her. "She doesn't have anything more to say to Seb or anyone else—including you."

Mom tries to block Maisie from getting into the elevator. Maisie ducks under her arm and snakes her way through the suitcases until she's against the back wall.

"You don't have anything to say to Seb now," Maisie says, somehow ignoring Mom's searing stare, "but you will within an hour. You know you will. Don't leave. Stay with me tonight. We can talk it out."

The elevator door opens in the lobby. Dad pulls the suitcases out and heads toward the door.

"Maisie," Mom says, trying to smile. "You know I love you like a daughter, but Sophie's leaving. You need to back off."

"No," Maisie says, trying to stretch her five-foot-four body up to meet Mom's eyes. "I'm sorry, Deb, but you need to back off. You're wrong about this."

"Wrong about what?" Raine walks over with Millie two steps behind her. She looks at the suitcases, and then up at me. "What's happening? Are you leaving?"

Mom says, "Yes," just as Maisie says, "No." They continue glaring at each other.

"I'm going back to Miami," I say to Raine. "It's all gotten to be too much for me."

"Uh." Raine looks between Mom and Maisie who look like they're seconds away from throwing down. "Millie and I need to talk to you before you leave."

"No!" Mom says, pointing at Raine. Raine squeals and jumps back from her. "Enough. We'll be late for our flight. Come on, Sophie. We're leaving."

"Mrs. Banks," Millie says, pulling Raine behind her. "We need to talk to Sophie before you leave. Why don't you wait in the car?"

"Excuse me?" Mom's head tilts slightly to the side like it does before she's about to lose it on someone.

Millie takes a step toward her and looks directly into her eyes. I hear Raine whimpering behind us.

"You'll be more comfortable waiting in the car," Millie says, her voice suddenly becoming deep and terrifying. "If you'll excuse us, this is a private conversation."

"Mom," I say, stepping between them. "Go. I'll be right out."

Mom tries to back Millie down with one more withering look. When Millie doesn't budge, she whips around toward the exit door. "Two minutes, Sophie. That's it."

"Is she gone?" Raine peeks around Millie. "I've only seen Deb lose it once. I don't want to see it again."

Millie pulls me to the corner of the lobby. Raine and Maisie follow.

"What's this big secret?" I ask. "Make it quick. We need to get to the airport."

"We know who the *Twitter* user is," Millie says.

"What *Twitter* user?" Maisie asks. "The miamibballbabe one? Oh my god, it's Deb, isn't it?"

"It's not Mom." Millie and Raine are staring at me—eyes not blinking. "Wait, it's not my mom, right?"

"It's not your mom," Millie says. "It's Evelyn."

"Evelyn who?" I ask.

"Evelyn Marks," Raine whispers as a group of Miami team employees walk by us. "From the team."

"What?" I take a step back. "No way. Why do you think that? It doesn't even make sense. You have to be wrong."

"First of all, I'm never wrong," Raine says, looking over her shoulder to make sure we're alone, "and second, we know for sure. There's no doubt."

"Who's Evelyn?" Maisie asks.

"She works for the team," I say, squinting to try to make my brain work faster. "She loves Seb. And she loves me. There's just no way."

"We-l-l-l," Millie says. "I think you're right about half of that. She definitely loves Seb—so much that we think she's trying to get rid of the obstacle to them being together. That's you, by the way."

"That's insane," I say. "She's known him for like a decade. If she wanted him, she would have made a move long ago. Why do you think it's her?"

"We don't think it. We know it." Raine points to Millie's phone. "Millie basically has control of Evelyn's phone right now. She can see everything Evelyn's texted, tweeted, posted—everything."

"What?" I look between them. "How?"

"Never mind how," Millie says. "Here, I'll send you a text from her phone right now."

I look down at my phone as it vibrates. There's a text from Evelyn.

Millie and Raine are right. Believe them.

I look back up at her. "How?"

Maisie grabs my phone, reads the text, and then looks at Millie. "How did you do that? Are you magic?"

Millie ignores her. "Evelyn is miamibballbabe. End of discussion. Sophie, you need to decide what you want to do about it. Or you can pass it to me and I'll take care of her."

"Please choose option two. Please," Maisie says, still staring at Millie with wide eyes. "Let Millie take care of her and please, please, please let me watch."

Raine nods her head toward the door. "Head's-up. Evelyn just walked in."

"Which one is she?" Maisie looks around the lobby. "I'm about to end this bitch."

"Stop, Maisie," I say. "I'm still not convinced. It doesn't make any sense."

Millie grabs my hand and pulls me over to a couch. "Sit with me and observe. I'm going to text her from her own number."

Raine sits on Millie's other side and points at the screen. "Text 'I'm watching you.' It's overused, but it really does cause the most amount of panic coming from someone's own phone."

Millie types it out and sends it.

I'm watching you.

Raine directs my gaze to Evelyn who's standing about thirty feet from us, talking to a few team employees. Evelyn looks at her phone. Her face melts into confusion. Her head starts turning back and forth as she takes a few steps away from the group.

Who is this?

Millie shows her phone to me when the text comes through. "Do you need more convincing?"

"Kind of."

Millie types out another text.

It doesn't matter who I am. What matters is that I know you're miamibballbabe. Very bad tweets, Evelyn. I'm guessing they could get you fired.

Evelyn reads the text, then squeezes her eyes shut as her chest starts heaving. She finally opens her eyes. Her thumbs fly over her phone's screen.

I don't know what you're talking about. Leave me alone. I'm blocking you.

Millie laughs as she shows the screen to Raine.

"Well, we know we're not dealing with a criminal mastermind," Raine says, grabbing the phone and typing a reply.

I'm texting you from your own number, dumbass. Pay attention, Evelyn. Or am I distracting you??

Evelyn reads the text, spins around a few times, and then runs out of the lobby.

Raine laughs. "I love a good virtual takedown. All of the fun without actually having to talk to anyone."

"How are you inside her phone?" I ask. "I don't get it."

"Soph," Raine says, patting my leg, "I know you have some idea of what I do for a living. Millie does the same thing. Millie cloned Evelyn's phone at the game tonight. Evelyn's the user. I haven't had time to do a deep dive of the phone, but I searched her history with Ricky and—"

"What history with Ricky?" I close my eyes as my brain tries desperately to keep up with the new information. "She barely knows him."

"She had an affair with him five years ago," Raine says. "It ended his marriage."

"What?" My eyes pop open as I move away from her on the couch. "There's no way."

"Sophie," Raine says, grabbing my shoulders, "it's time for you to move beyond the disbelief stage. Everything I'm telling you is fact. Keep up with me. Evelyn met Ricky when he was visiting Seb. They started talking. Then they started hooking up when Ricky visited Miami. Evelyn wanted more. Ricky said no. She texted Ricky's wife from an anonymous number. Ricky's wife left him. I don't think he has any idea that Evelyn was the one who texted his wife. Their affair ended, but they've remained friends. Ricky has given her all kinds of information about you and Seb, but I don't think he knows she's the *Twitter* user."

"I, uh," I say, looking at her blankly. "I don't even know what to say. I mean, how is the affair my fault? I didn't know any of them—including Seb—when that went down. Why would she be coming after me?"

"Don't overthink it, Soph," Millie says. "She just wants to be with Seb. Jealousy is always the most powerful motive."

"Wait," I say, looking back at Raine. "Did she have something with Seb at some point? Did they hook up?"

"I don't think so. She doesn't even have Seb's number in her phone. I need to dig a little deeper, but I really don't think they ever had anything."

"This is crazy," I say. "It can't be just jealousy. How does she think something's going to happen between them now if it hasn't already?"

"Didn't you tell me Seb hasn't had a serious relationship since high school?" Raine asks. "Maybe Evelyn was playing the long game, and then you appeared out of nowhere and swept him up in a few months."

Maisie finally stirs from next to me. She's been sitting there with her mouth open for a strong minute. "The long game? Holy shit. That's taking unrequited love to a whole new level."

Millie shrugs. "It happens all the time. People don't want to make a move because down deep they know they'll be rejected, and then the fantasy will come crashing to a halt."

"Un-fucking-believable. Even the people we trust want us to be miserable." I look up at the ceiling for a second, and then back at Millie. "If you have control of her phone, can you delete the *Twitter* account?"

"Yep," she says, showing me the screen. "Watch me do it. We're on her account. I'm changing the password so she can't get back in. Hold on. Okay, done. Now I'm deleting the account. There it goes. It's gone. Try to find the account on your phone."

I pull up *Twitter* and search for the account a couple different ways. Nothing.

"Huh, I like having control of her phone. Don't give it up just yet. I might want to fuck with her more later." I stand up and look around the lobby. "But now it's time for action. What did you say, Maisie? That I need to fight back? Done. Does anyone see Evelyn? It's time for us to have a little chat."

"That's probably not the best idea." Raine tugs on my hand to try to get me to sit back down. "There are other ways to handle this."

"Maybe," I say, pulling my hand away, "but I choose violence."

"But we don't have the means to track her. She could be anywhere—"

"Raine Nira Laghari," I snarl as I point at her. "Get your little spy surveillance network working and tell me exactly where she is. Right now."

"She used your full name," Maisie whispers, nudging Raine. "Give up the information before the rarely seen, but greatly feared Storming Sophie appears."

Raine buries her head in Maisie's shoulder and squeaks out, "She's already here. I'm so scared. Save me."

"Evelyn's at the pool." Millie stands up and points across the lobby. "Follow me."

"Fuck," Raine says, springing up. She starts jogging to keep up with Millie and me. "This is not a good idea."

"What's not a good idea?" Elle suddenly appears next to us, followed by Kit. "We're headed to the bar. Come with us."

"Later," Maisie says from behind me. "Sophie's about to kick someone's ass."

"Ooo, fun!" Kit grabs Elle's hand and starts pulling her along with us. "Can we watch?"

As we charge across the lobby, a man jumps in front of our group.

"Hey. You're Seb Miller's wife, right?" he asks, grabbing my arm.

"Keep your hands to yourself, asshole," I say, pulling my arm away from him, "and my name's Sophie, not Seb Miller's wife."

"I just asked you a question. No need to be a bitch."

Maisie lunges at him. "You did not just call her a bitch!"

I pull Maisie back and swing my purse, clocking the guy in the head.

"What the fuck!" The guy winces as his hands fly over his face.

"Purse to the head wouldn't have been my choice. Maybe try palm to the nose next time," Millie says, showing me the technique. "It's very effective."

I push the guy out of the way and herd our group toward the pool. "Maybe I'll try that on Evelyn."

When our group bursts out onto the pool patio, Evelyn's the only one out there. She's sitting on a lounge chair, typing furiously on her phone. Her head jerks up when she hears us.

"The account's gone, Evelyn?" I say as I charge toward her. "Or should I call you miamibballbabe?"

Chapter Twenty-Six

SEB

November 3, 2022

"I changed my mind."

"What does that mean, Seb?" Joe's jogging behind me down the hallway. "Changed your mind about what?"

"I'm stopping Sophie. Either she's staying here or I'm going back to Miami. I'm not letting this bullshit separate us—even for one night."

Joe tries to block me from the elevator doors. "Seb, she said she needed time—"

"Tough," I say, pulsing the down button repeatedly until the door opens. "She's not getting it. We're a team. We handle our problems together."

The elevator doors close so slowly that I want to grab them and pull them shut. "Move faster! Why does my room have to be on the top floor?"

"Because that's the safest floor." Joe stops when I hiss at him. "Oh. That was a rhetorical question? My bad."

My head almost explodes when the elevator stops on the tenth floor. Alex is standing there when the door opens. I grab his arm and yank him inside as I attack the lobby button with my other hand.

"Damn, Seb," Alex says, "ease up. Where's the fire?"

"No time to explain."

"Nine more floors to explain," he says, looking back at Joe who's shaking his head.

"Sophie's trying to leave to go back to Miami. I'm stopping her. I've been texting her. No answer. I need to find her."

"That's weird," Alex says. "I've been texting Raine, too, with no answer. I'm headed to the lobby to look for her."

When the elevator doors open, I burst out and scan the lobby. I see Bob and Deb standing by the exit door. They look panicked.

I run over to them. "Where's Sophie? I thought you left for the airport."

"We can't find her," Deb says, her voice shaking. "She was just here talking to Raine. We were waiting in the car. We came back in and they were gone."

"Gone where?" I ask, growling. "Have you texted her?"

"Texted, called," Deb says, her eyes getting glassy. "She's not responding. What if someone took her?"

"No one took her," Bob says, his voice much deeper than usual. "Everyone needs to settle down. She's probably just using the restroom."

I start to text Sophie again when I hear a whistle. I look up to see Butch waving me across the lobby to where he's standing with Mason, Nash, and Alex.

"Have you seen Sophie?" I ask, closing in on them.

"We're looking for our women too," Butch says, holding up his phone. "None of them are answering texts."

"Hey, Miller!" A man runs up to me and points his finger in my face. "Your wife just clobbered me in the head with her purse."

"Put that finger in my face again and I'm removing it." I grab his t-shirt collar. "When did this happen? Speak!"

"Like a minute ago," the guy says, his eyes getting wide.

"Where?" I demand as I tower over him.

"Right over there," he says, pointing across the lobby. "She went out to the pool after she hit me."

I push him out of the way. Mason, Butch, Nash, Alex, and Joe fall in behind me as I start running across the lobby.

When we clear the door to the pool, I see Sophie shoving a woman away from her.

"Don't try to deny it!" Sophie yells. "We know it's you. We shut down the account. Yeah, look at your phone. It's gone. Try to post shit about me now."

"Sophie!"

The other woman turns to me when I yell. It's Evelyn Marks. "Seb, thank God you're here. Sophie's gone crazy. She's hurting me. Please make her stop."

"Shut the fuck up," Sophie says, shoving her again. "You're the crazy one."

"Sophie!" I pull her back. "Stop. What are you doing?"

"Seb," Evelyn says, her voice getting softer, "I was just sitting out here by myself, trying to get a little alone time, and Sophie came running out here, followed by her group of mean girls. They're yelling at me about something. I don't know what I did. Please make them stop."

Sophie looks up at me. "She's miamibballbabe. She's the one tweeting all that bullshit about me."

"What?" Evelyn and I say at the same time. I look at Evelyn. She's nodding at me—her eyes imploring mine for understanding.

"It's crazy, right?" Evelyn walks around Sophie and puts her hand on my arm. "Seb, I would never do anything to hurt you."

"Don't touch my husband," Sophie says, yanking her hand off me.

"Sophie, stop," Evelyn says. "You're hurting me. Please stop attacking me. I don't know what I did."

"That's not attacking," Sophie yells as she lunges for Evelyn. "This is attacking."

Sophie slams her shoulder into Evelyn's chest, sending them both flying into the pool. They surface and start swinging at each other as they try to get their feet underneath them.

"Enough!" I yell, marching down the stairs into the pool. I trudge through the water until I get to Sophie. I grab her arm and pull her away from Evelyn. "Sophie, settle down. Tell me exactly what's happening."

She points at Evelyn. "She's the *Twitter* troll. She's been calling me a whore for months behind the safety of her keyboard. It's time for her to say something to my face. I dare you, Evelyn. Say something."

Evelyn's mouth drops open. "What are you talking about?"

When Sophie tries to get around me, I lean down and put her over my shoulder. "Stop!"

"Put me down!" Sophie starts pounding on my back. "I'm not even close to being done with her."

"You're done." I march back up the stairs with her still over my shoulder and point to Raine. "Tell me what's going on."

"Evelyn Marks is miamibballbabe," Raine says, nodding to Millie. "We're one hundred percent sure."

"That's not true!"

"Shut up!" I turn to Evelyn who's still in the pool. "Don't speak again or I will put Sophie down and let her at you again."

"Yes!" Sophie yells as she continues to pound on my back. "Do that. Put me down!"

I wrap my arm tighter around her legs as she tries to slip down my body. I turn back to Raine. "Do you have proof?"

"Tons of it," she says. "She also had an affair with your friend Ricky. I'm not sure if you knew that."

"No," I say, turning back to Evelyn who looks away from me quickly. "I definitely didn't know that."

"We need to dig a little deeper," Raine says. "I'm sure there are a lot more sorted details. I'll let you know what I find."

"Please don't. I don't want to hear another thing about her." I glare at Evelyn, and then turn to Joe. "Joe, Raine and Millie are going to send you some evidence that Evelyn has been slandering Sophie on *Twitter*. Do you think that's enough to get her fired?"

"More than enough. Dottie won't like that at all. Get me the evidence. She'll be gone by the morning."

Millie taps on her phone. "Sending it now."

"Seb," Evelyn says, whining. "I can explain. Sophie's ruining you. You deserve so much better than her."

"Shut up." I hold up my hand. "Just shut up. If you ever get near my wife or me again, I'll have you arrested."

Joe pulls Evelyn out of the pool and points her toward the exit door. "We're talking to Dottie right now. Raine and Millie, please join us."

"On it," Raine says as she and Millie follow them to the door.

"Seb," Sophie whispers, her body suddenly going limp on my shoulder. "Too much blood rushing to my head. I think I'm going to pass out."

"Sorry, babe." I slide her down my body a little bit so she can get her head upright. "Are you okay?"

"Dizzy."

"Wrap your legs around my waist and put your head on my shoulder."

"You can put me all the way down," she says. "I think I can stand."

"I'm not putting you down," I say, kissing her forehead. "You're a flight risk."

"A flight risk or a *fight* risk?" She scrunches up her face and starts silently laughing at her joke.

"Are you on the Paloma juice again?" I ask, smiling. "Because that joke wasn't even close to being funny."

"It was hilarious." She closes her eyes and laughs again. "And not drunk. Just dizzy."

"Put your head on my shoulder, baby."

She lays her head down and whispers, "I'm sorry I walked out on you, Seb. I don't want to go back to Miami. I'm staying here."

"Don't apologize. You didn't do anything wrong." I kiss the side of her head. "Can we go up to our room and talk about it there?"

"Yes, please." She wraps her arms around my neck. "Can we order pizza? Fighting makes me hungry."

"Yeah, baby. We can order pizza—"

Her head pops up. "And cheesy bread."

"Soph." I shake my head. "We've covered this a hundred times. Pizza and cheesy bread are the exact same thing."

"False," she says, tilting her head. "Cheesy bread doesn't have toppings."

"Then it's just like ordering cheese pizza."

"Seb, no." Her eyes get wider. "It's thicker than pizza. It's totally different."

"Fine. We can order cheesy bread too. But you can't eat as much of it this time. It always makes you sick."

As we walk back into the lobby, Deb and Bob run over to us.

"What's happening?" Deb puts her hand on Sophie's back. "Is she hurt? Who is that woman with Joe? Did she attack Sophie? Why is everyone wet?"

Sophie lifts her head. "Mom, I'm fine. I've decided not to leave. You can go back if you want, but I'm staying."

"Seb, put her down," Deb says, looking up at me. "I don't know what's happened in the last ten minutes, but

Sophie needs separation from everyone right now—including you."

"Deb, I respect you," I say, "but that's the last free shot I'm giving you. You need to get off me. I'm a good husband. You know Sophie's my entire world. I barely even look at other women."

"Barely?" Sophie raises her eyebrows, a smile covering her face. "Just for that, I get to order double cheesy bread."

"Head back down."

"Fine," she says, nuzzling her face into my neck.

Bob pulls Deb back from us. "We'll stay here. I want to see your game tomorrow. Come on, Deb. Let's get the luggage out of the car. Soph, we'll keep yours in our room. Text me when you need it."

"Thanks, Dad."

As we continue across the lobby, I notice some people snapping pictures of us. "I wonder what story they'll make up about this. We're dripping wet and I'm carrying you up to our room."

"Seb Miller saves wife from drowning after she attacks an innocent bystander." Sophie laughs as I carry her onto the elevator. "I'm sure it will be good, but at least we won't have to read Evelyn's take on it. Millie changed her password and deleted the account. I guess she can start a new one, but she'll have to start from scratch. She's lost her thousands of followers. Can you believe it was her? I couldn't have guessed that if you gave me a million tries."

"Nothing surprises me anymore. Seriously. I thought I built the wall around me high enough, but apparently I need to build it higher. No one's allowed in the innermost circle anymore except you." I press her against the wall of the elevator. "I mean, if you still want to be there."

"I never left there," she says, weaving her fingers through my hair as my lips move to her neck. "It's my favorite place in the world."

Chapter Twenty-Seven

SOPHIE

November 4, 2022

"Seb. Too tight. I can't breathe."

When I wake up, Seb's spooning me. Actually, it's less of a spoon and more of a wrestling hold. He has one arm looped under my neck, the other around my chest, and his legs knotted around mine.

"What?" He slowly stirs out of sleep and starts uncoiling himself from my body. "Oh, sorry. I was having a nightmare."

I roll over on my back and stroke his cheek. "Oh, baby. What was the nightmare about?"

"You were trying to leave me," he says, pressing my hand to his face. "I think that's why I was squeezing you."

"I'll never walk out on you again. No matter what. I promise. I'm so sorry. I wasn't thinking straight."

"I told you not to apologize. With everything that's happened, I can't believe you stayed strong as long as you did." He leans over me and gives me a slow kiss. "Just tell me we're good."

"We're perfect." I groan as my stomach starts to roll. "Oh no, I think the cheesy bread is attacking me."

"I told you. You can't keep eating that crap. You have the most sensitive system in the world." He starts running his fingers over my belly. "Do you want me to order ginger tea with cinnamon? It always makes you feel better."

"Yes, please. Thanks, babe. You take such good care of me."

"And I always will." He kisses my stomach before he pushes himself off the bed. "What else do you want?"

"I don't want any food right now, but there are a few things that I want—like life things. I've been thinking about it all night."

"Oh," he says, looking back at me. "Okay. Anything, Soph. You know that. You can have anything."

He holds up his hand for me to pause while he orders his breakfast and my tea. When he's done, he crawls back into bed with me.

"Tell me what you want," he says as I lay my head on his shoulder.

"I only want two things."

"Fine. Done and done."

I hold up my hand. "No wait. Three."

"And done."

"You haven't even heard what they are yet," I say, smiling.

"Doesn't matter. Done, done, and done. Anything. Just tell me what they are."

"Well," I say. "I've been thinking we should spend less

time in Miami. It's really where your fame is the most intense. Keep a small place there—like a condo on the beach—but move out of our house. Maybe we can make our primary residence somewhere we can live a little more normally."

"Done. We'll start packing right when we get back. Where do you want to go?"

"I was thinking about Michigan. You've always said you want to buy your own lake house there. Maybe we can get something south of where your parents are—halfway between Chicago and Grand Rapids. We would be close to both families, but not too close."

"That sounds perfect." He starts rubbing my back. "And it's a good place to raise kids when we get to that point. We can start looking for a house when we're up there next week. Done. What's number two?"

"I want to buy a house in Blitzen too," I say, looking up at him, "and start spending the majority of our summers up there when you retire."

"We're on the same page. I've already asked Nash about houses. He said the houses right on the lake don't come on the market very often. He's keeping his eyes open for us. We can look when we're up there for their wedding in December."

"Yay! That makes me so excited. I think it will be the perfect summer getaway when we have kids—which brings me to request number three."

"Tell me."

I sit up so I can look him in the eyes. "I want to start trying for a baby within the year. You can pick the exact date, but I want it to be in the next year even if you're still playing. Okay?"

He puts his hands around my face and pulls me in for a kiss. "Yeah, baby, it's okay. Let me think about the timing a little more, but we'll start trying at some time in the next year."

"Thank you," I say, beaming at him. "That's the end of my requests. Tell me what you want."

He traces my lips with his fingers. "This. Just being with you as much as possible."

"That's a given, but there has to be something else." I climb on top of him and wrap my arms around his neck. "Tell me. What do you want?"

He smiles, pulls my tank top out, and peeks inside.

"That's a given too," I say, swatting his hand away. "Be serious. Relationships are about give and take. I just asked for a bunch of stuff. You get to ask for stuff, too."

"Well first, I want all the stuff you asked for, so it's not like I'm giving anything up," he says, stroking the stubble on his chin. "But there is something I've been thinking about."

"Tell me."

"When you said you wanted to fly commercial yesterday," he says slowly, "did you mean forever? Or can we keep the private plane? Like I will literally live in a shack if we can just keep that plane."

"Oh, God. I don't want to fly commercial. No one does. We're keeping it. We can even live in the plane if it comes to that."

"Oh, look. They're alive."

When we walk into the lobby, our parents are sitting in the lounge having cocktails.

"Stop, Mom," Seb says as we walk over to them hand in hand. "We needed some alone time."

"I'm not saying you didn't," Adie says. "I'm just glad to see you're breathing. We haven't heard from either of you since you went to your room last night. Deb told me you were fully dressed and soaking wet. Care to explain?"

"No," Seb says. "Mind your business, and don't grill Sophie about it today. Everything that happened yesterday is forgotten."

Joe points Seb toward the door as the team bus pulls up.

"I'll see everyone after the game," Seb says, turning to me. "Are you sure you want to go to the game tonight? I won't be mad if you watch it from here."

"I'm sure." I get on tiptoe to give him a kiss. "I'll be fine. They can pour an entire keg of beer on me if they want, but they're definitely getting one back in their faces. I'm ready for a fight."

"After what I saw last night, I'm putting my money on you." He gives me another kiss and then turns back to our parents. "Take care of Sophie for me."

"Always," Adie says. "Good luck, honey. Your dad and I are so proud of you. Soph, do you want to join us for a drink?"

"Yeah, and food too. I haven't eaten all day. I'm starving," I say as Seb pulls me toward the door. "I'll be back in a second."

"No cheesy bread," Seb says, smiling. "Or cheese of any kind. Promise?"

"I'm never eating cheesy bread again."

"Liar," he says, pointing at me as he backs toward the door. "But none for at least a week. Say you promise."

"I promise," I say, blowing him a kiss.

I watch him until he disappears into the bus. As I turn around, a man approaches me.

"Hey," he says. "I read Seb's tweets last night. I'm sorry you've had to go through all that. I had no idea. I don't think most people did. I hope things get better for you."

"Uh, thanks," I say, squinting my eyes as he walks away.

I pull out my phone to look at *Twitter*. Seb didn't tell me he posted anything. I'm thinking it must have been his social media coordinator until I start reading the thread.

Twitter @realsebmiller
(November 4, 2022)

Last night at the game, a man threw a beer in my wife's face. He screamed that she was the reason Miami was losing. I've never been angrier in my life.

The man who threw the beer was echoing what's been going around the entire week. Is my wife distracting me from playing my best? I'm distracted and I haven't played my best because of it, but my wife is not responsible.

Let me repeat that. My wife is not distracting me. Do you want to know who is? The man who followed her to her car in a dark parking lot a few weeks ago to ask her for my autograph. He distracts me.

And how about the man who pulled her out of her seat and grabbed her while she was watching me play in June? If someone did that to your wife or daughter or mother, would you be distracted? Damn straight you would. I was too.

Do you need more examples? How about the men and women who yell obscene things at her when she walks to her seat to watch her husband play baseball. They really distract me.

The social media idiots who hide behind their keyboards to smack talk my wife. They distract me. And the media who writes bullshit stories about how my wife is a distraction. They distract me too.

The only thing my wife does is love me better than I've ever been loved—way better than I probably deserve to be loved. And how do I repay her? I expose her to this world where everyone blames her for my mistakes.

God, it's just baseball. I love this game, but is it so important to you that you're willing to destroy a person's life? If it is, I don't know what to tell you. You need help, man. It's just a game. Maybe examine your priorities a little bit.

All I want to do is play baseball and go home to my wife at

night. That's not too much to ask. Thanks to the fans who just want me to do that too. I know there are more of you out there than the idiots.

Chapter Twenty-Eight

SEB

November 5, 2022

We won last night 9-2. I had three RBIs and even more important to me, I didn't make an error. I felt completely like myself for the first time in weeks. We only need to win one more game to clinch the championship.

After the game, I saw Sophie for a few minutes before she headed back to Miami with our families. She said that for the most part, the fans at the game were pretty chill. I think my tweets might have helped.

With our postgame obligations, the team didn't get in the air for about three hours after Sophie left. It's eight in the morning when I finally pull into our driveway in Miami.

Deb's sitting on a bench underneath our portico. She glances up from her book when I pull in. I take a deep breath as I see her headed my way.

"Seb," she says before I can even get my door fully open, "I owe you an apology."

I shake my head as I crawl out. "No you don't, Deb. If anything, I owe you an apology—you and Bob both."

"You don't owe us anything," she says, blocking her eyes from the sun with the book. "Thank you for taking such good care of our daughter. I'm sorry I interfered."

"Deb, seriously," I say, putting my arm around her shoulders, "don't apologize. You were just being a protective mother. I'm not mad at that."

"I was being too much of a mother, especially where you're concerned. Tell me you forgive me. It will make me feel better."

"I forgive you," I say, squeezing her shoulders. "Really. It's not a big deal."

"Thank you," she says, nodding toward the house as Bob walks out carrying suitcases. "We're headed down to Roman's hotel with your parents. We thought you and Sophie could use some alone time."

"You don't have to do that. There's plenty of room here for our family."

"We kind of want to," Bob says as my parents follow him out with their luggage. "We thought we would party it up for a few nights."

"Watch out, South Beach!" Mom says, throwing her arms in the air. "The Bob, Deb, Jack, and Adie Show is coming at you!"

"No one's ready for that," I say, rubbing my temples. "Just try to stay out of jail, okay?"

"No promises," Mom says as she puts her arm through

Deb's. "Are you two good? Or are you going to force me to choose sides between my son and my best friend?"

"We're fine," I say. "No choosing. We're going to need all grandparents on deck when we start having kids."

"And just when can we expect that?" Deb asks, smiling up at me.

"There she is," Mom says, pulling her toward the car. "Team Grandchild is reunited."

Deb pats my arm as they walk by. "Sophie's sleeping. She's up in her dressing room. I tried to get her to move to the bedroom, but she clinging to that crazy pink couch like it's Rose's door from *Titanic*."

"Yeah." I laugh. "We both like sleeping on that couch."

"Seb." Dad lingers behind as the others get into the car. "Is everything good between you and Sophie?"

"Yeah, Dad. It's perfect."

"Glad to hear it." He nods. "That will help you focus over the next two games."

"Two? There's just one more game. We're ending this thing tomorrow night."

He pats my shoulder as he starts walking away. "That's my son. Get it done, Seb."

Sophie didn't even stir when I carried her from the couch into our bed. I'm curled up behind her watching her breathe. Every time she inhales, the top of her golden hair catches the one ray of light coming through the blinds. The shimmer has been mesmerizing me for almost a half an hour.

"Seb," she finally whispers, turning her head to look back at me. "When did you get home? What time is it?"

I spoon her closer to me. "I got home about an hour ago. It's like nine or so."

"Why didn't you wake me up?"

I put my nose into her hair and inhale. It still smells like oranges. "When I carried you in here, you barely moved a muscle. I don't think I could have woken you up even if I tried."

"Probably not," she says, wiggling her butt back into me. "All of this has been so exhausting. And not just lack of sleep, but like full-body exhausting, you know?"

"Yeah. I can't wait to get to the lake and just sleep for like a week straight."

"That sounds like pure heaven." She rolls her face back into the pillow. "When do you practice today?"

"Not until two." I snake my hand under the blanket and run it over her butt. She's wearing a pair of my boxers. "Just a light workout for the off day. And then back here for the night."

"Are you sure you get to stay here?"

"Positive."

I massage her butt for a few minutes, and then tug at the waist of the boxers. She shimmies them down her legs and over her ankles. She tries to roll over on her back, but I hold her tightly in the spoon.

"Huh uh," I say, wrapping her arms in front of her. "I'm doing all the work this morning."

I slide my fingers between her legs and start exploring. Her butt jolts back against me when I touch the spot. I figured out where it was the first night we were together.

When I get my fingers anywhere near it, her body's pretty much mine.

She moans into her pillow as her butt starts pulsing against me. "How can you touch me once and my body just loses it?"

"Because the universe loves me."

As I lean over her body to take one of her breasts into my mouth, I slide an arm underneath her and start massaging the other one.

"You're like an octopus," she says as her body bucks back into me again. "Too many arms. Too many things happening."

She buries her mouth into the bed as it starts making those little purring sounds I love. When I flick my tongue over her nipple, she gets louder. Once she starts moaning, I always make it my mission to see how loud I can get her.

I let her build a little bit before I move my mouth to her neck. I discovered the neck thing our first night together too. It makes her crazy. She pretty much goes into heat the minute my lips touch it. When I start nibbling, her hand shoots between our bodies. She tries to pull me out, but I take her hand away and fold her arms in front of her body again.

"What did I tell you about letting me do the work this morning? Patience."

"Stop teasing me like that, Seb," she says, trying to reach for me again.

"Okay, baby," I say, smiling. "How would you like me to tease you?"

"Stop using my words against me," she says, starting to pant. "God, I think I'm going to come already."

"Let go, baby. I'm feeling this is going to be a multiple morning for you."

I put a few fingers inside her as my thumb starts rubbing. Her feet start twitching. For some reason, her orgasms start there. I still haven't figured out why, but I know she's almost there when the feet start moving.

When I start pumping my fingers faster, the twitching moves from her feet up to her legs. Her body gets tight against mine as a string of sounds erupts from her mouth. She vibrates against me hard—one last moan rumbling out.

I hug her tighter to me. "Do you need a little recovery time before we try for another?"

She shakes her head. "This one isn't even over. It's still tingling through my body."

"Maybe we can stack them on top of each other," I say as I slide into her from behind.

I start slowly moving inside her. It only takes a few seconds for her to reengage. When her body starts moving with mine, I turn up the speed. I place my hand on her belly and press her harder into me.

She looks up at me—her lips reaching for mine. I slide my tongue into her mouth as I continue to rocket against her body. I groan into her mouth as my body gets rigid against her. I thrust hard one more time. When I explode inside her, our moans blend as we slowly ride this one out together.

Chapter Twenty-Nine

SOPHIE

November 6, 2022

"Are you ready?" Mom asks as we start walking toward the door that leads out into Miami's stadium. "We can still sit up in the suite."

"I'm so ready," I say, smiling. "Everyone was cool in L.A. for the last game. I think Seb's tweets helped a little bit."

"Well," she says slowly. "Not everyone."

I shrug. "It was a lot better, though. No one was yelling stuff at me at least. I'm done hiding. I'm going to sit in the box seats and watch my husband play baseball. The haters can bring it. I don't even care anymore."

As we walk to the seats, the fans in our section start stirring. I glance to the left. Everyone seems to be smiling at me or ignoring me. It's a start. I look to the right to see an entire section of familiar faces.

"Oh, look," Maisie says, "you're not wearing your Unabomber costume. I can see your entire face."

Maisie, Ryan, and the entire Blitzen crew are sitting about twenty rows behind my seats.

"Did Seb get these tickets for you?" I point at Butch and Mason. "I told him I didn't want bodyguards."

Butch nods his head back to Sam who's sitting in the row behind him. "Seb didn't get these seats for us. Sam's girlfriend did."

"Really?" I raise my eyebrows. "Sam, do you have a girlfriend now?"

Millie puts her arm around him and lays her head on his shoulder. "He has so many girlfriends."

"Yes, he does." Elle mimics her action from the other side of him.

Sam puts his arms around Millie and Elle—his sweet face beaming with joy. "I have enough love to go around. Sophie, do you want to sit with us?"

"I would love to sit with you, but I promised our parents I would sit with them. I better get down there," I say, pointing to where Dad's waving at me. I point at Mason and Butch. "No interfering if someone tries to get to me. I have to learn to fend for myself."

"Okay, killer. Do your thing," Butch says. "There's no pool here, though. Maybe you can tackle them onto the field. Just make sure you land on top of them so they take the brunt of the fall."

"Noted. Thanks for the tip," I say. "Enjoy the game. Party at our house after if we win tonight."

As I keep walking down the stairs to my seat, people are taking pictures of me, but no one's saying anything. I think I'm in the clear when a burly, bald man stands up and points at me.

"Hey, Sophie," he says, a thick Brooklyn accent pouring out of his mouth. "I saw Seb's *Twitter* stuff the other day. It pissed me off. I have a wife and three daughters. If anyone came after them, I'd feel the same way he does. If you have any trouble tonight, just yell out my name and I'll take care of them. I'm Bob, by the way."

"Thanks, Bob," I say, stopping to give him a fist bump. "I appreciate the backup."

"My pleasure. Seb's my second favorite player ever."

"Oh yeah?" I smile at him. "What does he have to do to move into that number one spot?"

Bob laughs. "Die and come back as Derek Jeter."

"Fair enough. I'll let him know."

"Hey, Sophie." Another guy stands up. He looks at Bob. "My name's Tariq. I'm not quite as big as Bob, but I'm a middle-school teacher. If I can deal with those little assholes all day, I can take care of anyone who tries to get at you. Just let me know what you need. Not all of us are idiots. Most of us just want to watch the game."

"Thanks, Tariq," I say, nodding. "That means a lot to me."

A woman stands up in front of him and holds up her hand to show me her manicure. "I'm Bonnie. I'm old and weak, but I have daggers for nails. If Tariq and Bob get them down, I'll absolutely claw their eyes out."

"Nice. Now I'm kind of hoping someone attacks me so I can witness that."

I give her a high five and continue walking to my seat.

As I walk into my row, the fans around me echo the sentiments.

"We've got you, Sophie."

"Just enjoy the game."

"Thanks, everyone," I say, smiling and giving them a little wave as I slide into my seat.

Adie grabs my hand and squeezes it. "That was so lovely," she says, a tear rolling out of her eye.

"Adie, stop." I pat her hand as more tears escape. "No crying in baseball, remember?"

She squeaks. "I just love it when strangers support each other. It's my crying kryptonite."

"Everything's your crying kryptonite. Mom, make her stop."

I turn to Mom. She has tears streaming down her face, too.

"Both of you, stop." I put my arms around their shoulders and hug them to me. "What are you going to be like when we tell you that we're pregnant?"

"Stop it, Sophie." Adie waves her hand in front of her face. "Stop. There's too much emotion right now. If you tell me you're pregnant, I will absolutely pass out on the spot."

"I'm not pregnant. One major life event at a time." I point their faces toward the dugout. "Look, the players are coming out for introductions. Concentrate on that."

When Seb walks out of the dugout, he looks back at our section and smiles when he sees me.

"All good?" He mouths.

I nod and blow him a kiss.

"Don't worry, Seb," someone yells from behind me. "We have her back. Just play ball."

Seb laughs as he turns around to take his spot in the line. When the announcer says his name, the crowd goes wild. He usually gets the loudest cheer, but I've never heard anything like this.

He takes his cap off and turns around a few times to acknowledge them. On his last turn, he looks back at me and winks. Just from the look on his face, I can tell we're going to win tonight. The feeling sweeps all the way through my body. Seb told me once that some games just feel right—almost like everything's moving in slow motion. I think that's happening for him right now.

It's the top of the ninth inning. We're up 5-4. The other team has the bases loaded with two outs. The tension is so high in the stadium that I feel like I'm about to pass out.

Both teams have played hard, but Seb has been the star of the game. He had a two-run homer in the fifth, and he's thrown out two runners attempting to steal second. Last inning, he snagged Jack's throw from center and blocked a runner from tying the game. The runner slammed his body hard into Seb to try to get him to drop the ball. Seb didn't budge. The guy bounced off him like a little kid.

He's deep in the zone. Nothing seems to be bothering him. It's the most important game of his life but he looks like he's playing a game with his friends at the neighborhood lot.

I take a deep breath as the other team's cleanup hitter walks to the plate. He's played great tonight too. He could easily clear the bases with one swing.

"You're going to twirl the hair right out of your head."

Mom grabs my hand and lowers it to my side for the fourth time. It's my tick when I'm anxious, and I'm about to lose my mind right now.

"We're only one out away from winning the World Series." I cover my eyes with my hands. "I can't look."

She pulls on my hands. "You can look and you will look."

I peek through my fingers to see our team's manager, Bud, walking out of the dugout. He calls a timeout.

"Oh, damn," Dad says, "I think he's going to pull Manny. There's not a chance I would do that. You have to let him finish the game."

"Agree," Jack says. "Despite this current predicament, he's dominated. What do you think, Soph?"

"Uh, I didn't see Bud motion to the bullpen." I look out there again. None of the relievers are headed out onto the field. "I think Bud's just trying to calm everyone down—remind them that the play's at the plate."

"Okay, Miss Baseball," Mom says, laughing. "When did you learn so much about the game?"

"Mom, I'm married to a professional baseball player. He teaches me stuff." I look between Jack and Dad. "Do you think the guy on third is a threat to steal home? He's so fast."

Dad shakes his head. "I don't think so. He's too jumpy. I don't think he has the confidence to do that."

"Agree," Jack says again. "What if Bud's telling them to put the batter on? Prevent the grand slam."

"I hope not," I say, looking out at the field. "Seb would

hate that. He's way too competitive to give anyone an intentional walk."

"Agree. Agree. Agree." Jack points out at Alex who's making his way to the mound. "I'm guessing Alex has a plan. He usually does."

"Maybe, they're going to try to pick the runner off at third," I say. "Seb told me Chick mentioned that guy to him. Chick thinks his leads off base are too big."

"Huh," Jack says. "You know what? Chick's right. Wouldn't that just be something if that's the way the series ended?"

Chapter Thirty

SEB

November 6, 2022

Sometimes you just know you're going to win a game—even before it starts. It doesn't happen often, but when it does, the certainty is so strong that it almost feels like the game is moving by itself toward its pre-arranged outcome.

I felt it when I woke up this morning. I felt it again when we took the field. I still feel it now—even with our backs against the wall. It's the top of the ninth. We're up 5-4. L.A. has two outs with the bases loaded.

Their cleanup hitter, Derek Woods, is coming up to bat. He's seeing the ball really well tonight. He's already two for three with two RBIs. The runner on third is their fastest player—the kid Chick warned me about after the first game. I know he can score even on a deep infield hit.

Manny's on the mound. He's pitched a brilliant game, but I can tell he's getting tired. I'm about to go out there and talk to him when Bud walks out of the dugout. He calls a timeout and motions me to join him.

"Let's put Woods on base," Bud says as I get out to the mound. "He's too dangerous tonight. I would rather walk in the tying run than have him connect and put this game out of reach. Take the tie and win it in the bottom of the inning."

"No." Manny shakes his head. "I want to end it here. I won't give him anything good. I can get him to pop it up."

"I agree with Manny," I say, pulling up my mask. "Let's work the count a little bit and see what happens. The last thing we want is extra innings."

"No," Bud says, "the last thing we want is to lose this fucking game and have to go to game seven."

"Well, uh, candlesticks always make a nice gift," Alex says as he walks over from short. "And maybe you can find out where she's registered—"

"Never gets old," I say, laughing. "I've seen that movie a million times, and it just never gets old."

"We're one fucking out away from winning the World Series and you're quoting movies," Bud says, pointing at Alex. "Get your head in the game, Molina."

"I'm just trying to lighten the mood, Bud. Settle down." Alex looks at me. "You know that kid's going to take a big lead off third. Should we try to catch him sleeping?"

Dom joins us from third. "I was just thinking the same thing. He might even try to steal home."

Bud shakes his head. "Dom can't hold him at third. We need him to cover an infield hit."

"Let Manny pitch the ball. Dom can distract the kid by

charging the plate," Alex says, kicking the dirt. "I can get over to third and cover for Seb's throw."

Bud whistles. "That's dangerous if Woods connects."

"We won't give him anything to hit." I cover my mouth with my mitt in case anyone's trying to read lips. "First pitch, intentional ball to see what kind of lead the kid's taking. Second pitch, low and away. Dom distracts the kid by charging the plate for a bunt. Alex sneaks over to third from short. I throw him out."

"I don't know—"

"Come on, Bud. The batter's a lefty. I have a clear path to third."

The home plate ump starts walking out to us. "Wrap it up, gentlemen. Let's play ball."

Bud shakes his head. "I don't want to lose this game on a wild throw or an error at third."

"I promise I won't have a wild throw," I say, my mitt still covering my mouth. "Alex, you promise you won't have an error?"

"Scout's honor."

"Manny, you good?" I ask.

"All good." He whips the ball into his glove. "Let's end this bullshit now. I've got a taste for champagne."

"I'll flip up my mask after the first pitch if we're on for the pickoff at third," I say. "If not, the plays at the plate whatever happens. Let's end it here."

The ump gets out to the mound. "Bud. Off the field."

I look at Bud. "You heard the man. Let us do our thing."

Bud shakes his head and turns to walk off the field.

"Get it done. I'll need an entire case of champagne after this."

"Are we good?" I ask. Everyone nods. "Alright. See you on the other side, fellas."

Derek nods at me as I make it back to the plate. "You figure a way to get me out? You haven't yet tonight."

I flip my mask down and crouch into position without replying. I hold my glove out to the side. Manny throws one wide.

"Seriously, man?" Derek steps off the plate. He clinks his bat on his cleats a few times to shake off some loose dirt. "You're going to put me on? Come on, Miller. You're way more competitive than that."

I stand up and throw the ball back to Manny. I flip my mask up and act like I'm wiping sweat off my forehead. Alex and Dom nod slightly as we watch the kid make his way back to third base. He took an enormous lead—almost halfway down the line.

I flip my mask back down and crouch into position. Derek sighs and steps back into the batter's box. Dom starts charging the plate.

I hear Derek mutter, "I'm not going to fucking bunt."

I flash a sign to Manny for low and away. He rears back and throws. Then it all happens in slow motion.

I see the ball coming in. It looks as big as a basketball. I put my glove down to catch it. Out of the corner of my eye, I see Alex moving toward third base.

The ball lands in my glove. The kid's halfway to home plate again. He starts to turn when he sees me spring up. He looks at Dom who's about even with him then spins around to see Alex closing in on third base. He hesitates toward home, then heads back toward third. He takes a few quick steps and launches his body into the air as he tries to dive back into the base.

As Alex closes in, I throw a bullet to him. It comes in right at the bag where Alex's glove is waiting. Alex closes his glove over the ball and swipes it across the kid's hands as they desperately reach toward the base. When Alex holds his glove up to show he has the ball, the ump windmills his arm toward the bag and punches the kid out.

As the stadium erupts all around us, I pat Derek's shoulder. "You're right. I'm way too competitive to put you on base. Nice series, man."

When I turn back to third, Alex is charging at me. I flip up my mask and prepare for impact. He launches his body into mine, his glove held high with the ball still in it.

As the rest of the team starts piling on us, I grab the ball out of his glove and bury it into my pocket. That ball's going on his mantle somewhere right next to his series MVP trophy.

The scene keeps getting crazier as more people join us on the field. Photographers are shoving cameras at us. Our PR staff is passing out caps and t-shirts that say "World Series Champions." Reporters are trying to pull us aside for interviews. But all I can think about is finding Sophie.

I look over to where she's sitting but don't see her. I'm guessing she's somewhere in the middle of the celebration huddle of our friends and family. I take a few steps in that direction.

A big, bald guy nods at me and yells, "You looking for Sophie?"

"Yeah," I yell back. "Who are you?"

"I'm Bob," he says, waving. "Nice to meet you. You're my second favorite player ever."

"Uh, thanks," I say, laughing. "You see my wife in that?"

He nods. "Yeah. Give me a second."

"Sophie!" he yells. "Seb's looking for you."

I watch as Bob peers through the huddle. I see two slender hands reaching out through the bodies. Bob grabs the hands and pulls. When Sophie pops out, he points at me. When she sees me, a huge smile erupts on her face.

I point toward the dugout and yell. "First person I see when I come off the field."

"Always!" she yells back as she blows me a kiss.

"Seb." Ray Franklin is headed over to me—pen and pad at the ready. "Congratulations, man. What does it feel like to be a World Series champion?"

"It feels unbelievable. I'm floating right now."

"Whose idea was the pickoff play to end the game? I'm assuming that was planned."

"Yeah," I say, nodding over to Alex. "It was Alex's. He's the brain, the heart, the everything of this team. He better get the MVP award."

"I've got the scoop," Ray whispers. "He's getting it. I don't think he knows that yet, so just between us."

"I've got you." I wave to Dottie who's motioning me up to the stage they just erected behind second base. "I have to go, Ray, but I want to give you a story in the next few days if you promise not to publish until January 1."

"That's called an embargo," he says, raising his eyebrows. "And I give you my word, just between you and me until January 1. Do you want to give me a preview?"

I look over my shoulder as I walk to the podium. "I'm guessing you already know what it is."

He nods and smiles as he heads over to interview a few more players.

As I get up on the stage, the commissioner's handing the championship trophy to Dottie. I jump over and help her hoist it over her head. She's beaming underneath it as the crowd starts chanting her name.

"Take it from me, Seb," she says, laughing as she looks up at me. "It's too heavy and it's more yours than mine anyway."

I lift it over my head quickly and then hand it off to Alex and Manny. I take a look around the stadium and try to take it all in. The last ten years of my life flash through my mind. It's been a good ride, but I've known for months that it's time for the next chapter.

Alex walks off the podium after accepting the MVP award for the series. He shakes his head. "This should have gone to you."

"No way, man," I say, hugging him. "That trophy is all yours. You played out of your mind. The perfect way to end your career."

"Yeah," he says, nodding. "I'll miss this, but I'm so excited for what's next. I get to spend almost every day with Raine. Nothing's better than that."

"Totally agree. I can't wait to get there myself."

He pats my back as we walk toward the dugout together one last time. "You thinking next year is your last?"

"Not sure. Maybe this year."

"What? You can't quit now. You're one of the best ever to play the game. You have to let the league give you a going away party. You know the fans across the country will want to give you love on your last year."

I roll my eyes. "You know me better than anyone. What about me makes you think I would want a farewell tour?"

"Damn," he says, shaking his head. "Are you a hundred percent on this?"

"Not yet. Let's concentrate on celebrating this win. Plenty of time for the decision later." I pull out the baseball I've been holding for him in my pocket. "This is the ball from the last out tonight. Put it next to your MVP trophy."

"I thought I dropped it during the celebration," he says, smiling as he takes it. "How did you get it?"

"I took it out of your glove when you rushed me. I know you can only concentrate on one thing at a time."

"Fuck you," he says, laughing. "And by the way, your throw to third was high."

"My throw was perfect. Your glove was too low."

Chapter Thirty-One

SOPHIE

November 7, 2022

When Seb and I finally get back to our house past midnight, the party's in full swing on our back patio. When we walk outside, a roar erupts as everyone lifts their glasses to toast Seb.

"World Series Champion, Seb Miller!" Stone yells as everyone continues to scream.

Seb tucks me against him as his buddies run over and start body bumping him.

"Release me, Seb," I say, laughing. "This is between you and them."

He gives me a quick kiss, then lets me go as they mob him.

I take a few steps back and survey the scene. Our family and friends are spread out from the boat dock to the pool. My brothers are grilling hamburgers. Roman's making drinks at our outdoor bar. Mom and Adie are huddled in a corner with Seb's sister. Dad and Jack are on the dock night fishing under the close supervision of Butch. The strings of white lights above our deck are blending with the stars to form a twinkly ceiling above it all. It's really the most beautiful, welcoming thing I've ever seen.

"Sophie!" Raine yells at me from across the deck. She's sitting with our Blitzen crew.

"Hey," I say as I close in on them. "Did everyone get their flights changed to head back to California tomorrow? I was serious when I said you can stay free at Roman's hotel as long as you want. The victory parade is on Tuesday."

"We already changed our flights," Millie says, pouring me a glass of champagne. "We leave tomorrow morning. I really want to get back to the little man as soon as possible."

"Please give Mo all of my kisses," I say. "Is he coming to Blitzen for the wedding in December?"

"He is." Millie laughs. "That's going to be the first time he sees snow. We're bringing the entire family for a winter getaway—Dad and his girlfriend, and our best friend, Chase, and his wife. Will you be in Miami until then?"

"No," I say, taking a deep breath. I feel completely relaxed for the first time in weeks. "We're headed to Michigan right after the parade. We'll stay at the lake house until we head up to Blitzen."

Elle looks at Sam, her face scrunched up. "Sam, I'm trying to check you in for our flight back to L.A. tomorrow. It's not coming up."

"Actually," he says, patting her shoulder. "I canceled my flight. I'm staying in Miami for an extra week."

"What?" she asks as we all look at Sam. "Why are you staying here?"

"Stop prying, babe," Nash says, putting his arm around her.

"No," she says, sitting up straighter. "Samuel Nicholas, tell me right now what's going on."

"I think the jig's up, man," Butch says, tapping Sam's arm as he walks up to the group. "You need to come clean. I'd like to save you, but they're going to keep gnawing at you like little rats until you break."

"Damn right we are," Millie says, pointing at Sam. "Speak."

Sam shakes his head—a glimpse of a smile forming on his face. "If you must know, over the last week, I've been getting to know Dottie Morris. We've found that we have a lot in common. I'm staying in town to get to know her a little bit better without the distraction of the World Series."

"Eek!" I say, clapping my hands. "That's so amazing. Dottie is just the sweetest person. Just like you. You're perfect for each other."

Sam smiles. "I enjoy her company very much."

"You can stay with us if you're done with the hotel. Seb and I will be gone in a few days, but you're welcome to stay at our house as long as you want."

"Thank you, Sophie," Sam says, "but I already have a place to stay."

Butch nods. "You shacking up with her?"

"Butch!" Elle says, pointing at him. "Stop."

"Nope. Sam knows the rules of this group. Everything out on the table." Butch turns to Sam. "Let's have the dirt, Sammy. You have a girlfriend now?"

"I'm a little too old to have a girlfriend. Let's just say I have a lovely companion."

"Companions with benefits?" Butch asks.

"*And* we've just crossed the line. Next topic," Nash says. "Our wedding is New Year's Eve in Blitzen. Who's coming?"

Everyone raises their hands as Seb walks up.

"What are we voting on?" he asks as he pulls me out of my chair, sits down, and then pulls me onto his lap.

"We're voting on who's more handsome—me or you," Butch says. "Sorry, man. Looks like you lost by a landslide."

"I asked who was coming to our wedding," Nash says, ignoring Butch. "Looks like everyone is. Come in right after Christmas if you can—spend the week celebrating with us."

"Maybe we'll even have time for bachelor and bachelorette parties," Elle says.

"Fun!" Kit looks at her. "I'll start planning your bachelorette party. Where's everyone staying? Holly House?"

"That's really the only place in town," Elle says. "We have a bunch of rooms blocked out for that week, but it's not very big. Speaking of, the Holly House owner, Hank, texted me last night. He said Roman called him and was inquiring about investing in it to make it bigger."

"Really?" Raine asks. "Roman wants to invest in a new resort in Alex's hometown in Puerto Rico too. They've been talking about it for months. How much money does Roman have?"

"Roman has enough money to buy a hotel in every city in America," I say. "Seriously, he's loaded."

"Make your reservations now for the wedding," Elle says. "If Holly House sells out, we have friends who have extra rooms."

"Including me," Sam says. "Anyone's welcome to stay at my house."

"Sophie and I are looking to buy a house in Blitzen," Seb says. "If we find a place before the wedding, anyone's welcome to say there."

Sam looks at us. "I might know of someone willing to sell. It's the house on the other side of mine. The owners are never there. They moved to Florida years ago. It's a rental right now, but I don't think they really want the hassle anymore. Do you want me to ask them?"

"Yeah," Seb says. "Please do. We're ready to buy immediately for the right place."

"Are you moving to Blitzen full time?" Kit asks. "Butch and I talked about moving there after we retire."

"Just summers for now," I say. "We're moving to a house on Lake Michigan when Seb quits playing. Both of our families are near there. It will be a great place to raise our kids."

"So no Miami when the playing days are done?" Mason asks. "I kind of like it down here."

"We'll keep a condo on the beach," Seb says. "We have a lot of friends down here. When we're not in town, any of you can use it. Same with the Blitzen house."

"So," Raine says, "this group now collectively has places in Blitzen, San Diego, Miami, Lake Michigan, St. John, and Puerto Rico. It looks like we're set for vacations for years to come."

I circle my arm around Seb's neck. "What do you think,

baby? When you retire, maybe we can just travel around to all of those places."

"Sounds amazing. It can't start soon enough for me," he says, pulling me against him. "Only two more days until we're at the lake house."

Chapter Thirty-Two

SEB

Lake House in Michigan

November 9, 2022

As I'm making my third cup of coffee, I hear the old wooden stairs start to creak. I poke my head around the corner to see Sophie's feet—covered in my big athletic socks—inching downward.

"Good morning," I say as the feet suddenly stop. "Be careful. Those stairs are crazy slick."

She sits down on the stairs, grabs a banister spindle in each hand, and presses her face between them. "Why are you up so early? We didn't get in until midnight."

"I couldn't sleep. You know how excited I get to be here. I've been up for a few hours." I smile at her scowling face. "The sun's about to rise. Do you want to come out on the deck and watch it with me?"

"The deck faces west. We can't watch the sunrise from there. Come back to bed."

"Then we can watch the lake come to life." I walk over to the bottom of the stairs. "If you come all the way down, I'll make you the pumpkin coffee stuff you like."

She tilts her head as she considers my offer. "Do we have that pumpkin pie spice stuff?"

"Yep. Mom stocked the house before we got here." I turn around and motion for her to get on my back. "Come on. I'll carry you."

She plods down the rest of the way, throws her arms around my neck, and lays her head on my shoulder. "Fine, but it feels like it's cold outside. I need lots of blankets."

"It's not cold. It's crisp." I circle my arms under her legs and lift her onto my back. "And we have plenty of blankets."

I carry her into the kitchen and set her on the counter. When I turn around, she's looking at me through the strands of hair that have fallen over her face. I push them back and kiss her forehead. "Your morning grumpiness is cute."

She grunts.

"You wearing my sweatpants is also cute." I tug at the waistband. "But we can get you some of your own so you don't have to roll the waistband down like five times."

"Huh uh," she says, shaking her head. The strands fall back over her face. "I like wearing yours."

She takes the hair tie off her wrist and twists her hair into a crazy pile on top of her head.

"You should know," I say, putting my hands on her knees and leaning down to kiss her. "When you wear your hair like that—especially when you're wearing your glasses—it really turns me on."

"Are there things that don't turn you on?" she asks wrapping her legs around my waist.

"Not with you. Pretty much everything works." I run my hands down her arms. "Do you want hot, iced, or blended?"

"Are we talking about sex or coffee?" She closes her eyes and laughs to herself. "How am I this hilarious even when I'm tired?"

"It's one of life's great mysteries."

"Iced, please," she says as I walk over to the Keurig.

"Are you sure?" I glance back at her. "That's going to make you colder."

She smiles. "Then you'll just have to warm me up."

"Challenge accepted."

When I get done mixing her coffee, I turn around to find her curled up on the counter—almost asleep.

"Get up, sleepyhead. The fresh air will wake you up." I grab her iced coffee and my mug. "Do you want a piggyback ride or can you walk now?"

"Walk," she grumbles as she slides off the counter. "I'll get the extra blankets."

She follows me out onto the deck and crawls between my legs as I spread out on a lounge chair. I cover us with three blankets until only her face is showing.

"Enough? Or do you need one more?"

"Enough." She leans over to the table and sucks some of her coffee out of the straw, and then settles back against my chest. "When did you wake up? I didn't even notice you leaving the bed."

"Around five. I've been out here thinking."

"About?"

"Two things." I take a deep breath. "First, I've played my last inning as a professional baseball player. I'm announcing my retirement in January."

She sits up and looks at me. "Are you sure? Do you want to play one more year so you can have a farewell tour or whatever?"

"I definitely don't want a farewell tour. The less attention, the better. I just want to fade away with no commotion."

"Seb," she says, raising her eyebrows, "there's going to be commotion—a lot of it. People are going to freak."

"Let them." I pull her back against me as a shiver runs through her body. "I'm done. Not because of you or all the bullshit that happened this season, but just because I'm done. I wanted to play in a World Series before I retired. I did. We won. It's a great way to go out."

She sits up again. "But you're going to miss playing so much."

"Yeah, I will, but that will be the case whenever I retire. I've thought about this a lot. I know it's the right decision. My head's not in it anymore. It's time to move onto the next phase of my life—of our life—which brings me to the second thing." I pause for a second to try to prepare for impact. "I'm ready to start having babies whenever you are."

She jumps out of the chair—blankets flying everywhere. "What? Like now?"

"That's up to you. I'm ready when you are."

She straddles me and takes my face in her hands. "I'm ready now. Like right now. Can we start this instant?"

"Yeah. Any time. Stop taking the pill."

She squeals and starts wiggling around on my lap.

"Oh, you mean, right now," I say, laughing. "Because if you keep going with this lap dance, I'll be ready for attempt number one in a few seconds."

"I didn't take my pill yet this morning," she says, placing kisses all over my face, "but I don't think it happens that fast. The pill probably needs to get out of my system or something."

"We'll take as many practice runs as we need."

She shivers again as a little gust of wind comes off the lake.

"Grab the blankets," I say. "Let's get you warm again."

She hops around the deck picking them up, and then settles back between my legs. "I'm so excited. I can barely breathe. Let's not tell anyone we're trying, okay? Until we really have something to tell them."

I laugh as she snuggles against my chest. "I never tell anyone anything. But are you really going to be able to keep it from Maisie?"

"Well, I'll tell Maisie, yeah. I don't count her as anyone."

I tilt her head up. "Babe, you can't tell her about my retirement. I trust her, but it's too dangerous. I haven't even told Dottie yet. I'm going to tell her just before the end of the year, and I've already embargoed a story with Ray Franklin to drop on January 1."

"Embargoed?" She laughs. "Look at you with your fancy PR talk."

"You taught me well. Ray will hold the story, right?"

"He definitely will, and I promise I won't tell anyone, not even Maisie." She settles back against my chest. "Have you told your dad?"

"Yeah, he knows. He helped me make the decision. He won't tell anyone—even Mom. It's just the three of us. And Ray."

"I'm excited for you, baby," she says, snaking her arm out of the blankets to grab her coffee. She takes a long sip. "Do I have to stop drinking caffeine when I'm pregnant?"

"I think so, and booze, of course."

"Coffee will be way harder for me than liquor." She wiggles around on me again and squeals. "I don't even care. I'll give up everything."

"Do we need to get a book or something about pregnancy?" I ask as I wrap my arms around her. "I seriously don't know anything except the how to get pregnant part?"

"I guess," she says. "I mean, we'll have all kinds of advice once we announce it, but maybe we can find something to look at before that. I'll ask Millie."

"So now Maisie and Millie are going to know we're trying?"

"Millie won't tell anyone, but I'll have to tell Raine too, because she would kill me if Millie knew before her."

"Then Ryan, Mason, and Alex will know. Should we tell our parents?"

She sits up. "No! Are you crazy? What if it takes us a while? I can't enjoy sex if they're constantly nosing in."

"Then we're definitely not telling them. Let's just wait until the baby pops out to tell them, so we can keep enjoying sex." I look down at her. "Wait, we can still have sex when you're pregnant, right?"

"Seb, stop. Of course we can." She tilts her head. "I mean, right? But maybe not right before I give birth. Oh my god. Why do we know so little? We need to start googling this right away."

I pull her back against me as she tries to stand up. "Settle down. We have plenty of time for all that, especially now that I'm retired. We'll figure it out."

She takes a deep breath. "Have you thought about what you want to do when you retire? You said you wanted to amp up your foundation, right?"

"Yeah," I say, kissing the top of her head. "In fact, Alex invited us to Puerto Rico the last week of January to help him with a baseball skills camp that he's hosting free for some underserved kids down there. Do you want to go?"

"Definitely. We're in Blitzen for the wedding on New Year's Eve. Maybe we can stay there for a week after and do some skiing at Big Bear, then head to Puerto Rico."

"I don't know about the skiing if you're pregnant," I say, pulling her closer. "Maybe we'll just hang out in Blitzen and then make a quick stop at Roman's place in St. John to warm up our bodies before we head to Alex's camp."

"That sounds perfect," she says, sighing. "I already love your retirement so much."

"You know, I'm thinking I want to start doing free camps like Alex's back in Michigan—around Grand Rapids. Will you help me figure it all out?"

She nods against my chest. "Absolutely. I've missed doing work stuff anyway. I can plan the camps and other events. You'll just need to show up and work with the kids. Maybe we can expand them to Miami too."

"That would be great. And Alex said Manny wants to do some around his hometown in the DR. We can travel around doing camps until our kids are school age."

"Kids?" She sits up again, her eyes wide. "You know that's plural, right? Like more than one kid."

"Yes, I know," I say, smiling. "I'm ready to have more than one."

She starts dancing around on top of me. "Eek! How long do we have to wait after kid one to get pregnant with kid two?"

"Let's just concentrate on kid one," I say, pulling her tightly to me. "We have all the time in the world now, baby."

Epilogue

SOPHIE

Two Months Later

December 26, 2022

"Shh! Someone will hear you!"

Maisie looks up at me from across the bedroom as she pulls the pregnancy tests out of the shopping bag. "Who? Who's going to hear me? Seb's at the stadium. He said he wouldn't be home for a few hours. There's no one else in the house."

"Did anyone recognize you at the store?"

"Recognize me as whom?" She shakes her head. "No one knows who I am. That's why you had me buy the tests. Frankly, I can't believe you waited until you got back to Miami. You're almost a week late."

"How am I going to take a pregnancy test in

Michigan?" I whisper. "Both of our families were jammed into the lake house. I didn't have any alone time."

"Quit whispering, weirdo," Maisie says. "You're being so paranoid."

"I know," I say, looking around the room like someone's about to pop out of the closet. "But if it's positive, I don't want anyone else to know until I tell Seb."

"I'll know!" Raine yells from the phone. She's looking at us from where I have my phone propped up on the pillows on the bed. "Wait, you're going to tell me, right? I need to see every move you make from this moment forward. If you get the result and don't tell me, I swear I'll fly to Miami and go through your trash."

"I'm taking the pee sticks home with me," Maisie says, "because God knows someone will root through their trash and tell the world the results. I'll have to tell Ryan they're not mine. He'll freak if he finds them, especially if they're positive."

"He's still not ready, huh?" Raine asks.

"No. Neither am I. We only want one kid. We have plenty of time," Maisie says. "And I can practice on Sophie's kid."

"What?" Raine screams. "Do you already have the result?"

"Settle down. We're still unwrapping the tests. Did you really need to buy four, Mae? I'm only a week late."

"You're never late." Maisie points a pee stick at me. "Not even by an hour. Your body is freaky OCD about your period. I know you're pregnant."

Raine squeals. "Eek!"

"Raine, quit yelling. Alex is going to hear you. I don't

want him to know before Seb." I grab the tests and go into the bathroom. "Besides, we just started trying. I'm not going to be devastated if I'm not pregnant yet."

"Where are you going?" Raine says as she sees me pass by the phone. "Pick me up and carry me with you."

"You don't need to see me pee on the sticks," I yell over my shoulder.

"Yes, I do," she says. "Maisie!"

Maisie walks into the bathroom carrying my phone. Raine's face is covering the screen. "There she is, Raine. Do you want me to zoom in so you can see her urine stream?"

"Maybe," Raine says. "Do you have enough pee for four sticks?"

"Go away. Both of you," I say, holding in my pee as I reach for another stick. "Stop watching me, perverts."

"I'll take her back to the bedroom," Maisie says, laughing as she walks out of the bathroom with my phone. "So, Raine. Let's talk about you and Alex. When can we expect a baby from you?"

"Shut up, Mae," Raine says. "I'm on your plan. One kid at a later date."

After I complete the four tests, I lay the sticks neatly in a row on the bathroom counter. I take a deep breath and look at myself in the mirror as I wash my hands. I'm trying to play it cool, but I want to be pregnant so badly. My entire life I've felt like I was put on this earth to be a mother, and I just can't wait to get started.

When I walk out into the bedroom, Maisie's lying on our bed with the duvet pulled up to her chin. She has Raine propped up against her legs.

Raine smiles when she sees my face come onto the screen. "Did you ever think this day would come? We've literally known each other since birth. And now you're getting ready to have a baby of your own."

"Don't jump the gun," I say. "We still have eight more minutes until we know."

"Yeah, but even if you're not pregnant today, you will be soon," Raine says. "And I'll probably be married soon—"

"What?" Maisie and I scream at the same time.

"Since when will you be married *soon*?" I ask, pointing at the screen.

She shrugs. "It's been a pretty great two months with Alex living out here. Everything's falling into place."

"Have you talked about marriage?" Maisie asks.

"A lot," Raine says. "He's ready. He asked me to keep him up to date on when I become ready."

"And?" Maisie and I say together.

Raine takes a deep breath and blows it out. "I think I'm ready."

Maisie and I start screaming and dancing on the bed.

"When are you going to tell him?"

"When we're up in Blitzen."

"Tell him now so he can buy a ring and propose to you there," Maisie says. "That would be so romantic in the pretty snow."

"He already has the ring—"

"What?" Maisie and I say together as we start bed dancing again.

"How have you not told us that yet?" I ask, my face getting serious. "Raine, that's unacceptable."

"I just found it yesterday," she whispers. "He has it packed in his bag for Blitzen."

"What does it look like?" Maisie asks. "Show us."

"I'll show it to you when it's on my finger. It's gorgeous. I told Millie what I wanted. She must have gone shopping with him."

I jump as the alarm goes off on my phone.

Maisie grabs me and hugs me to her chest. "Good luck, sweetie."

"Do you want us to come in there with you?" Raine asks.

"No," I say as I roll off the bed. "I want to do this by myself."

"Make sure she doesn't try to destroy the tests before we can see them," Raine says as I walk into the bathroom.

I close my eyes and take a deep breath.

"I can feel it," I say to myself as I open my eyes. "I know they're positive."

Epilogue

SEB

Later That Night

December 26, 2022

I'm stretched out on the couch in Sophie's dressing room watching her pack for our trip to Blitzen Bay. We're headed there tomorrow.

She puts a sweater in her suitcase, but then pulls it back out and sighs. "I seriously don't know what to pack. What are we supposed to wear to the wedding? Raine said they're getting married in that cute little chapel. Remember the one that's just down the street from the Holly House? It had the honeysuckle growing over the archway last summer. It smelled so good that I almost wanted to eat it."

She looks over at me as I start laughing.

"What?" She throws the sweater at me. "What did you pack to wear to the wedding?"

"Something that makes me smell just like honeysuckle."

"Shut up," she says, collapsing down on the chair at her makeup table. "You know how I get. I like to pack perfectly."

"Anything you wear will be perfect because you're perfect."

She shakes her head. "Even when I'm having my travel breakdowns you always say the right thing."

"We take turns calming each other down. That's why we work." I point at her suitcase. "Keep going. You can do this."

She stands up again and looks into the walk-in closet. "We probably should have brought our big coats back from Michigan. Elle said they're expecting a major snow storm this week."

"We can buy coats when we get there." I adjust the mound of pillows that surround my head. "Nash said that little store in Blitzen has everything we need."

"But then we'll each have two winter coats," she says, her hands on her hips as she frowns at her suitcase again.

"So?" I pull the blanket off the back of the couch and throw it over me. I can feel a major nap coming on.

"So, we don't need two winter coats." She looks over at me again and smiles when she sees the blanket on top of me. "You know your mom begged me to send her a picture of you napping on that couch."

"Don't even think about it. It's impossible to look manly surrounded by all this pink."

"I think she was counting on that," she says, forming a frame with her hands and pretending to line me up for a picture. "I'm sure the media would love this picture too."

"Sophia," I say, pulling the blanket up to my chin. "Behave. Don't make me abandon this couch. You know it's my favorite place in the house."

She tilts her head and lets out a long sigh. "You're so cute. I wish everyone knew this side of you."

"The ones who matter know enough," I say, motioning her over to me, "but this Seb is just for you."

She walks over and lowers her body on top of mine—her head resting on my chest. "I love this Seb so much."

I kiss the top of her head. "If we buy coats there, we can leave them in Blitzen at our new house. They can be our California coats."

She looks up at me. "I seriously forgot we bought a house there."

"Yeah. It will be interesting to see it in person."

"We probably should have waited until we got there to buy it." She lays her head back down. "What if it's horrible?"

"It's not. We did the video walkthrough," I say, rubbing her back, "and Nash checked it out. He said it's solid. The best part is that it's already furnished, so we can stay there this week. You know how I like my privacy."

"How much privacy are we really going to have with Sam, Nash, and Elle living right next to us? And not just them. Honestly, the entire town seems like they're going to be in our business from day one."

"But in kind of a cool way, right?" I start stroking her hair. "Blitzen has that comfortable small-town thing going for it."

"It does. When we were there over the summer, I swear my body de-stressed completely the minute we drove into town." She raises her head again. "Do you remember that Raine and Alex are staying with us. Holly House was sold out. Is that still okay? The master suite is upstairs by itself so we should have plenty of separation."

"It's fine. Honestly, I'm happy about it. It's only been a couple months, but I miss hanging with Alex."

"Agree," she says, laying her head back down. "It will be nice to see everyone again. Kit, Butch, Mason, and Millie are staying at Holly House. And they're bringing Mo. And Millie's dad and best friend are coming with their ladies. It will be crazy."

"I can't wait to get there. I told our pilot wheels up at ten tomorrow morning." I tap her butt a few times. "Are you still good with that? Or do you need more time to stare at your suitcase?"

"Shut up," she says, rolling off me. "Or you're not going to get your present."

"What present?" She walks to her makeup table and pulls a little wrapped box out of the top drawer. "Soph, you already gave me too much for Christmas. I don't need another gift."

She walks back over and straddles my body. "This isn't a Christmas present."

"What kind of present is it? My birthday's in August."

"There doesn't have to be a special occasion for presents," she says, holding the box out to me.

I give her my sternest look. "I agree, but that only applies to me giving you gifts. You know you never have to buy me anything."

"It only cost a couple bucks," she says, trying unsuccessfully to stop a huge grin from coming to her face.

"What is it?" I narrow my eyes. "You're making me very suspicious."

"Open it."

"Fine." I give her another stern look, and then untie the ribbon. I crack the lid and peek in. "Is it alive?"

"Kind of," she says, giggling. "Open it."

I lift off the lid and stare at it for a full thirty seconds before it registers what I'm looking at.

"Are you pregnant?" I look up at her. "Is this a positive test?"

She nods as tears start rolling down her face.

"Soph, you're pregnant? Really?"

"Really."

"But, we just started trying."

"Well, apparently," she says, smiling as the tears continue to fall, "we're really good at it."

I pull her down, squeeze her tightly to me, and then release immediately. "Wait, was that too hard? Did I just squeeze the baby?"

"The baby's the size of a pea right now. And believe me, she likes the squeezing as much as I do."

"She?" I tilt her head up. "Is it a girl?"

"Seb," she says, shaking her head, "I haven't even been pregnant a full month. We won't know that for a while, but I don't want to call the baby 'it.' Maybe you say 'him' and I'll say 'her.' One of us has to be right."

"Man, I have so many questions," I say. "When are you due? Do you feel sick? Did you go to the doctor? Do you need to go? Should we cancel our trip? Do you need to rest?"

"Seb," she says, rubbing her forehead against my chest. "I'm fine. I actually feel really good so far. I called my OB. We have an appointment with her when we get back from Blitzen, but she said the due date will probably be in August."

I nod as my brain tries to catch up. "Okay, that will give us plenty of time to move to Michigan. They said the renovations to our house will be done in March. Since this house is a rental, we'll need to buy all new furniture, but I'll take care of that. You don't have to worry about anything except for you and the baby."

"You're not picking out furniture for our new house," she says, laughing. "You wouldn't even know where to start. I can do it with our moms. They already said they would camp out at the Michigan house while everything's being delivered and set up. And when they find out we're pregnant, they're going to turn into super grandmas. All we need to do is pack up our clothes and move. We'll be moved in way before the baby's born—plenty of time for nesting."

"I'll do the packing. If you do it, we'll never get out of here," I say, nodding.

"Shut up," she says, sitting up. She pats the back of the couch. "We should probably take this, right? I'm not sure I can nap on anything else."

"Oh, yeah. The cozy pink couch is definitely coming with us. If the baby's a girl, maybe we can put it in her room."

"Look at you," she says, smiling. "You're more of an interior designer than I thought."

"It might be my new career now that I'm retired."

She crawls off me. "I better start packing again or we'll never make it to Blitzen."

I grab her hand as she starts to walk away. She looks back at me.

"Soph, this is the happiest I've ever been in my life. We're having a baby. Our next chapter is already starting."

She smiles and squeezes my hand. "And it's going to be the best chapter yet."

What's Next?

The entire gang's headed to Blitzen Bay in my next book, *Pretty Close to Perfect*. Nash and Elle from *The Runaway Bride of Blitzen Bay* will narrate the story of their impending wedding. And, there just might be another wedding. Blitzen Bay is a magical place. You never know what will happen.

Pretty Close to Perfect will be out December 2022. You can preorder it on Amazon. Sign up for my email newsletter at donnaschwartze.com to be the first to know when I publish it.

- Have you read the first two novels that take place in Blitzen Bay? *The Runaway Bride of Blitzen Bay* and *No One Wants That* are both set in this charming town.

What's Next?

- Millie, Mason, Butch, and Raine are introduced in The Trident Trilogy (*Eight Years*, *The Only Reason*, *Wild Card*). Read one of the first chapters of *Eight Years* below.

All of my books are available on Amazon and free on Kindle Unlimited.

A chapter from *Eight Years:*

Mason

I see her the minute she walks in. She opens the door and it's like someone shines a flashlight into my eyes. Her long, blonde hair is glowing through the haze of the bar. She's tall and slender, and from what I can make out from this distance, her legs go on forever. I immediately think about how they would feel wrapped all around me.

She starts maneuvering her way expertly through the drunk men. They're leering at her. It makes me want to pull out my rifle and shoot a round of warning shots over their heads. I watch as they brush up against her on purpose. She deftly changes direction every time it happens, ignoring their filthy eyes and hungry greetings. There's no doubt in my mind this happens every time she walks into a room.

She's only about twenty feet from me now. I get a better look at her. She looks like she just came off the beach—cutoffs, T-shirt, flip flops. Her skin and hair are still radiating the sun's glow. She takes a stool at the bar with her back toward me. Her hair sways back and forth as she settles into her seat. I'm hypnotized by it. I want to dip my hands deep into it and feel it flow over me like water.

She says something to Pete. I think she ordered something other than beer or whiskey. That's really the extent of his bartending skills. Pete leaves to get her a drink that I'm sure is going to be nothing like what she ordered. She turns her stool around and looks right at me. She sees me looking. I don't try to hide it. She smiles to acknowledge, but not to encourage, and looks away. The disappointment shoots all the way through my body.

I've seen her type before. Not often. Certainly not in this town. A woman like her is like a mirage—an illusion sent to trick you into thinking something on the horizon could actually quench your thirst. But in the back of your head, you know it's not real. You'll never be able to even get close to it.

I don't look away though. I'm not sure I physically can. My eyes dart up and down her body not sure where they want to land. There's so much to look at. I'm enjoying the subtle curves peeking out of her loose V-neck T-shirt when she crosses her legs, drawing my eyes all the way down to her ankles. As I'm thinking about how I'd like to start there and run my hands up her legs until they disappear under her shorts, I notice that the legs have started walking toward me.

"I'll play," she says to us, to me, to the team.

Seeing what we see every day, it takes a lot to bring us to a firm stop. But here we are, seven grizzled operators frozen in place—leering at the mirage.

Butch is the first to recover. "You'll play with us? Not sure you know what you're getting into, ma'am." He extends out the word "ma'am" to highlight his Southern drawl. It's one of his go-to pickup moves.

"Oh, I think I probably do." She doesn't look too concerned.

"We're like professional pool players, darlin'," Butch continues. "You ought not to mess with us."

"I'll take my chances, but I get to pick my partner."

I watch as my team straightens up like they're in the operator version of a beauty pageant—pumping out their chests and trying to smooth their beards.

"I want curly back there." She points at Mouse. As usual, he's the only one not seeking the spotlight. Currently, he's trying to blend into the wall.

"Mouse? All this on display and you want that?" Butch is flexing so hard, I think he might pop a bicep.

"Women are always suckers for the strong, silent type. Am I right?" she says, turning to Clark, one of the naval analysts assigned to our team. Clark rolls her eyes. She's about as interested in us as we are in her.

"Well, she's not going to say anything because she knows y'all, but trust me, she looks at those curls," the mirage says, nodding toward Mouse, who's about to keel over from all the attention being leveled at him.

She smiles, picks up a cue, and walks past us on her way over to Mouse. Our heads turn one at a time as she slowly passes by. Our eyes linger on her perfectly curved backside, as her sweet, heady scent fills our nostrils. It's fucking intoxicating. All of it. The entire show.

Her eyes lock with mine for a second. She does a double-take. I'm used to it. No one expects that color of blue coming out of my stern face. She recovers quickly, but she knows I noticed.

She finally gets over to Mouse. She presses her body

lightly to him and whispers into his ear. I'm filled with an unwarranted jealousy. I want to rip her away from him. I don't hear what she's saying, but I hear Mouse reply, "Yeah, do your thing. I've got your back if you miss." He puts his hand on her waist and pulls her a little closer as he answers. My jealousy's overflowing now.

"What in the damn hell are you doing?" Butch brings me back to reality. "If you get any closer to him, you're going to render him useless as your teammate. Mousie won't be able to walk soon."

"I'm discussing strategy with my teammate. You're familiar with strategy, right?"

Damn, does that mean she knows what we do for a living? It kind of disappoints me.

"The only strategy Mouse is going to need is how to hide what's going on in his pants right now," Hawk says from the corner. We all laugh at the honesty of it. The rest of us are getting hard just watching her. I can't imagine what it would feel like to touch her. I'd really like to find out, though.

"Do y'all want to talk all night or play pool?" she purrs, suddenly throwing in a Southern accent. She knows who she's dealing with. A lot of us are Southerners or Texans. She's using all of her ammunition.

"Okay, Strawberry Shortcake, let's see your stuff," Butch says.

It's not until now, as she moves directly under the light, that I notice her blonde hair has streaks of red running through it. Her hair, like the rest of her, is perfect. She looks like an angel to me.

She puts a hundred down on the table and waits for the

rest of us to follow. I'm so mesmerized. I temporarily forget that I'm expected to play in the game. I fumble for my hundred and put it on the table.

"Y'all okay if I break?" she asks as JJ picks up the money and starts to rack the balls. I'm back in game mode now. I nod to the table without saying anything. Ladies first.

She walks over to the head of the table and bends over slightly. Thank God I'm not standing behind her. I would be rendered useless. Bryce's eyes are laser-focused on her ass. I think he might be in shock. I look up to see her about ready to break. Her eyes lock with mine. She breaks without looking away from me. It's so fucking sexy.

"Stripes," she says. I finally look at the table. Perfect break. I think we're about to get hustled.

She moves around the table with military precision. The striped balls are falling into the pockets like obedient soldiers. It takes her about five minutes to clear the table. I'm guessing she's done it faster, but I can tell this is more of a show to her than a competition. And all of us are enjoying every last minute of it.

"Eight ball, top left." She gestures toward the target pocket.

Straight in. I'm not even sure it touched the sides. She straightens up, puts her stick on the table, and walks over to JJ to collect her winnings. He's fanned the bills out like playing cards against his chest. He's going to make her work for it. She looks at him directly in the eyes and plucks the bills out of his hands slowly, one by one. God, she has balls. There aren't many men who would stare at JJ for that long.

She walks over to Mouse and gives him his two hundred and a little wink. He winks back. I'm not liking where I think this is headed. But then, just as suddenly as she approached us, she walks away.

"Thanks for the game, boys," she says, the Southern accent gone.

"What? That's it?" Butch says. "We don't get a chance to win our money back?"

"Maybe another time. I need to get some rest. I have a big meeting in the morning." She looks right at me when she says it, knowing I should have figured it out by now.

She hands her two hundred to Pete. "I'm picking up their drinks tonight," she says, nodding over to us as she walks out of the bar.

And then it hits me, like a grenade blowing up in my face. Her meeting tomorrow is with me, with us. She's our new CIA agent.

Well this is just going to be fucking inconvenient.

Buy or download Eight Years on Amazon.

About the Author

Donna Schwartze is a graduate of the University of Missouri School of Journalism. She also holds a Master of Arts from Webster University. She is an avid yogi and plans to still be able to do the splits on her 100th birthday. Her favorite character from her books is Mack from The Trident Trilogy.